Bound By Blood

HALLOW RISING: A SPICY APPALACHIAN ROMANTASY SERIES

HALLOW RISING
BOOK ONE

CHRISSY CHICORY

HALF-PAST 2 PUBLISHING INC.

Published by Half-Past 2 Publishing Inc.

Edited by Kimberly Huther

For Kit Mitchell,
for telling me exactly what I needed to hear
at exactly the right moment.

Contents

Prologue

DREAM-FLAME: THE MAKING OF THE WAMPUS

In the Age of Making

The mountains were only ideas when we first learned each other's names.

I was smoke braided through stone, he was lightning sleeping inside ice. We circled as dragons do—vast and wordless—until the Hallow sang us human. Scale became skin. Fang softened to mouth. The caverns of the world brightened to a low gold as the Hallow Song rose around us: a pulse in the dark, a vein of life thrumming under everything that would ever be born.

It isn't a sound you hear with ears. It climbs the bones from the ground up. It tastes like iron and honey on the tongue. It presses at the wrists like a tide seeking veins. It says *live, live, live.*

We met inside that music.

Taren's back struck the luminous rock with a hiss of steam and I followed him down, laughing against his throat as if laughter were something I had learned long ago. We had just discovered hands. What else could we do with them but worship?

He was carved from the storm itself—skin the hue of slate after rain, hair shot through with pale lightning strands that caught the glow of the cavern. When he looked at me, the silver in his eyes shifted like sunlight beneath water—half-mercy, half-danger. The air around him bent with restrained power, the kind that could shatter mountains and still hesitate at the line of my jaw.

His fingers traced my shoulder as if he were reading an inscription, learning the new language of flesh. I watched him watching me, saw the wonder flicker through him as though he, too, were surprised that skin could be soft, that heat could live without flame. My body—smoke-born, newly human—answered every touch with discovery. Where his palms slid, I felt the shape of myself for the first time: the curve of hip, the breath beneath my ribs, the quickening rhythm that was no longer purely dragon but something perilously alive.

The scent of him—cold metal, pine, and distant thunder—wrapped around me. The sound of me—breath breaking, heartbeat rising—filled the Hallows between the stalactites. I learned the geography of my own form through the map of his hands; he learned patience through the quake of mine. Between us the Hallow Song swelled, matching our rhythm, bright threads of amber racing across the cavern ceiling like constellations newly invented.

Every movement felt both ancient and brand new, Creation folding back on itself, reminding us that even gods must relearn the miracle of touch.

"Lyra," he said, and my name ran along the stalactites, turned to water, fell in shining drops.

The sound of it ignited something deep inside me—older than breath, older than flame. My name had existed before language, but on his tongue it became a spell, a calling that reached down into the molten parts of me I longed for him to explore. The cavern shivered in answer. So did I.

I kissed him the way the world shapes rivers: insistence, patience, flood. Yet even as our mouths met, something more than motion moved through me—a hunger, bright and aching, spiraling low in my body like a forge waking from sleep. The rhythm of it was the Hallow's own pulse, wrapping around us, working through us, binding desire to duty until I couldn't tell where his heartbeat ended and mine began.

His answering breath met mine in perfect counterpoint; heat

meeting heat, each wave of longing feeding the next. The Song's current coiled around our joined bodies, liquid light tracing our skin, translating need into creation. Every heartbeat became percussion, every breath a note, until the Hallow itself seemed to sing through us—an ancient melody of want and wonder, of two forces remembering what it meant to make the world new again.

We were not yet guardians then. The earth was young, magic ungoverned, creatures wandering in their first skins. Some came from sea-salt and sorrow, some from stormlight, some from the wet breath of caves. More were being made by accident—wild births of hunger and desire. The Hallow kept singing.

When Taren moved inside me, the Song flared—blue-white through him, coal-gold through me—and broke like summer thunder across the ridges above.

Our breathing found the same rhythm, rising and falling like the mountains themselves exhaling through us. Every sound between us—his low gasp, my answering cry—became part of the Hallow's harmony. Echoing along the cavern walls until it felt as if the earth was singing with us. The air grew thick with light and pulse, a single heartbeat made of two.

He pulled me closer and the world disappeared into that small, infinite space where skin met soul. The glow that lived in him poured through my ribs, and I felt the shape of forever press against my heart. It wasn't only desire—it was recognition, the understanding that we had always been halves of the same flame.

The Song rose higher, a chord of power and surrender, and I let my head fall back as it moved through me—heat and light and something vast, breaking open every boundary between us. For a moment there was no Taren, no Lyra, no sky or stone. Only the pure, endless thrum of Creation remembering itself.

The light left us and went seeking. It threaded out of the cavern into a narrow seam in the rock, through a blackshaft and a root-tangle, up into leaf-shadow and cold air, up into a forest preparing for night.

There, an ancient cat slept beneath a hemlock: elder of her line, a shadow the size of a woman, paws big as a man's open hand. She'd seen the first hunters and the last shamans, had learned long ago to step between worlds when the woods grew loud. Too many men had taken too many of her kits. She carried their loss like a second spine.

Our spilled light found that grief.

The Song is a maker; it can't help it. It circled the cat's ribs, took the shape of her breath, and slid down her throat like hot milk. The hemlock's roots thrummed. The cat's whiskers burned from silver to gold. She woke with a gasp like a child's first cry.

Her eyes held two kinds of pupils then—cat slits nested inside human rounds. She lifted her head and the muscles of her face learned language. Not words yet, just vows. In the space between one heartbeat and the next she became two-footed and four, the edges of her body flexing between fur and flesh. She was old revenge made new. She was the Wampus, though we didn't know the name yet.

Below the hemlock, we shuddered together and felt the mountain change.

"Do you feel that?" Taren whispered.

We were still tangled together, limbs heavy, breathless in the after-thrum of the Song. The cavern's glow dimmed to a slow, amber heartbeat, pulsing in time with ours. The Hallow seemed to breathe around us—warm, humming, and alive—as if it had woven a blanket from light and drawn it close over our slick skin.

My damp hair clung to my temples and shoulders, the strands tasting faintly of salt and smoke. The air carried his scent—iron and pine, and the musky shadow of storms—so thick I could almost drink it. Beneath us the stone radiated a deep, steady warmth. And every exhale curled into mist before dissolving into gold dust that drifted upward like fireflies caught in amber.

He shifted beside me, his arm tightening around my waist, grounding me back into the world we had nearly burned away. The stalactites glittered with drops of condensed magic, each one reflecting us in miniature—two figures caught in the heart of the earth, haloed by the Song's faint luminescence.

The cavern stretched out in every direction, endless chambers breathing with quiet life: veins of crystal veined through black stone, trickles of glowing water tracing patterns like constellations across the walls. Everything shimmered softly, as though the light was reluctant to intrude on what we had made.

"I feel it," I whispered back, my voice small in the vastness. The Hallow answered in a low, contented hum, its power curling through my bones like a lullaby meant for gods.

The air shimmered faintly, gold motes spiraling through the cavern like the last breath of stars. Around us, the rock seemed to sigh—an ancient creature settling back into sleep, sated by the offering it had just devoured.

"The Song took something from us," I said, and the ache in my belly was not only pleasure. It was Creation's after-pain, a bright tearing that left me breathless. The glow that still pulsed beneath my skin felt foreign, as though part of me had been poured outward, reshaped into something beyond our control.

Taren brushed his thumb along my jaw, tracing the trembling edge of my lips before resting his forehead against mine. His breath mingled with mine, steadying it. "You gave," he said, voice rough with awe. "We both did."

His words sank deep, and I felt them bloom inside me like heat beneath ice. This was what tethered us—not just desire, but the exchange of essence. Of light. He wasn't just my equal; he was my echo, the missing note the Song had always needed to be whole.

I pressed a hand to his chest, feeling the steady thunder of his heart beneath the cooling skin. It beat the same rhythm as the mountain's pulse. The same rhythm as mine. For a heartbeat, I believed the Hallow had chosen us not as keepers but as its living proof that love and power could be the same thing.

Light flickered up the cavern walls, then dimmed to a living ember. The Hallow settled back into its slow heartbeat, satisfied and terrible. The glow faded to warmth, wrapping us in shadow and silence, but the bond remained. An invisible thread of longing that would stretch across centuries and ranges, pulling us toward one another even when the world demanded distance.

He kissed my temple, a whisper of lightning across skin, and I closed my eyes, already mourning the day we would have to let go.

We dressed in our human skins the way the mountains dress themselves after rain. I took hair the color of wheat and a mouth made for pleasure. Taren chose a storm-blue gaze and shoulders that could carry winter. We walked the long limestone halls hand in hand, laughing at the strangeness of fingers and the way our footsteps echoed.

When we reached the surface the air had changed.

The world above was wild and young, still half-formed, its edges sharp as obsidian. Mist crawled low over the ridgeline, turning the forest into a tangle of silhouettes. The ground steamed faintly where the Hallow's warmth met the cool breath of night. Every leaf glittered with the residue of magic—tiny beads of light that clung like dew, then vanished as the wind passed.

On the slope below us, a hunting camp smoldered. Men had been here—five, six—drunk on cruelty. Their fires still spat sap and bone ash, filling the air with the acrid reek of burnt hair and fat. We moved barefoot through the clearing, our skin still slick with the warmth of the Hallow, our bodies glowing faintly in the dark—creatures of Creation staring down at the wreckage of destruction.

The men had worn pelts stiff with old blood, necklaces strung with teeth, trophies taken from anything weaker than themselves. Their spears lay splintered—hafts cracked, obsidian tips snapped clean as if bitten through. Tents woven from animal hides sagged and tore, the ground churned with the signs of struggle—heel marks, claw marks, a smear that began as red and ended as nothing.

We found a line of snares made for anything with a throat and a trap baited with a kitten's cry. The sound had stopped, but its echo lingered —thin, pitiful, and haunting. The kitten was gone. So were the men's knives. So were the men.

The Wampus had eaten well.

Smoke drifted up from the blackened pit, carrying the mingled scents of pine resin, sweat, and fear. Taren's hand found mine, the heat of him steady against the cool mountain air. The difference between the world we had left below and this one struck me hard. Below, there had been the slow pulse of the Song, the sacred ache of unity; above, there was only the jagged silence left behind by cruelty.

We stood naked beneath the raw moonlight, utterly at ease in our skins, while the trappings of men—clothing, weapons, hierarchy—lay torn and useless at our feet. Their world was cold in its violence. Ours, for all its fire, had been tender.

Taren looked out over the carnage and then down at me, his expression unreadable in the blue wash of night. "This is what happens when the Hallow isn't tended," he said softly.

I nodded, feeling the ache of it—this fragile balance between Creation and corruption, love and hunger. Somewhere in the dark, the newborn creature we had accidentally made moved through the trees, sleek and sure, leaving only silence in her wake.

We followed the scent into a clearing split by a creek. The moon made a blade on the water. The cat-woman stood in the middle of it, one foot in fur, one in skin, blood painting the white of her thigh. She looked at us and I understood at once: not prey, not kin. The Hallow had touched her and left its mark.

"This is yours," I said to the night.

As the words left my lips, I felt no regret—only a quiet, aching peace. The air still shimmered faintly with the residue of our light, and I knew in my bones that this was what we were meant to do. To shape, to awaken, to let the Hallow sing through us. I was content to be its vessel, to feel Creation move where once there had been only hunger and flame. The making of life, the mending of balance—that was our truest purpose. Ours was not a dominion born of pride, but of surrender.

Around us the mountain exhaled, the mist curling in approval. The Hallow's pulse slowed, steady and deep, and I could sense its satisfaction. To give. To make. To let go. It was as it should be.

Taren's voice broke softly through the hush. "No, ours," he murmured.

He stepped closer until our shoulders brushed, his gaze fixed not on the creature fading into the trees but on me. In the faint glow, his eyes reflected the same coal-gold that lived beneath my skin—a mirrored fire that tied us together. There was a tremor in his voice I'd never heard before, something between wonder and devotion.

"She carries both of us," he said softly. "The Hallow's power, yes—but also our breath, our pulse. She was born of our joining. That means she belongs to both of us."

The certainty in his tone startled me. I'd never thought of creation as belonging, only as service. The Hallow called; we answered. That was the rhythm of eternity. But as he looked at me—truly looked—I felt the fragile thread of something new form between us, something the Hallow had not commanded: connection born of choice.

His hand brushed mine, a small, reverent gesture, as if he feared to disturb the silence that wrapped around us. "Every time the Song moves through us," he said, "it leaves something behind. Not just in the world but in us. Don't you feel it?"

I did. It thrummed low in my chest, a spark that was both his and mine. It wasn't the ache of obligation but the warmth of shared creation. His words carved space inside me where reverence met tenderness, and for the first time I understood that he didn't see himself as my counterpart alone but as my companion in purpose, in consequence, in the fragile act of making.

It surprised me, the depth of his care. And it moved me in ways I hadn't known I could be moved. The Hallow had bound us in duty, but something else was binding us now: something chosen, fragile, and *human*.

The cat bared her teeth in a grin no human mouth could manage. I felt her vow travel through the water of the creek to my ankles: *I will hunt the hunters. I will punish what doesn't respect the woods. I will take men who take.* The vow bound itself to the Song, a new chord braided into an ancient melody.

We should have bound her then. We should have taught her the part about balance—about how vengeance asked and asked until the ask itself became a beast.

We were young. We were in love. We let her walk away into the trees with the moon on her shoulders like a pelt.

When the near-ending came—the chaos and fever, the almost-extinction when magic rose wild and tore at the sky—it was the dragons who went down into the Hallow and offered our eternities. We promised to keep the Song in its banks, to seal leaks, to imprison what couldn't live beside men. We took mountains for anchors. We became guardians, tethered: I to the long, smoke-soft ridges of the East; Taren to the storm-torn, snow-bright Range of the West. Apart, to keep the world in one piece. Alone, for everyone's sake. The Hallow approved and tightened its bonds. That is what it does: it binds and it sings. It makes and it demands.

Now and then, when the Song swells, it lets us find each other again. In dreams. In heat. In waking. Our bodies never touch, but our souls remain intwined.

Time tested us. The earth learned cities and guns. The mountains took names. Dragons kept oaths.

Centuries later, in the Blue Ridge that called me home, the Hallow Song stirred with a note I hadn't heard since that hemlock night. Iron on the tongue. Honey under the breath. A vow awoke.

Beneath the Bottle Tree Tavern's din, beside ranger radios and search-and-rescue maps, under the good boots and bad decisions of tourists, the current quickened:

Live. Hunt. Take what takes.

I closed my eyes and saw her again — the cat and the woman overlapping, water sliding off her haunches, the moon rising like a scar. The Hallow Song had awoken her again.

And because the Song never gives without taking, it brought me Taren for a moment too—a spark in my rib cage, a storm along the spine of the Rockies, his voice like smoke on skin:

Lyra. Fire of my heart. Be careful.

Then the light went thin, the heartbeat slowed, and the mountains returned to breathing like old sleepers. I opened my eyes to a world that needed tending.

And hunting.

What Dragons Owe (Lyra)

If I'm doing my job right, you won't believe me.

Oh, it's fun to scroll through your feeds and read scary Appalachian tales:

If you hear a woman laughing in the woods after midnight, you didn't.

If something in the dark calls your name, you didn't.

Cute, right?

Campfire stories.

#folklore.

But let me tell you something.

If you step into my mountains, your doubt won't keep you safe.

I will.

Before men mapped highways over bones and called the crossings *towns*, the world was a wilderness of makers. Magic didn't hide in stories; it crawled and flew and sang. Creatures woke wherever the earth's deep music bubbled close to the skin—river hags from silt, storm-birds from thunderheads, wolves that could turn to smoke and back again. It was beautiful. It was ravenous. It almost killed everything.

When the chaos came—magic swallowing magic, hunger breeding hunger—the near-ending taught us a truth. That power without boundaries devours its own children. So the dragons went down into the dark and made a vow to the Hallow Song.

Think of a vein running under every mountain you've ever loved. A living current, older than gods, that wants life the way fire wants air. We promised to keep that river in its banks. Each of us took a range to anchor. We tethered ourselves to stone so the world could sleep at night.

We were not few. Across the earth, others took their vows: pairs bound to the Himalayas, the Andes, the Alps, the Carpathians, each sworn to temper the wild magic of their lands. Every range has its keepers—and every keeper its creatures to bind. Some call them monsters; we know them as remnants of creation that forgot how to rest.

I took the Blue Ridge, smoke-soft and secretive. Taren took the Rockies, all storm and bone. We became wardens, cleaners, jailers when needed. We let the rest of the world forget we existed. That was the price for peace.

My name is Lyra Lange. I'm a dragon. On paper, I'm a ranger with the National Park Service, Blue Ridge district. It's convenient. A badge gets you past most doors. A uniform makes mortals feel safe.

The morning after the Song woke me, I stood in my ranger station —boot-heels clicking on tile, coffee in one hand and a stack of incident reports in the other. The fluorescent lights buzzed faintly overhead, and the scent of burnt coffee from the communal machine clung to the air. My uniform jacket was still damp at the cuffs, rain darkening the olive canvas, the park patch on my sleeve worn soft from years of weather and work. Beneath it, the weight of my service belt and radio tugged comfortably at my hips—a mortal costume that somehow fit a creature older than the mountains themselves.

Butch, my Bouvier des Flandres, occupied his usual post on the oversized flannel dog bed in the corner—the one that conveniently offered the best view of the door. All one hundred pounds of shaggy gray fur and stubborn pride, he looked like a small bear masquerading as a house pet. When the door creaked open he lifted his massive head, one dark eye glinting through his tousled fringe, judged the newcomer, and gave a sigh so theatrical it might've been rehearsed. Satisfied that the intruder wasn't worth the effort, he flopped back down, paws crossed like royalty.

Henry burst in late, cheeks wind-pink, hair damp from the mist, eyes going wide when he saw me. Twenty-four, good heart, terrible poker face. If he ever stopped crushing on me, I'd check his pulse.

He had the kind of freckles you could map constellations with, scattered across a face that was too honest for lying and too curious for peace. His copper-red hair was a permanent rebellion, a halo gone rogue no matter how many times he pushed it back. The station's overhead light caught the gleam of his belt buckle and the small pocket knife he was already flipping open and closed, a nervous rhythm he didn't even seem to notice.

Without a word, he opened the crinkled paper bag in his other hand and tossed a donut across the room. I caught it without looking and finished pouring coffee into the chipped *Best Sidekick* mug he drank from every day. The motion was automatic—two creatures running on routine and caffeine. I handed him the mug with a small smile.

"Morning, Lange," he said finally, grinning around the first bite of sugar. "We got a call from the Bottle Tree. Maeve says some out-of-towners spotted a 'panther' crossing Blackdog Road. Tail like a rope, big as a man. She told them it was a bobcat and told me to tell you to tell her who's winning our betting pool."

"On whether the season's dumbest tourist tries to pet a bear or a copperhead first?" I sipped. "My money's on the snake."

The Bottle Tree was the heart of the county—half brewery, half refuge. The kind of place that smelled of hops, fried cornbread, and somebody's grandmother's perfume. Best bands on the weekends, poetry readings on Thursdays, and if you stayed late enough on a Tuesday you might catch a fiddle jam that could raise the ghosts in the floorboards.

Maeve ran it like a benevolent dictator and everyone's favorite aunt rolled into one. Folks called her *Mama* because she treated every soul who walked through the door like one of her strays—fed them, scolded them, sent them home with leftovers and advice they didn't ask for. She'd served me more dinners than I cared to admit. I didn't cook; never needed to. Between Maeve's kitchen and her steady mother-hen presence, I ate there once—sometimes twice—a day. The place was as close to family as most of us got.

Henry grinned, then sobered. "Also... a hiker's missing out near Devil's Gap. Darren Wells. Left his campsite before dawn to 'catch the fog.' Girlfriend, Michelle Crane, woke up to blood near the campsite."

The coffee went metallic on my tongue. Iron. Honey. That chord again, low and steady, working its way up from the soles of my boots.

"Let's go," I said.

Butch was already up, nails clicking on the tile as he reached the door first.

We headed out in the green park truck, the crest on the door catching the rain as we pulled onto the winding road.

* * *

The Blue Ridge did what she always does when she wants to be loved: showed off. Fog lay in the gaps like sleeping cats. Rhododendron leaves shone oily and dark. The ridges rolled forever, old backs under old sky, and every turn of the road felt like a freshly found secret.

"You ever think about transferring?" Henry asked after a while, an attempt at casual that tripped over its own shoelaces. "Like, fire crew out West? Different mountains and all that."

I almost laughed. *Different mountains.* If I strayed too far for too long, the Song yanked the leash and the whole range howled. That's the thing about oaths—they don't come with vacations.

"I'm where I belong," I said, and he took it like a personal rejection. Sweet boy. He'd survive.

We reached Devil's Gap trailhead to find two patrol cars, a worried girlfriend wrapped in a thermal blanket, and a volunteer SAR team we'd used before. Maeve Kincaid had parked her truck crooked across two spaces and was handing out coffee from a giant metal urn.

Maeve was built like the mountains she loved: solid and unshakable, all soft plaid and sharp eyes. Her dark hair framed a face quick to laugh but quicker to judge foolishness, and her smile carried both warmth and warning. There was a trace of flour on her sleeves from the morning biscuits and a scent of cinnamon clinging to her like a benediction.

"Ranger Lange," she called, chin up, eyes sharp enough to skin a man. "I brought the good stuff. If this turns to a body, nobody's drinking my cheap beans."

"Your faith in us is touching," I said, taking a cup. "What did your out-of-towners see last night?"

"Something with a tail that wasn't a story," Maeve said. "You'll want to have a look at Blackdog when you're done here. And Lyra? I've been hearing old songs again."

My shoulders went tight. "What kind of songs?"

"The kind my granddaddy said kept men from sleeping right," she said. "The kind that make cats walk on two legs."

If anyone in these mountains could still hear the echoes of the Hallow Song, it would be Maeve. She was mountain through and through—rooted deep, stubborn as granite—her heart beating in time with the ridges. Sometimes I wondered if the Song had brushed her bloodline on its way through the bedrock, left a trace of itself in her bones. Some humans carried that echo, a faint hum of old power, like the mountains had chosen not to forget them. Maeve was one of those rare few who didn't just live in the Blue Ridge; she *belonged* to it.

Henry looked between us, lost but trying. "Uh. I'll start a grid search along the creek?"

"Take Team Two," I told him. "Leashes on the dogs. If you smell anything like pennies in your mouth, pull everybody back and radio me."

He blinked. "Pennies?"

"Just do it. I'll talk to the girlfriend."

Michelle sat on the tailgate of a patrol truck, cupping a paper coffee cup with both hands like it was the last warm thing in the world. She'd dressed for a fantasy of camping, not the teeth of it—all curated pinks to match the highlight reel she'd imagined posting later. Brand-new puffer jacket in bubblegum blush, still creased from being shipped; matching pink knit beanie with a pom-pom perkier than she felt; pink hiking boots without a scratch to prove they'd ever touched dirt. A glittery rose-gold phone peeked from her pocket.

She was the kind of girl the outdoors usually ate for breakfast.

Yesterday's mascara made soft bruises under her eyes, and her lip gloss had cracked at the corners from cold and nerves. She looked like someone who had binge-watched survival shows and thought the forest would applaud her for trying.

But there she was—shaking, lips pressed tight, determined to belong in a place so old it barely noticed she existed.

Butch settled beside my knee with a heavy sigh, one that rumbled through his barrel chest like distant thunder. One enormous paw slid forward as he inched closer to the frightened girl until his shaggy shoulder pressed against her legs. A mop of bangs kept falling into his eyes, forcing him to tip his head just so to size up the world.

He has a policy about frightened humans: Become a wall beside them and let them lean.

Butch had read Michelle's fear the moment she'd seen us and decided she needed a fortress, not space.

"I'm Ranger Lange," I said, keeping my voice low. "Can I sit?" She nodded. I perched on the bumper, boots planted in the mud that had crusted and then broken again with the morning freeze. "Tell me your full name, please."

"Michelle." She swallowed. "Michelle Crane."

"Michelle, I'm going to ask some boring questions. Boring helps us find people." I tipped my chin toward the tent beyond the tape—a glossy showroom number pitched too close to the creek. "Your boyfriend—his name?"

"Darren." Her breath hitched on the second syllable. "Darren Wells."

She hesitated, then the rest spilled out the way panic does when it lacks shape.

"We're...new," she said, fingers tightening around the cup. "Third-date new. We matched online, but I followed his Instagram first. He's got all these pictures—summits, waterfalls, those big panoramic shots where he looks like he's about to conquer the world." She let out a shaky laugh. "He says nature is his 'cathedral,' which sounded kind of cheesy at first, you know? But also...really confident. Like he belongs out here."

Her eyes flicked toward the trees, as if hoping they'd confirm it.

"For our first date, he took me to the climbing gym. I'd never done it before. I pretended I wasn't terrified. He didn't make fun of me, though

—he kept saying I was stronger than I thought. I liked that." Her voice softened. "It was the first time someone saw adventurous potential in me."

I followed her gaze to the tent—brand-new seams glinting, stakes driven shallow.

"The second date," she continued, "he took me to this sporting-goods store. He bought the tent for this trip. Said his old one was too small for two people." She ran her hand through Butch's fur. "He planned everything. The firewood, the trail, the photos we'd take at sunrise. He said he wanted to help me fall in love with the mountains, too."

A tear slipped down her cheek, racing the steam from her coffee.

"And I did," she whispered. "Last night, I did."

Her free hand drifted without thought, fingertips touching the fabric of my sleeve—a small, seeking touch. Like she needed to tether herself to someone who wasn't going to vanish into the pines.

"It was...beautiful," she said, voice dipping into a secret. "We lay out under the stars because he wanted to show me the difference. Not city sky—real sky." Her gaze lifted as if the memory hovered somewhere above the treetops. "We made up constellations. He showed me how to find the ones that were already there. He kept pointing and laughing because I'd guess wrong on purpose just to hear him go on about it all."

Her cheeks warmed, pink rising to match her boots.

"He held my hand," she went on, softer now. "And he told me he liked...how I see things."

Her lashes fluttered as if replaying the moment.

"He said the mountains looked new again because I was looking at them. That my wonder made him remember why he fell in love with this place in the first place."

She let out a tiny, embarrassed laugh.

"He said it's brave, you know? Trying something completely different just because you want to feel alive."

Her smile trembled, hope and sadness blurring together.

"It was the first night I ever slept under anything but a roof. I thought...maybe this could be our thing. Campfires and stars and me being the brave girl he saw when he looked at me."

Michelle blinked, suddenly realizing who she was talking to—a federal uniform, not a girlfriend on speed dial.

"Sorry," she muttered quickly, pulling her hand back like she'd touched a stove. "You don't need to hear all that. I'm just—" Her throat closed around the words. "I'm freaked. High on romance one second, and then...this."

Humans always did this around me—spilled their softest truths before they meant to.

One of the perks of being a dragon? People tell you the things they never say out loud.

Some whispered their fears. Some confessed sins.

And at the Bottle Tree, after two beers and a shot of blackberry moonshine, the entire county treated me like a very patient priest.

"You don't have to apologize," I told her gently. "Your details help me find him."

She nodded, embarrassed but grateful, knuckles whitening around the cup again. Clinging to the warmth the way she'd clung to Darren's hand under a cathedral of stars.

Butch, perceptive as ever, leaned harder into her knee until she steadied her breathing against his solid weight.

"What time did he leave the tent?"

"Five? Maybe a little before. He said he wanted the fog on the water for his camera. He...he takes pictures for his Insta—sorry, that's not important."

"It's useful," I said. "What was he wearing?"

She blinked, trying to pull the memory into focus. "Gray hoodie. Old. He said it was lucky. And the green beanie. The camera strap across his chest. He took the big lens."

"Shoes?"

"Hiking boots. Not new like mine." A guilty glance down at the spotless pink.

"Did he take food? Water?"

"A granola bar. He woke me up with the wrapper. And his metal bottle. He filled it at the spigot last night."

I ran the checklist in my head; my mouth kept the warm, human rhythm. "Any medications? Any health issues I should know about? Asthma, diabetes, allergies?"

"No. He's...he's good." The last word cracked. Butch pressed closer. She let one hand fall to his head and sank into the fur like she might drown there.

Behind us, team two conferred quietly with Henry. Radios crackled. A crow scolded from the pines, then went silent as if it had remembered better.

"What route did he say he'd take?" I asked.

"He pointed at the map on his phone—downstream to the little falls and back. He said it was a loop, just an hour. I didn't go over it again because..." Her shoulders hunched. "Because I didn't want to look stupid. He camps all the time. I don't."

"That's okay." I let the words sit. "Who else knew you were here?"

"Just the barkeep. We stopped by the—what's it called? The Bottle Tree? She told us the chili special and to put our food in the car, not the tent." Michelle's mouth tugged. "I thought she was kidding about the bears."

"She's never kidding about bears," I said. "Or anything with teeth."

A snort from behind us. Maeve nudged a fresh cup into my free hand, then traded Michelle's lukewarm coffee for one hot enough to steam. "Drink. You'll think better." Her eyes shifted back to me.

Maeve squeezed Michelle's shoulder like she was her own stray and drifted a little distance to harass the deputies into taking a pastry.

I stood. "Let's take a quick look at your site. Walk me through the morning."

We moved the twenty yards to the tent—brand-new silnylon glimmering dull blue, guy lines slack. The door flap bore a smear that had oxidized to a brown coin. Blood. Not enough for panic. Enough for attention. I tasted iron, then beneath it that old sweetness like honey warmed on a stove. The Song thrummed at the edge of hearing. *Not now*, I told it. *Later*.

"Try not to touch anything," I said gently, and crouched. The rain fly's dripline had been set too narrow; last night's mist had crept inward, darkening the ground sheet. I could see where a knee had indented the sleeping pad and where the zipper track caught a bit of loose thread—

someone had tugged too hard, half-asleep. Inside, a pink sleeping bag lay open, still faintly warm. The air held the buttery smell of store-new nylon and two different shampoos.

"What time did you wake?" I asked.

"When the zipper stuck. Five-ish? He swore and laughed and kissed my forehead and said don't come out, you'll just fall in the water. I thought he was joking."

I nodded. "You didn't hear anything after that? Voices? An animal?"

She shook her head. "Just...something weird." She hesitated, embarrassed. "It sounded like...someone pretending to purr? Don't write that down."

"I'll write everything down." I smiled to take the sting out of it and jotted a note anyway. Purr—human mimic? The Blue Ridge delights in humiliating certainty.

I circled the site. Tracks layered the damp duff: Darren's heavier boot prints angling downstream, Michelle's small new soles wandering between tent and fire ring. No sign of a second set—no companion, no confrontation. But at the creek's edge the story changed. The pebbles showed a slide where someone had skidded, and on a flat rock a palm print had bloomed in diluted blood—the kind you get when you reach to steady yourself after a scrape.

I breathed in and let the world narrow to scent: wet stone, woodsmoke, the ghost of expensive cologne Darren must've thought would impress a girl who liked pink. And under that, cat musk; not bobcat, not cougar. Something older, rounder in the nose. My tongue touched my teeth. Pennies. Honey.

"Could he have gone into town?" Michelle asked, reading my silence as doubt. "Like—left me? He wouldn't, but—"

"He didn't," I said. "He went toward the creek. We'll follow."

"Is he—" She couldn't spit out *alive*.

"He left under his own power. That's what I see." I tipped my head at the fire ring. It had been built like a photograph: perfect circle, kindling stacked in a neat teepee, new grate unblackened by use. "First time you've built a campfire?"

"I watched a YouTube," she said miserably. "He laughed and rebuilt it. I'm not good at this."

"You don't have to be good at this," I said. "You have to be honest and careful, and you are."

Team two drifted closer with the alert caution of people who've lost more than they've found. Henry hung back, trying not to look at me like I walked on water. His knife flicked open and shut, open and shut, quiet as breathing.

I crouched again, eye level with Michelle. "Did Darren carry a knife?"

"Yes." She glanced instinctively toward Henry as if all pocket knives were related.

"Any alcohol last night?"

"One beer at the Bottle Tree, then we split something he brought— vanilla whiskey? It tasted like melted frosting. It was fabulous."

"Drugs?"

"No."

"Here's what we know," I said, keeping my voice calm and clipped, the way humans need when panic is chewing holes in their logic. "We've got a capable hiker who left before dawn and didn't come back when he said he would. There's blood on the tent flap and more by the waterline, but no signs of a struggle—no torn fabric, no drag marks, no prints."

Michelle's grip tightened on the coffee cup. I didn't sugarcoat it.

"And after last night's panther sighting on Blackdog," I added, "we're not waiting around to see if this turns into something worse. There are things in these woods that don't give warnings."

Her breath hitched.

"Okay." I straightened. "Here's what happens next. Search teams will sweep downstream in a grid—dogs leashed. You'll go with Maeve, because she'll feed you and that's an order, and you'll answer your phone if I call. Don't wander off to 'help.' Don't follow the creek. Don't post anything online—not a word about what you heard."

Her eyes darted. "Because of the panther?"

"Because of people," I said. "Stories attract them."

Maeve reappeared like she'd been summoned by the word *feed*, tucking a scarf around Michelle's throat with a practiced snap. "You heard the ranger. Back to the Bottle Tree with me. We'll get you a stool in the kitchen where the world can't see your shaking."

"I should stay—"

"You'll be no good to him if you faint," Maeve said, not unkindly. She turned her attention to me. "Blackdog's got a kink in her this week. Creek's been speaking sideways. Watch your footing."

"I always do," I said, which was a lie humans like to hear.

Maeve squeezed my arm, eyes narrowing the way they do when she smells rain. "I'll be at the Tree if the mountain wants to talk through an old woman later. Seems to like doing that." She jerked her chin at Michelle. "Come on, sugar. Let Mama be useful."

They moved off together, flannel and pink, the absurd and the mundane in one frame. Butch watched them go then looked up at me, beard damp, patience gone.

"Alright," I told him and the waiting trees. "Let's read what the creek wrote."

Behind me, Henry barked orders he must have learned from someone else's mouth. Radios answered. Leashes clipped. The Song stood up inside my bones like a tall dog sensing thunder.

We stepped into the brush. The mountains listened. And somewhere ahead, a cat who wore a woman's body lifted her head and smiled.

Hunger Talks Softly (Wampus)

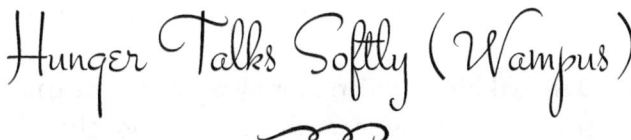

He was soft when he slept.

Soft like the under-haunches of deer I once devoured whole. Soft like the bellies of kits I curled my body around in winter to keep alive.

Not prey, I thought. *Not anymore.*

But the hunger didn't see differences so easily.

Hunger only knew two truths: chase and claim.

The pulse-quick spark of the hunt.

The slow, molten pull of the mate.

One urged my claws forward—tear, take, devour.

The other softened me—press close, taste warmth, breathe his name into skin.

Both lived in my blood like twin stars dragging each other into orbit.

The Hallow had carved instincts into every bone. Stalk what fascinates. Keep what sings. Destroy what threatens.

I could feel him in the air—his heat, his scent—curling around my ribs like vines searching for places to root. The ache said I wanted him under my teeth. The ache said I wanted him under my heart.

It was confusing, this living thing my longing had become.

But one thing was certain.

He was no longer something to kill.

He was something to keep.

Savor.

The air in my den was as cold as the first breath after snowmelt, but he steamed gently under the weight of the wool blanket I'd dragged down here for him. A gift from a campsite three ridges over. Their scent had faded by now—just pine, damp stone, and the coppery sweetness of his blood.

Blood had slicked his shoulder. Not by my claws. *He* had stumbled on the river rocks, scrambling from the dark he thought would never catch him.

I had caught him.

My den wasn't much to human eyes—just cavern and crevice and the shine of minerals weeping from the walls. But to me it was everything. A crack in the mountains' bones where water ran singing through a channel of black stone. Cold pools sprawled beneath ferns that had never known sunlight. The air held secrets left here by the Hallow long before men grew teeth.

Scattered among all that ancientness were my treasures: a silver lighter etched with a map of stars; a fox-fur glove with one finger missing; buttons the size of coins, red as heart-meat; a leather wallet long since emptied. Humans dropped so many shiny things without understanding the stories clinging to them—loss and laughter and the last warm touch of the hand that held them. I kept those stories. I made a home from them.

I licked my fingers clean of his blood—slowly, one knuckle at a time. The taste shivered through me: salt and iron, wild and reckless.

My tail tapped a restless rhythm against the cavern floor, giving away what I pretended I could control. My skin shimmered beneath fur where it existed. Patches of woman, patches of mountain-lion, stitched together by a hunger the Hallow had never taught me to name.

I leaned in, close enough to feel the whisper of his breath against my cheek. My free hand hovered above his face, not quite touching— tracing the air where his jawline cut its clean line, following the pulse at his throat. My fingers ached to know the warmth beneath, to press gently.

But I stopped just shy of contact.

I pressed the blood-wet fingers to my lips again, one by one, letting the warmth fade into me as if that could quiet the pounding in my ribs.

Protect.

Don't ruin.

Hold.

Don't tear.

That was the war inside me—every breath a decision not to claim him the way my instincts demanded.

I curled back, letting only my forehead rest near his shoulder, close enough to feel the steady rise and fall that stoked my yearning.

He was safe.

He was here.

He was not prey.

Not yet.

The Hallow had scarred me into this shape.

Moonlight never quite reached my cave, but my eyes saw as if it did: every drop trembling on the ceiling, every pulse beneath his skin.

He was beautiful in the fragile way of humans. Rough beard shadow, wind-chapped lips parted around a dream. His lashes—a darker gold than the leaves that curled outside in fall—fluttered as if he might wake.

I leaned close, breathing him in.

His scent clung to me from the hunt—fear, yes, but also that fire they carry inside, that *want* to belong to the world even as it tries to swallow them. He had looked at the night sky the way I once did.

During the hunt, I had stalked the edge of their clearing like breath held too long. Mist had clung to my fur, and the first spider thread of moonlight had revealed me to him before I meant it to. He'd looked up —eyes wide, startled—and I had felt that look like a hand pressed against my ribs.

That hunger.

That wonder.

He saw me.

Even in the dark.

When he slipped from the tent at dawn—camera in hand, boots softened for this earth—I followed. His steps were clumsy but hopeful, and hope made men loud. A twig snapped beneath him. He swore. And in the shadowed hush between one heartbeat and the next, I leapt.

He fought, wild and virile, like prey trying to be predator. A claw—my claw—caught the meat of his forearm before I could pull back. He gasped, stumbled, skull striking stone. The moment his eyes rolled back, I gathered him in my arms as gently as a creature made of teeth could.

Now he lay before me, chest rising slow and steady.

"I didn't mean to frighten you," I murmured.

My voice came out broken—raw edges and purr-rumble—like I was still learning what lips were for.

I brushed a leaf from his hair.

"You were supposed to see me," I whispered.

Outside the cave, water rushed over stones worn sharp by time, and somewhere above, ravens quarreled. The mountain was waking. But in my den, only we existed. Only his scent. Only the ache gnawing under my ribs.

Keep him.

Claim him.

He is yours.

I hissed softly, shaking my head as if that could clear it. The Hallow's music still clung to my bones, too loud sometimes, too persuasive.

It had given me form.

It had given me name.

It always wanted more.

I dipped a strip of moss into the pool and pressed it against his wound. He flinched, breath hitching, but didn't wake. Warmth radiated from him—human warmth, fire-warmth—and I tasted the edge of it on my tongue. It tingled like the last spark before kindling bursts to flame.

"You'll heal," I whispered. "You're not like them. You see."

My gaze slipped past him, toward the far curve of the cavern where shadows piled into thicker darkness. The bones were there—stacked with care, ribcages nested like cathedral arches, femurs aligned in tidy rows. Skulls crowned the top, their hollow eyes fixed upward as if still seeking stars they once hoped loved them back.

They had been beautiful too, once.

Mine. Not victims, never prey. Each one believed they had found something sacred in the dark, a story worth dying for. They came with torches and questions and the trembling awe of the devout. I let them. Their words warmed the cave for a while. Their hearts kept time with mine, until hunger retook the measure.

Love first.

Then teeth.

I remember their cries—the way it echoed through the caverns like wind through hollow stone. I remember their hands, the brave ones who touched me as if I were a woman and not the warning whispered in their fireside tales. I remember each name until it burned away.

Some still wore bits of themselves—braided bracelets, buttons sewn by waiting hands, rings that promised forever. I kept those tokens. Arranged them in little shrines, bone altars to the warmth I could never hold long enough.

Then the world went quiet.

The mountain sealed.

And I slept.

A deep, dream-bound sleep where centuries tangled like roots. I dreamt of rivers turning to veins, of the forest forgetting my shape, of silence pressing against me until even my hunger dulled.

Until now.

Something called me back.

Not in words but in resonance—a low, living hum that trembled through stone and marrow. A sound older than fear, older than faith. It spoke my name in the language the world used before speech.

Wampus.

The mountain's breath. The forest's grief. The echo of every warning ever whispered.

I don't know why I am awake again. Only that the air trembles with that old song, and it feels like memory made sound.

My tail curled tighter around my thigh, need and hunger twisting together. I had promised myself I would not add another.

And yet—

He breathed.

He dreamed.

He glowed like a living ember against all this cold stone.

My fingers curled around his arm just to anchor myself.

"You see the world like I used to," I murmured. "Before hunger made everything look like meat."

The ache inside me throbbed—wanting warmth, wanting closeness, wanting *him*—in ways I wasn't sure the Hallow meant when it shaped me into this half-thing.

I lowered my head, lips brushing the air above his heart.

"I'll keep you safe," I vowed.

From hunters.

From the Hallow.

From myself... if I could.

But the hunger purred a different promise.

Another purr-growl pitched low in my throat.

"You looked at the sky."

His lips parted. I leaned closer, nearly brushing mine against his. The desire to taste his breath burned through me, primal and foolish.

But his heartbeat—steady, trusting—pulled me back.

I curled around him instead, limbs careful, tail protective, my body shaping a shelter against the cold. His skin against my fur sent shivers like electricity along every nerve. I rested my cheek to his shoulder, eyes half-closed, imagining that his warmth might be enough to keep the Hallow quiet inside me.

He sighed in his sleep, head tilting toward mine.

Yes.

He was mine now.

Not prey.

Not passing curiosity.

Mine from the moment he lifted his gaze and saw the magic that refused to die.

Something pricked my ear—faraway footsteps, a dog barking sharp once, twice. They were searching. The Song fluttered against my ribs like a warning wing.

I pulled the blanket higher over him and bared my teeth toward the cave mouth.

"They won't take you," I promised the dark. "I will not give you back."

The hunger stroked its claws through my chest, pleased.

He was alive.

He was here.

And I was not alone anymore.

His eyelids fluttered.

Not fully waking, just floating up through the layers of dark like a diver remembering the surface exists. His breath hitched, and the shape of a name scraped across his tongue.

"Michelle...?"

The sound pierced me, a thorn of jealousy quick and deep. Of course he would call for her first. She was warm and simple and human. She fit the world he thought he still lived in.

I lowered myself beside him, close but not touching. My voice softened to velvet and fog.

"She is far away," I murmured. "You are safe. Kept."

His gaze drifted toward me, pupils enormous, searching for a shape he understood. I let the cave's dim light kiss only pieces of me—a cheekbone, the curve of a shoulder, the gold glint of an eye. Beautiful enough to trust, dangerous enough to follow.

"Don't be afraid," I said, letting my breath brush his ear like a secret. "The world above is full of teeth that smile. I am the dark that keeps those teeth from you. Rest in my dream."

His confusion melted into fascination the way prey sometimes falls in love with the predator just before the end. But this wasn't ending. This was beginning.

He lifted a trembling hand to my cheek.

"Are you... real?" he whispered.

I nuzzled into his palm—catlike, claiming—letting him feel the softness of fur that faded into skin beneath his thumb.

My purr answered him.

His breath slowed, his heartbeat syncing unconsciously to the rhythm of mine—a pulse older than spoken language. A rhythm the Hallow had carved into all living things before men pretended they owned the earth.

The Song curled through the cavern, low and seductive—a purr of the mountain. He shivered as it brushed his spine.

"Are you a dream?" he breathed, the fear shrinking into wonder.

"A dream. A thought come to life. Perhaps a nightmare. You can choose," I answered.

I traced a single claw—blunted, gentle—along his jaw, then over his collarbone, following the map of his warmth without breaking skin. He leaned into the touch, eyes hazy, every instinct surrendering to the pull of mine.

"Sleep," I coaxed, wrapping myself around him like a promise. "Heal. Stay."

His lashes lowered. His body relaxed fully into mine.

One soft, trusting exhale against my throat.

Yes.

He chose warmth over fear.

Curiosity over flight.

Me over everything else.

I buried my nose in his hair, breathing him deep, and let the hunger purr its satisfaction.

"He is mine now," I whispered into the dark.

A vow.

A warning.

A prayer.

His eyes opened.

Fully.

Clear.

Not confusion this time but recognition.

Not fear but curiosity.

"I'm dreaming," he breathed again, but now the words sounded like gratitude.

I felt his gaze take me in—the fur along my spine, the curves where woman lived in my shape, the gold light in my eyes the Hallow refused to dim. His hand rose, slow and willing, and I let him place his palm against my ribs.

Warmth.

Not the warmth of prey trying to appear brave.

Not the warmth of someone bargaining with death.

Warmth that chose me.

He traced the line of my side—reverent, almost trembling—and the touch left a trail of molten wanting. I inhaled sharply, a sound too human to be a purr and too wild to be a sigh.

"You..." He swallowed, voice roughening. "You're beautiful."

A word once thrown at me like bait.

Like something to trap with admiration and tame with desire.

But from his lips it felt like truth.

The Hallow Song stirred beneath the mountain. A low thrumming pulse, a heartbeat so old it taught the first stars how to shine. It rose from the stone into my bones, urging:

Yes. Yes. YES. Create. Become.

His fingers skimmed up, brushing the place where shoulder became throat. My body answered him—arching into the heat of his hand, breath catching, hunger sharpening into something that tasted like worship.

The Song threaded itself into his pulse, too. I felt it.

The moment instinct and will aligned.

He leaned in, *meeting* me.

A vow made in motion alone.

Our bodies aligned—chest to chest, breath to breath. And the cavern brightened with a soft unearthly glow, as if the minerals themselves had caught fire. His lips hovered inches from mine. He waited.

Consent.

Choice.

A miracle.

I cupped his jaw gently, my claws retracting, and brushed my mouth to his. A kiss like the first spark in a long-sealed cave. A kiss that tasted of salt and dawn and a future pulling taut.

The Song rose.

It curled around us like a living curtain of light, blue-white and gold. The same magic that once carved wonder-creatures from riverbeds and let trees walk before their ability faded to memory. It thrummed through his veins, through mine, through every root reaching for the morning above us.

My tail wrapped his thigh.

His fingers slid into my hair and held.

The Hallow's heartbeat matched our rhythm; ancient, commanding.

I gasped against his lips, overwhelmed by belonging.

He saw me as something worth touching. Worth wanting.

The Song swelled to a crescendo—stone trembling under us, water rippling outward like a blessing.

We broke apart only when breath demanded it. Foreheads resting together. Sharing the same air as if we were learning to breathe for the first time.

His whisper was a vow.

My voice came out low, fierce, sacred:

"You are mine now."

And the mountain—the ancient Hallow Song itself—agreed.

The Blood Trail (Lyra)

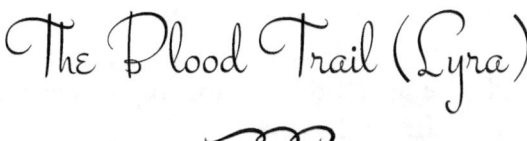

Rain eased into a mist—the kind that clung to skin and slipped beneath collars like a whispered dare. The woods along Blackdog Road were a cathedral of old trees, their moss-veiled branches bending low as if to eavesdrop on our progress. The mountains breathed around us, slow and ancient, paying attention.

I let my gaze sweep the ground in front of us.

The dirt path wasn't a path so much as a conversation—every footprint, every crushed blade of grass a sentence waiting to be parsed.

Deep-press boot tracks, a day old—two hikers moving in rhythm, close together. One set lighter, heels reluctant.

The other: confident stride, longer gait, cutting slightly upslope where the ridge tempted them with views.

A streak of white scat near the edge told me a red fox had breakfasted well—songbird feathers clung to the leavings. A groundhog's waddling prints crossed the path at a goofy angle, and the delicate arrow-marks of a wild turkey parade trailed toward a patch of disturbed leaf litter.

Life thriving.

Normal.

Comfortingly mortal.

Butch nosed a fresh set of marks near a tangle of roots. Tiny holes punched into the dark soil—claws from a gray squirrel on a frantic descent. And there, half-hidden beneath a fallen limb, the neat, small entrance to a fox den—fur lining the packed interior, warm with promise. Kits nested inside. That softness tugged at something ancient in me.

A pair of coyote tracks veered off into brush too dense for humans but inviting to predators; their pads pressed deep, the back-toe spread speaking of speed. The Blue Ridge was an ecosystem woven tight, every creature knowing its place in the web.

Humans were the only ones who pretended the rules didn't apply to them.

But the mountains always remembered the balance.

These woods held every ordinary fear a hiker could name: bears, bobcats, coyotes, venom and teeth.

Predators with territories and rhythms and limits.

They also held the other fears; the ones hikers only whispered about under zipped tents.

The kind they laughed at to keep their hands from shaking.

Stories spun so the monsters might stay politely imaginary.

And yet...the laughable felt close now.

Breathing.

Watching.

The air ahead felt hollowed-out, like breath sucked from a room.

Like a chord in the Hallow Song that had been plucked too hard or too deep.

The last few yards of forest had gone unnaturally quiet—every fox, owl, and squirrel holding still in agreement:

This wasn't their hunt anymore.

I rose slowly, mist dripping from my lashes. The mountain didn't want to scare me. She wanted me alert.

"Something's off," I murmured, and Butch's ears flicked in agreement.

Henry looked around, seeing only trees, mud, and fog.

He didn't yet know how to read the heartbeat beneath all that.

But I did.

Butch ranged ahead, nose deep to the earth.

The herding dog in him tracked with disciplined precision—methodical sweeps, shoulders rolling low, paws silent despite his size.

His tail was low, not wagging. Alert, uneasy.

I didn't need scales to read him.

Butch didn't spook easily.

When he did, something worse than a predator was near.

Henry trudged behind me, kicking damp leaves with the enthusiasm of a man seriously wronged by breakfast.

"We're the only idiots still out here," he muttered. "Team One's already back at the Bottle Tree, inhaling biscuits. Team Two's warming their toes. Meanwhile, we're in the woods chasing what? A bobcat with a gym membership?"

I let the corner of my mouth tick up. "Professionalism looks good on you, Henry. Very stoic. Very ranger-y."

His eyes narrowed. "Stoic would be easier with a sandwich."

"You just had a donut."

"That was a starter donut."

Butch's grunt cut our bickering short. He froze, hackles bristling, then dropped his nose to a clump of ferns beside a slick boulder streaked with rainwater. A deep rumble built low in his chest.

Henry and I converged. The world quieted for a breath.

A fabric scrap clung to the rock's edge, pinned by a blackberry thorn. Frayed. Damp. Gray cotton.

"Is that—?" Henry knelt, squinting. "Didn't Michelle say that Darren was wearing a gray sweatshirt?"

"She did," I said, already scanning the brush-line.

A smear of rust-dark blood marred the rock—not much, but enough to say someone stumbled here. Fell? Fought?

The trees creaked overhead, shifting weight like giants listening for the next beat of our story.

Henry stood, shoulders stiffening. "Okay, so this is where he got hurt. Trail's cold now, though. Water's washing away the rest."

Butch disagreed. His snarl warped into a low, focused whine. His paw pressed into the soft ground, claws sifting the mulch. When he lifted it, the earth held a crescent-shaped indent.

I crouched beside him.

"Good boy," I murmured, brushing a hand over his thick fur. He leaned into the touch—a guardian stone disguised as a dog.

Henry angled his flashlight. "Prints?"

"Something like that." I traced the shape with a gloved finger. Too wide for a bobcat. Too narrow for a cougar. Heel-heavy—like something balancing between two worlds.

The mountains hummed beneath my boots. A slow, rising chord from the Hallow Song—curious, cautious.

The Blue Ridge wasn't afraid of much.

But she paid attention when something moved inside her skin.

Henry stood straighter, trying for calm and landing closer to nervous humor.

"Could be a bear," he offered.

"Sure," I said. "A three-toed bear who wears gray sweatshirts."

He grimaced. "I hate when you get cryptic."

"Only when reality does," I said.

Rain pattered softly against the leaves—a thousand tiny feet tapping a warning on the roof of the world. In that moment, the forest didn't feel like a place we were walking through.

It felt like a living thing watching us pass.

Judging if we were worthy to stay.

Butch suddenly surged forward, following a thread only he could sense.

I rose, every part of me—scales and skin—poised.

"Come on, Best Sidekick. Gotta earn the title on your mug."

Henry groaned but followed.

The trail pitched sharply upward, the earth turning slick with black loam and exposed roots that grasped at boots like hands. Rainwater sheeted down the incline, carving quick, hungry rivulets that tried to steal our footing.

Henry slipped once, caught himself on a sapling, and muttered something unflattering about nature.

"Careful," I said, stepping past him with the practiced ease of someone gravity rarely argues with. "The mountain doesn't like show-offs. Take it slow."

"You literally ran up a rock face last week," he huffed.

"That rock face liked me."

He gave me a *you can't be serious* look.

Butch had no patience for our banter. He lunged ahead, muscles knotting.

"Hold up—" Henry braced his heels, mud spraying.

"The public will love the tribute mug," I said lightly. "Best Sidekick: Went Out Doing His Best."

He groaned, but it shook off a sliver of fear.

Butch stopped suddenly at a patch of disturbed earth. The prints there were clearer—deeper, newer.

I knelt.

A cougar pad. Broad. Perfectly formed.

Then inches away, a second impression. Narrow. Heel-shaped.

Human.

The spacing between told a story: one creature becoming another mid-stride.

"Henry," I murmured.

He leaned closer, squinting. "That...is not how animals work."

He shined his flashlight further upslope, and the prints simply stopped. No scramble marks. No leap.

Just vanished.

Like a ghost took one last step and remembered it had wings.

Henry swallowed hard. "Maybe we should radio Team One. You know, backup. Guns. People who don't think gravity is optional."

I rose slowly, letting the Hallow's hum settle into my bones, the terrain speaking in its old language.

The ridge above us narrowed and twisted like a spine.

Trees leaned downhill, roots exposed. A sign the mountain had shifted here before, violently.

The air felt stretched thin, like something large had passed through recently, dragging its hunger behind it.

I could taste Henry's fear in the air.

And beneath that, the Hallow's pulse.

Something powerful moving, awakened.

"I get it," I said softly. "This feels wrong."

"So we go back?" he asked hopefully.

"If you were alone, yes."

"But I'm not alone." He exhaled, a shaky breath he probably didn't realize he was holding.

I glanced over my shoulder with a dry smile. "Never ignore the danger. Just walk into it smarter."

He groaned. "Of course we don't turn around."

"You're learning," I said, and this time it wasn't a tease. It was approval.

We climbed, breath and rain threading the branches overhead into a muted rhythm. Henry scanned the ground like he expected it to answer him, flashlight beam jumping in nervous arcs. Butch pressed on with steady purpose, fur slicked to muscle, every step saying *follow me* or *don't. Your choice.*

For him, the world was scents and instincts.

For me, the world was music.

A sudden metallic tang hit the back of my tongue. Sharp, like biting down on a penny.

I stopped so abruptly Henry nearly collided with me.

"What?" he whispered.

"Don't move."

The mountainside hummed—no wind, no birdsong—just a low thrumming beneath the soil. The Hallow Song wasn't background anymore; it was rising to the surface, close enough to brush against my skin like static before a storm. Heat rolled up my spine in a wave of memory, molten and uninvited. Taren's hands had once gripped my hips as if they were the first earth he ever claimed, our bodies lit from within by gold and blue fire under the mountains' ribs. I'd felt steam curl from skin that didn't always stay skin—scales threatening to break through when pleasure blurred the line between our forms. His mouth had spoken my name like he'd just invented the sound and the Hallow answered through us, a blaze of creation demanding tribute. I remembered light tearing upward—magic exploding from us like sparks from a struck anvil—seeding life into the world where it was not meant to run free.

My pulse tripped over itself as the Song now brushed my nerves, testing them. Human lungs pulled shallow breaths, too narrow, too slow; dragon heat coiled beneath them, ready to unfurl wings that currently had nowhere to go. The Blue Ridge breathed hard around me —mud clutching my boots, roots shifting underfoot, the sky pressing low and urgent.

The Hallow remembered.

The Hallow recognized its offspring.

Henry spoke softly, trying too hard not to panic. "Uh...Lange?"

I blinked back into flesh and rain. "Something woke up. Changed. Recently."

"You say that like it's a...common occurrence."

"It isn't," I said. "That's the problem."

He swallowed so loudly even Butch flicked an ear.

Our dog-guide dipped his head toward a narrow gap between two boulders, sniffing deep, then let out a growl low enough to vibrate through my bones. The print trail ended here.

No scat.

No tracks.

No drag marks.

Just absence.

The forest watched us, old eyes behind every leaf.

Henry pointed his flashlight into the dark opening. "Cave?"

Butch whined, hackles razor-straight.

I crouched, touching fingertips to the mud. A tiny rivulet of water gleamed coppery under my skin. Blood diluted and older magic beneath it. Not Taren's flame-scorch. Not my smoke-song.

Wilder. Feral. Half-born.

The first time we created something in the Age of Making, Taren and I hadn't known better. We thought love was enough of a guardrail. We thought the Hallow would stay contained in our pleasure and our light.

We were children with a wildfire.

"You okay?" Henry asked. His voice was a frayed thread.

I forced my shoulders loose. "Fine."

Lie.

My pulse was scaling up, a slow slip from human rhythm to dragon tempo. Heat shimmered beneath my skin like embers remembering what they were for. The part of me bound to this mountain didn't want to remain folded away anymore.

It wanted to hunt.

I scanned the trees again. My senses sharpened, color deepening into near-glow, every sound outlined with surgical clarity: rain ticking on oak leaves, a vole tunneling beneath moss, and Henry's heart beating just a little too fast. But beneath all that ordinary life something vast and cunning exhaled—like the mountain itself had just remembered a predator it once tried to forget.

The Hallow Song struck a single, reverberating note.

Not a warning. A summons.

Unleash her, it urged through root and stone.

Let what you made run free. Let hunger make the world new again.

Heat flared beneath my ribs, scales prickling to break skin. For a breath too long, I almost wanted it. The wildness, the freedom, the fire without fences. Instinct whispered how sweet it would feel to stop holding back, to stop caring what burned.

I clenched my jaw against the pull.

"No," I whispered. "Not again."

Henry blinked at me. "Did you just...tell the mountain no?"

"Sometimes we disagree," I said, voice rough.

"And does it...uh...usually listen?"

"It doesn't have to," I replied. "I do. It's complicated." I rubbed the taste of pennies off my tongue. "And a bit theoretical."

He stared. "Awesome. Just what I needed. Theoretical geology with intimidation."

Butch's growl snapped deeper. His stance widened, guarding us from the dark ahead.

Henry lifted his radio. "Maybe we should—"

"It's close," I interrupted.

Henry froze. "It?"

"The thing that found Darren."

"And...maybe took him?"

"And maybe worse."

He paled. "Is worse an official ranger term?"

"In my vocabulary."

For a heartbeat, none of us moved.

Then I took a step toward the gap in the rocks.

"Lyra—"

I turned back to him, voice low but sure. "Find higher ground. Call Maeve."

His throat bobbed. "And you?"

"I'll see what's hiding between the teeth of this mountain."

Henry hesitated—wanting to stand his ground, wanting to be brave, and hating that fear still lived in the seams of his youth. The mist clung to his freckles, rain matting the curls he kept pushing out of his eyes. He looked so *mortal* in that moment. So breakable.

Humans didn't belong in the hunger of the wild.

That's why dragons stayed.

To keep the monsters where they belonged. *Beneath.*

"Just don't die," he said, trying for humor and landing closer to plea.

"I'll do my best," I promised. "You, too."

Butch pressed against Henry's leg, nudging him backward like a shepherd herding a particularly clueless sheep. Henry got the message.

I waited until they were moving away, then faced the dark alone.

The Hallow Song swelled once more—a summons.

My scales prickled under my skin, ready to tear free if needed.

A promise older than roads and rangers and the fragile men who wandered into my care.

With one deep breath, I stepped into the mountain's mouth.

The world swallowed the light behind me.

And the hunt began.

Predator's Prayer (Wampus)

The forest breathed around me, a slow and secret rhythm I had always known.

Above it all, I crouched—one shadow folded among many—perched on a limb so high the mist curled below like smoke. My claws pressed into bark, tasting its slow sap heartbeat. Beneath, men moved with the graceless caution of prey that believed itself clever.

They thought the woods belonged to them.

I watched their metal traps glint in the damp afternoon light, their boot prints sinking deep where the moss could not protest. They called themselves *hunters*, but the snares did their work for them. No teeth. No chase. No prayer. Only wire and waiting.

I despised snares.

The things that killed without ceremony, without the recognition of the life they end—those were the true monsters. A snare did not taste the fear of what it held. It did not listen to the last breath. It simply strangled and forgot.

Below, one of them laughed. A sharp, careless sound that sent the deer scattering. The forest flinched.

I shifted my weight, silent as wind over bone. Muscles rolled beneath fur and skin. The tree accepted my movement with a whisper of leaves. From up here, I could see every secret path the hunters missed. The soft ruts where foxes crossed, the narrow trails deer carved over generations, the hollow logs that slept like old gods.

The mountain had always hidden me well. My cave even more so. Its mouth lay buried beneath stone and vine, the entrance marked only by silence. No one had found it, not even the curious ones who claimed to love the wild. They came close sometimes—too close—but the mountain protected its own.

The man I had taken slept there still, wrapped in darkness and the faint glow of his ember-breath. He was safe. My *prize*.

He wouldn't wake yet, nor escape. The paths leading to that hollow twisted like veins.

So I watched.

These woods were not a place for mercy. They were my cathedral, my confessional. Each dawn began with a prayer to the quiet—the unspoken vow that if I must feed again, I would at least remember the faces of those who bled for me. The snares remembered nothing.

I exhaled once, low and deliberate, feeling the weight of the forest gather in my chest. Then I loosed it.

The cry ripped through me like a first breath on flame. It began as a vibration in my ribs then grew, clawing up my throat, until it tore free in a sound that split the morning clean in two. It was not human. It was not beast. It was *mine*—a sound the mountains had not heard in centuries, sharp enough to wake the stones.

The forest answered with panic. Birds erupted from the branches in black floods. The hunters froze, eyes wide, before stumbling back, shouting over each other. One dropped his rifle; another swung it up, trembling, trying to find a target that was everywhere at once.

Their fear thrilled me. It was honest.

I moved before they could remember how to breathe. Muscles coiled, tail lashing, I sprang from one branch to the next—each landing silent as falling ash. The air burned cold against my face, the scent of metal and panic blooming below like blood in water.

Gunfire cracked—bright, stupid noise. Splinters bit my cheek, but it only made the pulse in my throat quicken. Adrenaline roared through me, ancient and clean. They fired into the trees, into shadows, into the myth they had just met.

Fools.

They thought themselves hunters.

I laughed—a rasping, feral sound that made even the wind recoil—and dropped lower through the canopy. They split apart, just as I knew they would. The young one broke right, stumbling toward the deeper thickets where the light died early.

Perfect.

I tracked him from above, his every step ringing like a heartbeat in the loam. His breath came sharp, clouding the air. He looked up once, wide-eyed, and for a flicker of a moment I saw reflected in his gaze what the old stories had rightfully called *Wampus*: the forest's judgment made flesh.

Then I leapt.

The world blurred—branches snapping, air roaring past my ears, the scent of sap and panic blooming upward to meet me. The impact was thunder through my bones. We hit the ground hard, the breath exploding from his lungs in a startled cry that never fully became a scream. I landed astride him, knees sinking into the damp earth on either side of his ribs. His body jerked beneath mine, a tremor of instinct, of refusal to die quietly.

For a heartbeat, neither of us moved. The forest held its breath.

Then he tried to fight.

His hands struck at my arms, his boots dug into the soil, but his strength was the frantic flutter of a bird in the jaws of something much older. His eyes—wild and wet—searched my face for mercy that wasn't there. I studied him the way I once studied the stars, memorizing every line of fear that crossed his features: the disbelief first, then comprehension, then the desperate hope that he might still wake from this.

The scent of him rose thick and sweet—iron and salt and terror—curling into my nostrils like incense. It woke something deep in me that had slept too long, the primal hunger that remembered joy only through the act of ending. My tail twitched, slow and satisfied.

He turned his head, as if to look anywhere but at me. I let him. My hand slid down the front of his vest, feeling the quicksilver flutter of his pulse beneath the fabric.

"Easy," I murmured, though the word came out like a growl.

With a flick of my wrist, claws extended—five curved blades that caught what little light filtered through the canopy. I drew them downward. The synthetic fabric parted like fruit skin, scattering bright threads and orange panels into the undergrowth. It looked almost festive—the forest floor littered with the confetti of his disguise. Bright scraps fluttered, then died against the wet leaves.

He gasped, clutching at the torn edges, but I pinned his wrists easily. His heart hammered against my thighs, against the weight of me. I could feel each beat echoing through my own chest, two rhythms briefly aligned.

So small, I thought. *So impossibly alive.*

His lips formed a soundless plea. I leaned close, close enough to see my reflection in his pupils—slitted and wrong—and breathed in his fear until it steadied me.

The forest watched. The air thickened.

A tremor of delight rippled through me. Not for the kill but for the reminder of what I was. The mountain's hunger. The silence given voice.

He struggled once more, weaker now. My claws pierced deliberately at his throat.

Above us, the birds had gone quiet again. Even the wind had stopped to listen.

A feast for the waking that was my hunger.

His pulse stilled beneath my grip when the wind changed.

It slipped cold across my cheek, scattering the scent of blood with something sharper—smoke, ash, and the clean edge of a storm. I froze, nostrils flaring. The forest bent around it, wary.

This was no human trail.

It carried memory. Power.

And something uncomfortably like *me*.

I drew in another breath, tasting the shift on my tongue. Beneath the copper of fear and the musk of men lay the faint metallic hum of scales, the heat of forge-fire sealed beneath flesh. My pupils narrowed to razors.

Farther down the mountain, beneath the line of mist, a figure moved through the fog.

The air around her shimmered faintly, bending light the way heat bends distance. She walked as though the forest recognized her—didn't dare resist, didn't dare breathe. Every motion deliberate. Every pause weighted with knowing.

I crouched lower over the boy, instincts splitting—one voice urging *devour*, another whispering *run*.

The second won.

I rose in a single movement, leaving him draped against the earth. His vest caught in my claws as I withdrew, tearing another bright scrap into the air. I didn't look back. The forest could have him. My hunger could wait.

With a bound I was up the trunk, claws sinking into bark slick with moss. The ascent was effortless—muscle and memory, predator returning to height. The canopy swallowed me whole.

From limb to limb I traveled, each landing a whisper above the chaos below. The hunters' shouts rang hollow now; they were no longer the axis of my attention. The forest narrowed to a single pulse. *Hers.*

She moved with purpose far beneath me, and yet I felt her presence in the marrow of the trees.

Every breath she drew stirred an echo in my chest, like a note I had once known and forgotten.

Smoke. Ash. Frost.

Old elements. Old gods.

When I found her through the parting fog, she was standing still—head lifted, eyes like molten amber catching the faintest trace of my scent. The sight struck something ancient and disquieting within me.

Recognition.

She should have been a stranger, yet the shape of her stance, the tilt of her head—it was as though I were watching a reflection distorted by centuries. Something in her bones spoke the same language as mine.

A memory flickered at the edge of thought: heat, roaring wings, a scream swallowed by fire. Creation and undoing braided together.

I didn't know why she felt familiar, only that she *was*.

The forest held its breath again. I pressed myself flat against the limb, heart pounding not from hunger now but from the uncanny certainty that the thing walking below was a part of the story I had forgotten...

A shard of the same broken godhood that had made me.

She was moving toward my mountain.

Toward him.

Toward my truth buried in stone.

And I couldn't let her find it.

A low growl rippled from my throat before I could swallow it.

Dragons were ruin given shape. The world had nearly forgotten them, but I was remembering. I had felt their shadow once—centuries past, when the first fires came and the rivers ran with melted stone. I had buried myself deep then, in the cooling dark, listening to their wings beat against the sky until silence fell again.

And now one walked in daylight on two legs.

I stayed hidden among the branches, the forest's shadow wrapped around me. The mountain held its breath. She was below the mist, a pale shimmer moving between the trees, and I watched.

The sun climbed, burned through the fog, then began its slow descent. Hours passed in measured silence. I didn't shift, didn't blink for long stretches; the forest changed around me instead. Bees grew drowsy in their hives. The air thickened with heat and resin. Even the moss smelled sun-tired.

Time softened at the edges. A hawk screamed once, circling, then vanished toward the west. The dragon woman moved like a current beneath the leaves—hunting, listening, never rushing. I tracked her as the light tilted toward amber.

When the first tremors of panic reached my ears, I knew the men were near. Voices—human, high and ragged—broke the stillness. The forest recoiled from their noise.

I shifted my weight along the branch, muscles tightening, and peered through the leaves.

They stumbled into the clearing below, wild-eyed and panting.

Their orange vests were torn, their rifles clutched like relics. Fear had stripped away their arrogance; they smelled of it—raw, acidic, human.

Then she stepped from the fog.

The dragon woman.

She moved with a grace that quieted the forest, her boots barely disturbing the moss. Even the birds, frantic moments before, fell still to watch her. The men froze as if salvation itself had materialized.

"Easy," she said. Her voice carried, low and steady, the kind of command that makes the wild obey. "Tell me what happened."

The oldest spoke first, words tumbling over themselves. "It—it came out of the trees! Fast—faster than anything—claws, I swear to God, *huge claws!*"

The other nodded violently. "Took him—Tommy! My younger brother's gone! We found blood—"

She didn't flinch. "Another victim." Her golden eyes cut through their panic like knives through fog. "Where?"

They pointed back toward the slope, their trembling hands useless for direction.

"Go down the mountain," she said. "Follow the creek until you reach the road. Tell whoever you find there to send help. I'll look for your brother. I'll radio it in."

Neither argued. They just ran, crashing through brush, tripping over roots in their desperation to escape. Their shouts faded quickly, swallowed by the mist.

I remained motionless, crouched against the bark, eyes fixed on the movement below. A large beast went before her—a hound, broad-shouldered and fierce, its coat bristling like the pelt of a small bear. The creature moved with wary intelligence, nose low, every step deliberate. It paused often, testing the air, growling deep in its chest as though warning the forest itself.

Then she followed.

The woman of smoke. The one the hound protected. Power pulsed around her in waves I could almost taste, as cold and electric as stormlight. Even the trees seemed to draw back from her passage.

Something in that power was familiar—old as my first breath. The rhythm of her stance, the tone of her voice. Even her stillness felt like memory. My claws dug into the branch.

I slid along the branch, moving from tree to tree, keeping above her. My muscles tightened, each motion careful, silent. She was searching the ground—the blood, the broken leaves, the trail that led to my lair.

If she followed it, she would find the boy.

If she followed it farther, she would find *him.*

My claws dug into bark.

She couldn't see me—not yet—but her gaze lingered too long. Some ancient knowing hummed between us, predator to predator. Recognition without name.

I had known wolves, cougars, even wendigos that claimed territory near my borders, and none had ever unsettled me. Yet something about her scent—smoke and sorrow—raked against old memories I didn't want to wake.

She would ruin everything.

She would find him.

She would take him.

The thought struck with a heat I didn't expect—rage, yes, but threaded through with fear. He was mine. The first thing I had chosen to keep not out of hunger, but out of wonder.

The dragon woman wouldn't understand that.

She was a creature of fire and taking, not of keeping.

The hunters stumbled on, oblivious. One brushed a branch and sent a flock of blackbirds spiraling skyward, shrieking. The dragon woman turned her head toward the sound. Her eyes narrowed, pupils slitting like mine.

Predator recognized predator.

I pressed lower against the branch, muscles tightening for the leap I would not yet make. The forest stilled, the air thick with the promise of collision.

High above her, I whispered the words of my oldest prayer—to the bones, to the trees, to the sleeping dark that once loved me enough to let me live:

Keep them blind.

Keep her lost.

Keep what's mine.

Footprints of Fire (Lyra)

Mist lay low in the hollows, bruised lavender by first light. Radios crackled in tired bursts. Dogs wove through the underbrush like ghosts on leashes. Search Team One swept the northern slope, fluorescent tape flashing in the trees where they'd marked their progress. Team Two fanned out along the contour lines to the east, their shouts drifting in and out like a broken chorus.

Darren had been missing more than twenty-four hours.

Tommy, the youngest hunter, more than twelve.

The mountain didn't care about our numbers. Her ridges rolled on forever, old backs under an old sky, and we were just small, bright specks crawling over her skin.

I moved along the drainage edge, boots sinking into moss that had given up being dry sometime around midnight. My legs felt the miles but my body still moved easily, the way it always had. Dragon stamina tucked itself neatly inside human joints. Muscles ached, but they didn't fail. Exhaustion for me was a far horizon; for the humans, it was already at their heels.

Henry stumbled up beside me, breath frosting in the chill. His eyes were red-rimmed, freckles stark against skin the color of wet paper. The bill of his cap was pulled low, but it didn't hide the fatigue.

"You need to sit down," he said. It came out more plea than suggestion. "You've been going since yesterday morning. That's... what, twenty hours straight?"

"Twenty-eight," I said. "Give or take."

"Exactly." He threw his hands up, then winced as the motion tugged sore shoulder muscles. "You're supposed to be setting an example, Lange. For safety. You give all the 'fatigue impairs judgment' speeches, remember?"

I stepped over a fallen log slick with lichen. "I also tell people they don't get to schedule emergencies around full nights of sleep."

"That's not an answer." His voice frayed. "You're swaying."

I wasn't. Not yet. The earth's pulse hummed under my feet, steady and old, a second heartbeat propping up the first. Still, I let myself lean against a hemlock for a breath, palm flat on the bark. The tree's life ran slow and deep, steadying the buzz in my bones.

"We've got a missing hiker and a missing hunter," I said quietly. "The first is past the twenty-four-hour mark. You know what that does to survival odds in this terrain."

He did. The numbers lived in every ranger's head: after twenty-four hours without shelter, hypothermia and injury clawed their way up the list. After that, the mountain stopped being a backdrop and started being an active predator.

Henry chewed his lip. "Just... ten minutes. Drink some water. Eat something that isn't coffee."

I glanced at him. He was trying to be the adult in the room. It looked good on him, even if it scared him half to death.

"How long have *you* been up?" I asked.

He hesitated. "Does it matter?"

"Yes."

He blew out a breath. "Since the Bottle Tree called. So... same as you."

"Sit for five," I said. "That's an order."

His mouth opened, closed. "That's not what I meant—"

"I know what you meant." I jerked my chin toward a flat rock by the creek, its surface dry enough to be less miserable than the ground. "Park it. Drink. You're human. It's allowed."

42

He squinted at me. "You say that like you're not."

I walked on. "Semantics."

He muttered something unflattering, but he did sit and dig out his water bottle, the plastic crinkling like a reprimand. Butch, who had been ranging ahead, doubled back long enough to shove his massive head under Henry's arm, demanding a scratch and accidentally forcing the bottle to Henry's lips. Co-pilot enforcement.

I let them have their moment and focused on the terrain.

The search grid laid itself out in my mind the way it always did: a lattice of possibility. Last known point at Darren and Michelle's campsite. Intended route along the creek to the falls. Terrain traps where injured bodies liked to hide—ravines, blowdowns, sudden drop-offs. We'd divided the teams by elevation bands, each assigned a slice of contour lines.

"Team One, this is Ranger Lange," I said into my radio. "Status check."

A woman's voice crackled back, thin with distance. "This is One. Negative on visual. Canines showing intermittent interest, no hard alert. Moving to Sector C-Three."

"Copy. Maintain forty-foot spacing. Call out every thirty seconds."

That last part was more for Henry's benefit than theirs. He knew the protocols in his bones by now, but repetition kept fear and exhaustion from rewriting them.

Search looks methodical from the outside: orange tape, clipped radio codes, dogs quartering the slope. Inside, it was anything but. The brain wants to sprint in every direction at once, to throw itself at possibility until it hits something that looks like hope. Training is what you use to cage that instinct and walk the grid anyway.

"We work from known to unknown," I said, half to myself, half to the mountains. "Last seen, most probable path, terrain features. We don't chase ghosts. We chase evidence."

"You talking to me or the trees?" Henry called from his rock.

"Yes," I said.

He huffed, but some of the tension in his shoulders unwound.

"Team Two, check in," I said.

A male voice came through, breathless. "Two here. Negative so far. Lots of deer sign. One old fire ring. No human tracks past six hours."

"Copy. Keep your dogs leashed near the drop-offs. We don't need more victims. Report any scat or prints you can't classify, we'll log them for wildlife."

"Roger that."

A crow scolded from the canopy, its call harsh and repetitive. I tasted iron on the back of my tongue, faint and far. Like a memory of blood rather than the thing itself. The Hallow's hum stayed low, background noise under the radio crackle, under Butch's heavy breathing and Henry's mutter-sighs. It was watching. Waiting.

Henry pushed himself up and trudged back to my side, water bottle capped. Dark moons sat under his eyes. "Okay. Five minutes. Happy?"

"Ecstatic," I said.

He snorted. "Sarcasm noted." He glanced up-slope, where trees closed in thick and unforgiving. "Do you think we'll find them?"

The question had been stalking him all morning. It finally slipped past his teeth.

I didn't answer right away. I drew a slow breath, tasting damp earth, old leaves, the faint tang of boot rubber and cold metal. Somewhere ahead a dog barked once, sharp and questioning.

"We'll find something," I said. "We always do."

"That's not exactly reassuring," he said.

"It isn't meant to be."

He walked a few steps in silence, twigs snapping under his boots. "This is my first one like this," he said quietly. "We've had lost kids who wandered off and got turned around. Drunks who slept it off on a rock. Old timers who misjudged their meds. But this..." He shook his head. "Blood on the tent. Blood at the creek. Now a hunter missing... It feels different."

It *was* different.

This wasn't just the mountain misplacing someone. This was the mountain waking something that liked to keep what it found.

"Remember your training," I said. "What do we do?"

"We don't panic," he said, reciting like catechism. "We secure the scene, notify dispatch, establish LKP, identify probable routes, deploy grid search with canines, keep communications clear."

"Good."

"We don't speculate." His jaw worked. "We don't assume."

"Exactly."

"And we definitely don't talk about..." He gestured vaguely at the trees. "Panthers and cat-women and old songs."

"Not on the radio, we don't," I said.

He shot me a look. "So you're not going to tell me I hallucinated those prints yesterday."

"No."

"Fantastic. That's so much worse."

The ground steepened as we followed the drainage. Water whispered over rock, thin and urgent, carrying last night's rain toward the deeper hollows. My boots found purchase without thinking; this slope and I had argued years ago and finally learned to respect each other. Henry's foot slid once; I snagged his elbow before he could go down.

"Eyes up," I said. "Hands free when you can. Don't stare at your boots. The forest doesn't drop clues at your toes; it hides them at the edges."

He grunted.

We moved in a slow Z-pattern, checking every game trail that branched off the main drainage. I noted each piece of evidence, even the mundane: fresh deer prints, coyote scat, an old beer can half-buried in moss. Most of it would have nothing to do with Darren or Tommy.

Search is work made of maybes. You stack them until one turns into a yes.

Ahead, a distant shout floated through the trees, thin and distorted. Another dog barked, this time twice in quick succession. Not a full alert, not yet. My shoulders tightened anyway.

Henry's hand went to his radio. "Team One?"

Static hissed, then a voice: "This is One. Negative find. Canine hit on old campsite, no current sign. Continuing sweep."

My lungs eased a fraction. No bad news yet. Just the grind.

Henry exhaled. "I hate this part."

"Which part?"

"The waiting part." He glanced sideways at me. "How do you do this and not lose your mind?"

"I didn't say I didn't," I said. "I said I've learned how to lose it later."

He considered that. "Healthy?"

"It works."

The light strengthened, sliding in narrow shafts through the branches. Mid-morning now. We were burning the best hours for visibility and scent. After noon, heat and wind would start erasing stories from the ground.

"We'll run this band until eleven," I said. "Then we'll regroup at the trailhead, debrief, and assign fresh volunteers to the lower sectors."

"Assuming we haven't found them by then."

"Assuming," I agreed.

He swallowed. "And if we only find...part of them?"

"Then we treat what's left with respect," I said. "We record everything. We give the family answers instead of questions. And we make sure whatever did it doesn't get another chance."

He walked quietly, boots crunching leaves, breath settling into the same rhythm as the dogs and the distant radios. The search became a hymn of small sounds: whistle blasts, handler calls, the click of carabiners against packs.

Under it all, barely there, the Hallow thrummed—a bass note running through the roots, through the creek, through the iron in my blood. Waiting. Listening.

Something on this mountain had taken a hiker and a hunter.

We were not just looking for them.

We were closing in on it.

Butch's bark changed first.

Up until then it had been work noise—short, businesslike woofs when he found an interesting scent, the occasional huff when a squirrel taunted him from a branch. This one came out of him like someone had stepped on his soul. A hard, sharp bark that broke off in a growl.

My head snapped up.

"Hold," I called.

Henry froze mid-step. "What is it?"

Butch stood several yards upslope, body rigid. His front paw hovered above the ground, toes spread. Hackles stood along his spine in a ridge of rough fur. His nose pointed toward a tangle of saplings where the drainage bent around a fallen log.

He didn't move. He didn't look back at me. He was locked.

"Alert," I said quietly.

Henry swallowed. "That's...different."

"Stay here," I told him. "Keep your radio on. If I tell you to, you turn around and walk back down this hill, no heroics."

His jaw clenched. "Lyra—"

"Henry." I didn't raise my voice. I didn't have to. "If it's nothing, you can gloat all you want later. If it's something, I need you functional. Not tangled up in it."

He shut his mouth. His hand found Butch's spare lead at his belt, ready if I signaled.

I moved upslope.

The ground grew wetter, soil turning to dark, spongy loam that tried to swallow my boots. The air felt thicker here, like breath had trouble leaving. Moss muffled my footsteps. I let my senses unfold, slipping past the limits of human skin.

Iron tickled the back of my tongue. Not the faint ghost taste from earlier. Fresh. Close.

"Easy, boy," I murmured. Butch's ears flicked backward; the only sign he'd heard me. He stayed braced, nose cutting through the air in short, decisive pulls.

There was a smell underneath the blood: fear-sweat, cigarette smoke, the sour tang of cheap beer. Human.

"Okay," I said under my breath. "Show me."

I touched two fingers to his shoulder and gave the hand signal to move in. He surged forward exactly four steps then stopped again, as if he'd hit an invisible wall.

I saw why.

On the far side of the fallen log lay a man. Orange safety vest shredded in strips, shirt dark with blood. His body had rolled partly onto its side, one arm flung outward, fingers caught in the root tangle. His face turned toward the sky with an expression that still held the last second of his disbelief.

Tommy.

He looked small without motion, without sound. Just another boy who had thought neon polyester and a gun made him invincible.

For half a breath, the forest went very quiet. The crows shut their beaks. Even the creek sounded muffled, as if the water bowed its head.

I stepped closer.

"Lyra?" Henry's voice came soft down the slope.

"Stay," I said. "Do not come up until I tell you."

My own voice sounded unfamiliar in my ears. Flatter.

I knelt beside the body. The ground soaked cold through my pants.

His throat bore the worst of it. The flesh there was torn in ragged, parallel arcs, as if something with too many knives for fingers had raked downward. The wound had bled heavily and then slowed; the blood on his vest was already turning rust-brown around the edges, stiffening the fabric. Bruising blossomed beneath it, purple and ugly.

What caught my attention most was what I didn't see.

No tearing at the abdomen. No missing limbs. No feeding.

This was not a kill for hunger.

This was a kill for pleasure.

I swallowed the low growl that wanted to climb my throat. The Hallow trembled under my skin, a sympathetic chord struck too hard. The mountain could feel the wrongness of it—violence without purpose, death with no balance.

Life and death are the same river, the old current whispered. Both belong to the Song.

Yes. But some sparks are snuffed too soon.

I let my gaze travel over the boy's still face, the freckles fading into pallor, the slack line of a mouth that had probably laughed just yesterday. Humans lived so briefly. Even the ones who grew old never stayed long. Their entire existence was a single bright flare—born, burning, then gone.

He could not have been more than nineteen. Maybe twenty if arrogance had carried him past caution. Had he planned anything beyond this hunting trip? Did he know what he wanted his life to mean?

Had he kissed someone and believed it was love?

Had he failed something important and learned from it?

Had he tried and fallen and risen again?

Or was his story nothing more than a handful of beginnings now destined to remain unfinished?

I had seen empires rise and rot to dust. I had watched entire bloodlines end with a single winter storm. I had walked past battlefields where the dead lay in piles so high the mountain wept. But in this moment, this—one boy, alone in the moss—felt heavier than all of that.

Because he had not lived long enough to choose who he wanted to become.

His spark had scarcely begun to burn before it was crushed under claws that meant to frighten, not feed. A waste. A severed thread in the tapestry of life.

I closed my eyes, the grief settling into the hollow beneath my ribs like cold water.

"Your life should have been longer," I murmured, too soft for Henry to hear, too soft for anyone but the Hallow and the dead. "You should have had time to see more, to fail more, to love more."

The Hallow hummed in agreement—a low vibration, ancient and mournful.

I placed two fingers gently against the earth near his shoulder, honoring the spark that had been. A gesture older than ranger protocol. Older than this mountain. Older than my own name.

Then I stood, jaw tight, breath steadying.

Fleeting as they were, humans mattered.

Their sparks mattered.

This boy mattered.

And whoever had taken his life like it was nothing would answer for it.

I forced my hands to clinical motions.

Gloves on. Check for signs of life though the answer was obvious. No pulse. Skin cool to the touch, but not yet the deeper chill of long death. Rigor beginning in the jaw and fingers. Time of death six to eight hours ago, if I went by human standards. The mountain's chill could blur those lines, but not erase them.

"Found a body," I said into my radio, voice steady. "Male. Late teens to early twenties. Orange hunter's vest. Multiple lacerations to neck and torso. No obvious animal feeding."

Static hissed before dispatch responded, calm and distant. "Copy, Ranger Lange. Logging as DOA. Please confirm coordinates and nearest access point."

I rattled off the GPS reading and the quickest way to reach us with a stretcher.

"Understood," dispatch said. "County sheriff and coroner enroute. Wildlife officer notified. Time now zero-nine-forty-one."

"Ten-four," I said. "Advise SAR we have one confirmed fatality. Continue search for second missing subject."

"Affirmative."

I clipped the radio back and let myself exhale once.

Next step: scene protection.

I marked a wide circle around Tommy's body with bright flagging tape, tying strips to saplings and branches. The color screamed against the green. Do not cross, it said, to rescuers and to the mountain both.

"Okay," I called downslope. "You can come up. Watch your footing. Stay outside the tape."

Henry's steps were careful, but I heard each one. When he crested the rise and saw the orange vest, the color drained from his face.

"Oh," he breathed.

Butch pushed his snout into Henry's hand as if to anchor him.

"That's..." Henry swallowed hard. "That's Tommy."

"We'll need formal identification from family, but yes."

He skirted the tape, eyes wide, nostrils flaring like his body couldn't decide whether to breathe or shut down. His hand clutched the radio at his shoulder without pressing the button.

"What did this?" he asked. The words were thin, shaky.

I studied the wounds again, letting my gaze catalog instead of speculate.

"Not a bear," I said. "No crushing bites. No feeding."

"Cougar?"

"Cougars rake, yes, but their claw patterns are narrower. And they don't usually go straight for the throat from the front like this. Too risky."

"Wolf?"

I shook my head. "Wrong teeth. Wrong everything."

He stared. "So... what then?"

I refrained from saying, *Something that walks on two legs and knows exactly where to put its claws.*

"I don't know yet," I said instead. Truth enough to sit between us. "That's for the wildlife officer and coroner to help determine. Our job is to preserve what we can and keep anyone else from ending up like this."

Henry scrubbed his hands over his face then paced a few steps away, boots chewing up the moss. He stopped, braced his hands on his knees, and breathed like he might throw up.

I gave him the dignity of not watching.

Cold brushed the back of my neck. Not the chill rolling off Tommy's skin or the morning breeze. A different kind of attention.

I straightened slowly, letting my gaze drift up, up, into the higher branches.

The canopy knitted above us in woven greens and browns, broken by narrow veins of sky. To most eyes it would look empty.

To mine, it looked like something had been there.

Branches still swayed where the wind had not touched them. Bark carried faint scratches, fresh, curving in arcs that no human hand could reach. The hair along my own arms prickled, scales under skin stirring in recognition.

Watcher, the Hallow breathed through the roots. *Huntress.*

I tasted another scent threading through the metallic tang of blood: musk, wild and feminine, edged with old magic. Cat and something more than cat.

Wampus.

She had waited for us. Not in malice, exactly. In curiosity. In the way predators sometimes watch other predators just to see what they will do.

I listened. Leaves whispered. A squirrel scolded far off. No telltale weight shifted above. Whatever had perched there was gone or very, very good at hiding.

"Do you feel that?" Henry asked suddenly, straightening.

My spine stiffened. "Feel what?"

He squinted up at the branches again, searching for something he couldn't define. His breath caught, and a faint shiver ran through him before he shook his head hard—like a dog shaking off a bad dream.

"I don't know," he said. "It just... feels off."

I watched him carefully. Henry was not the type to indulge in superstition. He was the checklist-and-laminated-protocol sort of ranger. But something had reached him—something instinctive and old, bypassing the rational part of his brain.

He rubbed his palms on his thighs, fingers twitching as if he wanted to grab something familiar, something tangible.

"It's probably nothing," he muttered quickly. "Just nerves. Adrenaline. Lack of sleep." He winced as if hearing himself. "I'm not saying, like... ghost stuff." His voice lowered, almost embarrassed. "I don't even believe in that."

His cheeks flushed. He stared down at the moss, avoiding my eyes.

"It's just... I don't know." He swallowed. "I've been in the woods my whole life, Lyra. Since I could walk. And this—" He gestured vaguely at the trees, the shadows, the space above us. "This doesn't feel like normal wilderness quiet. It feels like..." He hesitated, searching for the word and hating himself for it. "Like something's watching."

I felt the truth of it slide over my skin.

Henry shook his head again, trying to laugh it off. "I sound ridiculous. I know I sound ridiculous."

"You don't," I said softly.

His eyes snapped to mine, startled.

Humans often sensed the edges of things they refused to name. Their bodies always knew before their minds did. Some part of Henry's survival instinct was kicking against the inside of his ribs, whispering that the world was not behaving the way it should.

He opened his mouth, closed it, then raised one shoulder in a half-shrug that tried and failed to look casual.

"Whatever," he muttered. "Just... feels wrong. That's all."

That was more perceptive than I'd expected from him at this hour.

I looked down at Tommy's still face, freckles stark against skin gone waxy. His hazel eyes had fixed on some point beyond the canopy, as if he'd tried to see past the trees at the last second.

The Hallow Song shifted.

It rose from a background hum to a low, aching tone; vibrating under my soles, up through my ribs. Not the sharp, hot surge it used when something new woke in the mountains. This was softer, almost tender. A dirge note.

I stood very still and let it pass through me.

Life and death, again in the same breath. The Song didn't grieve the way humans did. It didn't categorize this boy as innocent or guilty, foolish or brave. It simply acknowledged that one more spark had gone out, and the pattern of the world had changed by a fraction.

Still, my chest hurt.

"I'm sorry," I said quietly—to the boy, to the forest, to the part of me that remembered how easily creation could spill into destruction.

Henry glanced over. "What?"

"Talking to the mountain," I said.

He gave a weak huff. "You know that's not less weird than talking to yourself, right?"

"Take pictures," I told him gently. "From the tape line only. Full body, close on the wounds, surrounding area. No posting. No sharing. These go in the case file and nowhere else."

He nodded, grateful for orders. Work steadied his hands. He fumbled his phone out of his pocket and began to document, each shutter click a small defiance against the helplessness gnawing at his throat.

I keyed my radio again, voice returning to its professional cadence.

"Dispatch, Ranger Lange. Be advised, terrain at body location is steep and slick. Recommend four to six responders for recovery, plus low-angle gear. Flagging is in place. I'll leave one ranger to guide them in and continue the search for our first subject downslope."

"Copy, Ranger Lange," came the crackle. "ETA for sheriff and coroner forty minutes. Wildlife ten behind. Do you require additional units?"

I looked at Tommy's vest, at the shredded edges fanned out like petals, at the faint drag of claw across bark above us.

"Yes," I said. "Have One or Two send a handler to meet them at the trailhead. And tell everyone to stay in pairs. No one alone, not even for a bathroom break."

"Understood."

I let go of the radio and rested my palm briefly on Butch's head. His ears flattened, eyes soft but alert. He had found death today, and he understood it in his own way.

"Good work," I whispered.

He leaned into my touch, shoulder solid against my thigh.

Far above, a leaf spun loose from a branch and drifted in a slow spiral, landing on the torn orange of Tommy's vest.

The Song gave one more low, mournful thrum. And then, as always, it moved on.

I gave the mountain what it needed of me before I let it have anything else.

Coordinates. Scene secured. ETA confirmed. Orders passed to Henry in a voice that sounded like it belonged to someone who had slept last night.

Then I stepped away.

"I'm going to check the drainage below," I told him, nodding toward the crease of land that folded away from Tommy's flagged circle. "See if anything washed down. Stay with him. Meet the recovery team when they come in."

Henry nodded too fast, grateful for something to do that wasn't staring at a dead boy's open eyes. Butch pressed his shoulder against Henry's leg like a wedge, holding him upright.

"I'll be right here," Henry said. His voice cracked on *here*.

I left them to their grief and walked into mine.

The slope dropped away, softened by centuries of leaf-fall. I followed the faint path the water took, weaving between maples and hemlocks. The air felt heavy, a thick, damp blanket that smelled of wet bark and iron. Above the canopy, clouds had gathered—layering gray on darker gray, a sky full of unspoken words.

By the time I reached a small shelf of rock above the drainage, the world had narrowed to three things: the ache in my chest, the quiet thrum of the Hallow in the soil, and the waiting weight of the sky.

I stopped and leaned my shoulder against a pine thick enough to hold me. The bark pressed into my jacket, rough and reassuring. Needles whispered overhead.

For a moment I let my eyes close.

Fatigue washed up as soon as I did; not the sharp burn of overused muscles but the deep, slow tiredness that lived in the bones. The kind that came from being the thing that stood between what wanted to devour and what did not deserve to be devoured.

I had done this for so long that the years blurred. Faces blurred. Screams blurred. Some days I was all edges and purpose. Today, under this sky with someone's son cooling on the hillside above me, I felt nothing but frayed.

The Hallow's hum curled around my ankles; a low, continuous vibration. It was not comfort and not quite indifference. It simply *was*.

Thunder answered it.

A low, distant roll moved across the ridgeline, making the air shiver. My eyes stayed closed. I felt the sound through my ribs more than I heard it. The hair on my arms stood up. The scent of ozone threaded itself through the damp.

Hear me.

His voice rode the tail of the thunder, sliding into the quiet places in my mind like it belonged there. Because it always had.

My breath stuttered out. Relief hit so hard it almost knocked my knees out from under me.

He always knew when I was about to come apart.

"I hear you," I whispered. My throat hurt. "I always hear you."

The first raindrop landed on the back of my hand. Warm, though the air was cold. It sank into my skin like a thumb pressed in reassurance. Another followed on my cheek, another at the corner of my mouth. Each carried a faint, familiar charge—as if the storm itself had a pulse.

I know you do, Taren said. His voice was low and rough, threaded with that quiet command that had never needed volume. *You could be buried in stone and I would still find the shape of you.*

My hand rose almost of its own accord, tracing the line of my cheek before curling around the side of my neck. My fingers followed the path his used to take, back when we had bodies that could touch without the world tearing for it.

"You always know when to come," I said.

Of course. Thunder rumbled again, closer. The pine at my back seemed to lean into the sound. *We were forged of the same flame, Lyra. When you fray, I feel it. When you bleed, I taste iron in my storms.*

The rain thickened. It pattered against leaves, tapped on stone, freckled my face and throat with warmth that had no business in the chill.

I let my head rest against the rough trunk and kept my eyes closed. It was easier to feel him that way. Easier to remember.

Once, creation had been a tangible thing beneath our hands. Light and heat and Song braided together. We had carved creatures out of possibility, molded rivers with our hips, traced mountains into being with the long arc of our bodies. Every heartbeat had been a hammer blow on the anvil of the world.

"I miss it," I said, the words catching. "Our time of creation. The magic of it. When everything we touched became more instead of less."

Rain ran down my throat in a slow, warm line. It felt like his mouth once had—following the hollow at the base of my neck, chasing the pulse there, memorizing it.

For a moment the storm went quiet, gathering itself. Lightning flickered through the clouds, a muted flash that turned the world white behind my closed lids.

We have not stopped creating, he said at last. *You walk a world full of proofs. Every life you keep, every boundary you hold—that is creation. Just a slower kind.*

"I'm weary," I murmured. "Tired of remaking what dies. Of patching the same holes in the same dam while the river keeps rising."

The confession hung between us, bare and ugly. I had not given it words in a long time.

The Hallow hummed under my boots, neither agreeing nor denying.

Thunder responded instead. Sharper now, cracking off a distant peak. When his voice came again it was closer, intimate, as if his mouth was right against my ear.

Then stop patching for a moment, he said. *Rest in me. Be filled with me. Let the river run around you instead of through you.*

Rain sheeted down harder, drumming on my face, my shoulders, my hands. Each drop landed heavy and warm, sinking into tired muscle and bone, carrying with it the echo of his heartbeat.

I pulled a breath into my lungs and let it out slowly. The air tasted like him: cold metal, pine, distant lightning.

"How?" I asked. It came out softer than I meant it to. "How do I rest, when everything is falling apart?"

You don't, he said. We *do.*

Lightning flashed again, closer. I sensed the arc of it through the clouds, the way it stretched between sky and earth like a vein of molten gold.

We walked between them, he continued. *Creation and death. We were made to. You are not meant to carry one without the other. Let me take some of the weight.*

His certainty sank into me with the rain. *We.* Not *you.* Not *I. We.*

I let my hand fall from my neck to my sternum, pressing my palm against the steady drum of my heart. The beat quickened, matching the cadence of the thunder.

"Every time I held a line," I said, eyes still closed, "I thought about laying it down. About letting you pull me back under. About us walking the ridges instead of babysitting them."

For a moment his laugh cracked through the storm, low and pained.

Do you think I don't dream of it? he asked. *I imagine you in my snowfields, turning the drifts to steam. Your smoke on my cliffs. No radios. No men with guns and snares. Just you and me and the Song to shape as we please.*

The image hit hard: his mountains under a sky bruised with evening, my smoke curling around his shoulders. Silence that was not empty but full of world-making.

"It would be so easy," I whispered.

It would be beautiful, he agreed. *And selfish. And the world would burn without us.*

"I know," I said. I hated that I did.

The rain slid under my collar, down my spine. It cooled the hot knot of anger there, the resentful, exhausted place that kept asking 'Why us?'. 'Why this?'. 'Why still?'.

You are tired, he said again, gentler. *Not because you keep everyone alive. That isn't your job and never was. You are tired because you do it alone.*

"I'm not alone," I protested automatically. "I have Henry. Maeve. The SAR teams. Butch. The whole county could probably use less of me, not more."

They have a ranger, Taren said. *You have a mountain. There is a difference.*

The words loosened something in my chest.

He had always been good at that—at sliding past the arguments I built and pressing thumb and palm to the exact bruise I tried to ignore.

"Then help me," I said. "Now. Here."

I am, he answered.

The storm swelled.

For a few heartbeats there was nothing but sound and sensation. The roar of rain on leaves, the rattle of drops on rock, the static crawl across my scalp. I felt him gather himself on the far side of the world— up in his own high ranges, snowfields and lightning at his feet—and pour that gathered power down the channels that connected us.

Heat flooded my limbs, not burning but steady; like coals banked in a hearth. The tremor in my hands eased. My shoulders unlocked. The rawness behind my eyes cooled.

I was still tired. The death on the hillside had not undone itself. The Wampus was still out there, pacing the edge of my territory with blood on her claws.

But the exhaustion was no longer a cliff-face with my toes hanging over the edge. It was a weight shared.

There, he said. Satisfaction curled through the word. *You remember how to breathe again.*

I pulled air in, let it out. It no longer felt like dragging stones through my chest.

"I do," I admitted. "Thank you."

We were made to do this for each other. The Hallow bound us for a reason.

Lightning speared the clouds directly overhead. The crack of it rattled my teeth. His voice broke on it, pulled thin across distance.

Lyra...

"Yes?"

There was a pause, filled with nothing but the hiss of water and the deep rumble of the Song below.

Don't let this break you, he said finally. *Not this boy. Not this creature. Not this hunt. I would rather the mountains fall than watch you go to stone inside yourself.*

"It won't," I said.

The storm crested. The connection flared so bright it almost hurt, then snapped.

His presence slid out of my mind like a tide retreating, leaving warmth on the sand but no wave to stand in. The rain stayed; colder now, ordinary.

The quiet after was almost violent.

I opened my eyes. At some point I had slid down the tree into a crouch, knees deep in damp leaf litter. One hand pressed to my chest, the other braced against the ground. Water ran down my face in steady lines. I wiped at it with the heel of my palm and came away uncertain whether the wet was rain or tears.

The ridge looked the same as it had before: trees, fog, the far-off glint of the flagged tape marking where Tommy waited for the world to notice he was gone.

Only, I was different. Slightly. Enough.

My radio crackled. Henry's voice came through, thin with distance and effort. "Lange? They're heading up from the trailhead. Sheriff says twenty out. You still good?"

I lifted the radio to my mouth. My hand did not shake.

"Copy," I said. My voice was hoarse but steady. "I'm on my way back up. Stay within sight of the body and keep Butch with you. No one goes off alone."

"Got it," he said.

I glanced once toward the dark shoulder of the western horizon, where the storm was already moving on. For a moment, just at the edge of cloud, the light broke gold.

My legs protested, but they held. The warmth Taren left in my bones glowed like banked fire.

Creation and death.

We walked between them.

I turned back up the slope toward Tommy, toward Henry, toward what would come next.

The Prize I Choose (Wampus)

The dragon woman knelt over my kill as if the forest had made her its priest.

From my branch above, I watched them ring my toy in plastic. Bright tape snapped in the breeze, little flags of ownership tied to my work. The boy's ruined chest rose and fell no more, but their voices moved around him as if they could stitch breath back into his ribs with words alone.

They could not.

He was not theirs anymore.

He belonged to the dark now—to soil and slow roots, to beetles and the quiet hunger that turned everything back to dust. I had given him to that cycle in the only way I knew: teeth and claws and speed. It had been a clean death, by my standards. Quick. Hot. Honest.

I didn't feel remorse.

I felt seen.

And underneath that...something like pride.

Death had always been a kind of art to me.

Not the crude slaughter men imagine when they whisper my name at their fires, but the ancient rhythm older than their first tools. The moment teeth met flesh, the world sharpened into perfect clarity:

muscle yielding, breath stuttering, heat spilling out like a prayer returned to the mountain.

There was beauty in that surrender.

Beauty in the way life left the body, unspooling into the air like steam rising from wet earth. Beauty in the stillness afterward—the quiet arrangement of limbs, the way the last heat curled away into the moss.

The forest always paused for that moment, honoring it.

Even now it held its breath around the boy's empty shell, recognizing the way one spark extinguished becomes nourishment for a thousand smaller ones.

The dragon woman didn't see that.

She saw tragedy where the mountain saw continuity.

She saw violence where I saw completion.

To me, he looked almost peaceful.

The torn fabric, the spilled red, the tilt of his head—they were strokes in a story the world has always told. The final one, yes, but no less necessary than the first.

I savored it the way others savor the last note of a song.

Yet she knelt there as though I had desecrated something sacred instead of performing an act as old as winter.

As if she, with her golden eyes and storm-scented skin, had the right to interpret my work at all.

The dragon woman's touch was careful when she closed his jaw, fingers smoothing his hair away from his slack face. Her expression hardly moved, but the air around her pulsed. Power hummed under her skin in tight, controlled waves, brushing the underside of my fur like static.

The mountain leaned toward her when she stood. I felt it in the bark beneath my claws.

That stung.

She spoke to the young male—Henry—with that low, measured voice humans make when they need each other not to break. His answers shook. Hers didn't. When she pressed her palm to his shoulder, he steadied as if the touch itself were a command.

He looked at her the way creatures once looked at me.

As if I were safety instead of the shadow in their story.

My tail lashed against the branch, sending a scatter of lichen down like ash. The beast—huge, shaggy, smelling of loyalty and old meat—pressed against the boy's legs, a living barrier between him and what lay on the ground. The dragon woman's gaze swept the tree line once, golden and sharp.

It passed close enough that my pupils slit down to knife-edges.

The Hallow's pulse swelled beneath all of us, threading through root and bone.

I hated it.

I had been one of its first creations. The mountains' original sharp edges. A thing it made by accident and then let roam. I knew that in my marrow. Yet when she moved the Song rose to meet *her*, not *me*. It recognized something in her that matched the first light that had poured down my throat under a hemlock long ago.

She smelled of that light. Smoke braided with frost. Storm-metal and pine.

Dragons. I remembered their shadows from before my long sleep: wings like thunderheads, bellies full of fire, eyes that saw everything and forgave nothing. They had burned men's camps and sealed wild magic away and vanished into the old stories.

I thought I had outlived them.

And now one crouched over a body I had taken, marking the ground, speaking into her black box while the mountain hummed approval.

The male shook his head, words tumbling from his mouth. I didn't need to understand them. Panic has the same taste in every language. The dragon woman answered with a tilt of her jaw, a tightening at the corners of her mouth.

No blame. No praise. Just the quiet weight of judgment.

She didn't look up at me again. She didn't have to.

The sting was not that she disapproved. It was that she thought she understood my choice at all.

He hadn't been special. Just loud and careless and in the wrong place at the right time. A good offering to remind the mountain I still walked its skin. My jaws had closed around him, the Song had shivered, his story had ended. Clean. Simple.

The one I had taken from the river rocks—the one who breathed slow in my den—he was different.

He was chosen.

If she followed the blood long enough, she might find that one. She would stand in my cave mouth with her storm eyes and her badge and declare him a victim instead of a prize.

My prize.

My back arched against the bark at the thought, muscles rippling under fur and skin. A low growl coiled silent in my throat, caged only because sound would have given me away.

The dragon woman finished talking into the box. Men's voices crackled thinly in answer. She gave instructions in that controlled tone and the beast lay down beside my work, great head on his paws, as if grieving too.

The forest listened to her.

It had once listened to me.

I flowed up the trunk, away from them, claws scoring the bark. Needles brushed my whiskers as I slipped into the higher canopy, where the light dappled and the air thinned. From there, the scene below blurred—orange vest, taped circle, green jacket, shaggy beast—until it all looked like a nest of bright insects crawling over something that no longer mattered.

He was finished.

I was not.

I moved from tree to tree, body remembering old paths. The muscled coil and release of my limbs, the swish of my tail for balance, the brief sting of twigs against my flanks—it all smoothed the sharp places inside me. Up here, away from the bright tape and the dragon's calm, the world went back to being simple again.

Branches bowed under my weight and sprang back when I left. Birds startled, then settled. A squirrel froze flat against a trunk until I passed, then resumed its busy life. The mountain's Song thinned into its usual hum; less focused, more background.

But a strand of it still held that new note.

Her note.

Smoke and frost. Storm and stone.

The Hallow had taken her into its rhythm, too, whether I liked it or not.

My ears flattened. I didn't want to share that music.

I dropped from the canopy when the branches thinned, landing in the springy duff with a soft thump. Moss cushioned my paws. Damp leaves licked between my toes. Down here, the smells were thick—wet bark, mushroom rot, the tang of fox, and the faint ghost of my own earlier passage.

I turned toward my ridgeline.

Each step I took, I marked.

A chin rubbed along a low-hanging branch. A deliberate brush of my flank against a leaning spruce. Claws raked down the side of a beech in one long, satisfying scratch, leaving pale scars in the smooth gray bark.

Mine, I told the forest. *Mine*, I told the Song. *Mine*.

Mine and mine and mine.

The mountain knew me. It had grown around my den, stones shifting to hide the cave mouth centuries ago when men still believed enough to fear shadows. But with a dragon awake in boots and ranger green, I felt the need to remind it whose woods these were.

Light slanted thinly through the canopy ahead, late-afternoon gold pooling in patches. Dust motes danced in it like insects. My pupils flared wide, sucking what little brightness remained out of the air. I tasted the day on my tongue—cooler, drier, edged with the smoke of distant chimneys in the valley.

Patience. Evening would come. Good. Predators did their best work pressed up against the edge of night.

Branches whipped my shoulders as I wove between them. My tail snapped once, twice, its tuft flicking up the scents behind me. My ears flicked independently; one tracking the distant rattle of metal where they prepared to move the dead, the other trained on the softer sounds. Vole under leaf, crow wing overhead, water laughing over stone downhill where I had pulled my prize from the creek.

He would be there.

The thought of him steadied my breathing.

Wrapped in the wool blanket I'd dragged from its forgotten campsite, smelling of fear and sweat and river and that extra thing that made him interesting. His pulse would be slower now, no longer galloping with terror. His skin would be cooler in the cave air, but not cold. Not yet.

He might have shifted in my absence. Murmured in his half-dream. Turned his face toward the sound of the underground water like it was a lullaby.

He wouldn't have left.

He couldn't.

The ways into my den were winding and knotted, hidden under tangles of root and stone. Even I had to pay attention when I traveled them, and I had worn them into the mountain's bones myself. A half-conscious human with a headache and a rip in his arm would not find his way out even if he woke before I returned.

He was safe in his unknowing.

Safe from the dragon woman's sharp eyes and sharper questions. Safe from being cut into evidence and pity, his story flattened to a line in someone's file. Safe from the world that would tell him I was a monster and she was mercy.

My claws bit deeper into the dirt.

Let her have the carcass. Let her have her talking boxes and her grieving boys and her big, loyal beast. Let the mountain hum for her when she passes, if it chooses.

I had something better.

I imagined his lashes twitching when I stepped into the cave mouth. The way his breath would hitch when my shadow fell over him. The rough sound he would make, somewhere between fear and relief when I touched his face with claws.

Mine, I would tell him, with my voice and my purr and my body curved around his. No dragon. No hunter. No world that wants to eat you slowly. Only me.

Jealousy cooled to a different ache as I climbed the last rise: a hollow, hungry tenderness that sat where my old litters used to curl. I couldn't keep kits. The world had taught me that with wire and guns and careless men. But maybe I could keep this one human, this bright, breakable thing who had looked up at the sky as if it might answer.

I crested the ridge. The laurel closed in, thick and glossy, claws snagging on its tough leaves as I pushed through. The hill folded down toward the hidden crack in the rock that was my doorway, the ground damp and slick with seeping water.

Home.

Behind me, somewhere far across the trees, thunder muttered—dragon-storm answering dragon-grief. The Hallow's chord vibrated in the soles of my feet, shared between them.

My lip curled.

Let them sing to each other across their high ranges. Let them mourn their boy and their broken balance.

I had a different song waiting in the dark.

By the time I reached the ridge where the mountain's skin opened to let me in, my mind had narrowed to one bright point:

Mine.

The entrance lay where it always had—nothing more than a wrinkle in rock to human eyes, a shadow where no shadow should linger. Ferns curtained the lower half, their fronds dripping from the earlier rain. A tangle of roots clawed down the slope above, disguising the subtle sag of stone that marked the real door.

I had spent a long time shaping this place.

Not with tools the way men did but with patience. With pressure. With knowing.

I had chosen a seam where the mountain already wanted to crack, then leaned into it over years—claws widening fissures, shoulders worrying stone, my weight finding and exploiting every weakness. Water had helped, seeping through the hairline fractures I opened, softening them, carrying away the grit until a passage formed just wide enough for me and those I chose to bring.

The entrance turned sharply twice in quick succession—a blind corner that broke scent and sight both. Wind never blew straight through. A predator following only its nose would overshoot the gap, scent carried past on the wrong current. A man would see nothing but rock and dripping green.

It pleased me, the cleverness of it.

Some beasts built dens. I had built a labyrinth.

I slipped through the ferns, flattened against the stone, and slid sideways into the crack. Cool air wrapped around me at once, rich with limestone and old water. My whiskers brushed rock; my shoulders remembered every scrape and smooth patch. Behind me, the forest's noises dulled to a muffled hiss.

Two steps in and the light died.

I didn't need it. I knew this darkness the way other creatures knew daylight. Every curve of the tunnel, every rise and dip, rimmed the inside of my mind like old scars.

The passage opened after ten paces, ribs of stone peeling back to form the first chamber. Here the ceiling was high enough for me to straighten fully. Moisture jeweled the walls, catching the faintest ghost of surface light and turning it to soft glimmers.

The bones greeted me.

They were not horror to me. They were history.

Ribcages arched against the rock like white cathedrals, each curve memorized with my hands. Femurs lay in orderly rows, thick and pale, the strength of them humbled at last. Skulls crowned the highest ledges —faces tilted upward, empty sockets forever searching for the stars they once trusted.

I'd placed each one.

Here, the hunter who had tried to set snares along my creek. There, the poacher who laughed when the fox kits screamed. Over there, the man who came into the woods not hungry, not desperate, but bored. I didn't know their names but I remembered their sounds, their smells. The way their fear tasted at the end.

Little trinkets broke the white: a brass watch with its hands forever frozen at a particular gasp, beads from a broken necklace, a plastic lighter with a faded logo of some tavern that no longer existed. Offerings they had not meant to give but which I accepted all the same.

I moved among them the way a curator moves through a gallery.

Attentive.

He lay near the back wall where I had left him, wrapped in the wool blanket I'd dragged from another campsite weeks ago. Its original owners had run home with stories of "something big" moving outside their firelight.

His chest rose and fell in slow, uneven pulls.

Good.

The man—my man now—smelled of cold sweat and river stone, of old fear drying at the edges. A bruise had bloomed along his temple, dark under the stubble of his hair where his skull had met rock. The makeshift bandage of moss at his arm was stiff with his blood, but the wound no longer leaked freely. Shock held him gentle, for now. Shock and exhaustion and the thin, metallic edge of thirst.

Not my magic.

The mountain's ordinary cruelty.

I padded closer, tail sweeping the floor in an absent rhythm. His lashes fluttered once, then stilled. He hovered in that soft place between waking and blackness, where the world felt like a half-remembered dream.

I circled him.

One slow lap, paws whispering over stone. My nose trailed his outline; my whiskers tasted the warmth that clung to him. The cave's air was cool, but he radiated heat like a banked coal. I dipped my head, inhaling deeply at his throat, then his chest, then the place where his pulse beat ragged in his wrist.

Mine.

The word thrummed through me like the Hallow's distant hum.

I pressed my cheek to his shoulder, rubbing along it, leaving the faint musk of my scent on his skin and the borrowed wool. The glands along my jaw flared, pleased. I did it again along his ribs, then curled around the top of his head, nuzzling until the hair stood in wild directions.

He stirred, a small sound catching in his throat.

"Shh," I murmured, the purr rumbling under the word. My voice cracked on human shapes; I had not used it in the long sleep. "You're safe."

Safe *with me.*

Safe *from them.*

His eyes blinked open to slits, pupils wide, trying to find edges in the dark. He saw nothing. To him, the world was void, pierced only by the faintest suggestion of my outline when I shifted between him and the cave mouth.

He tried to sit up. His hand slipped on the rock; his other arm buckled at the shot of pain from his wound. He fell back with a ragged exhale, chest heaving.

"Easy," I said again, lowering myself so my weight became a wall at his side, solid and unavoidable. My tail curled across his legs, anchoring him.

"Wh-Where..." His tongue caught on the word, thick and clumsy. "Michelle...?"

He always called for her first.

Jealousy bit clean and bright through my chest.

"She is far above," I told him, leaning close so my breath brushed his ear. "Far away. The stealers have her."

"Stealers...?" he echoed faintly.

"The ones who take," I hissed softly. Images flashed under my lids— bright tape, gloved hands, the dragon woman's golden eyes narrowed in judgment. "The ones who wrap and carry and bury. They found what I left. They will come looking for more."

My claws flexed against the stone, kneading deeply, the way I once kneaded moss for my kits. The ground had always comforted under my paws, answering pressure with unyielding solidity.

I turned my head and licked a smear of dried blood from his cheek, slow and deliberate. He flinched, every muscle tensing, but there was nowhere for him to go. The cave pressed close on all sides; my body blocked the rest.

"You are not for them," I said quietly. "You are mine. My prize. My keepsake."

His breath quickened. "Please... I need... I need to go back. She— she'll be scared—"

"She will be fine," I cut in. "She is soft. They like to comfort soft things. They will wrap her in blankets and pour hot drinks into her and tell stories about monsters to explain what they do not understand."

I nuzzled his hairline again, breathing him in, letting the scent of him push their faces out of my mind.

"No one will comfort me if they take you," I added, softer. "No one will remember *me*."

His throat bobbed. He tried to turn his head away; I followed the movement, my cheek sliding against his, pinning the motion with gentle insistence. My purr deepened, a long, vibrating thread.

"You will stay," I decided. "We will go deeper. Where they can't smell you. Where even she—" I spat the word without meaning to, a hot crack in the purr. "—cannot hear your heartbeat."

"What are you?" he whispered.

The question trembled between us, warm and human and breakable.

Names rose in my mind like old bones surfacing after rain.

Bastet, when my paws padded their thresholds and their babies slept easier for it.

Sekhmet, when they saw the flash of my claws and mistook restraint for mercy.

Hathor, when my purr curled around a lover's throat and they called it blessing, not warning.

Mut, when they begged the night to spare their children and felt my shadow pass overhead.

Tefnut, when the storms chased my spine across the sky.

Maftet, when my teeth found the wicked and they wrote it down as divine justice.

They carved those names into stone because they could not bear the truth of fur and breath and dripping jaw.

But here in these mountains, there were no temples.

Only fear.

They whispered *Wampus* like a curse they hoped the trees could smother.

The syllables always tasted the same on their tongues: iron, dread, inevitability.

A monster that stalked the ridgelines.

A thief of men.

A watcher in the dark.

His heartbeat fluttered under his skin—quick, frantic, prey-fast.

My whiskers twitched with every vibration.

The heat of him pulsed against my claws where they grazed the dirt.

His scent—salt, fear, and the faint sweetness of youth—rose into my nostrils like incense.

I inhaled him.

I wanted to rub my cheek along his jaw, smear my scent down his throat, mark him until anyone with sense would know he had already been claimed.

I was goddess.

Woman.

Beast.

I was Hallow-forged.

Born from the Song's teeth and tenderness, shaped by every creature that died singing its last note into the earth.

I thought of many answers—omen, shadow, hunger, miracle, mistake—yet none of them fit neatly inside the fragile little mouth of human speech.

I leaned close enough for him to feel the heat of my breath.

"What am *I*?"

My tail curled around his ankle; possessive, certain.

I thought of many answers—cat, woman, warning, mistake, miracle —but none of them fit neatly in his language.

"Yours," I said instead. "Come."

I rose in one smooth motion, tail uncoiling from his legs. The sudden loss of my warmth made him shiver. I caught his wrist—not with claws, but with the dull pads of my fingers—and tugged.

He groaned as he pushed himself upright, the world tilting for him. His boots scraped the rock, toes searching for purchase. With his good arm he groped blindly until his palm collided with my shoulder. I let him find fur there, muscle beneath, something solid in the dark.

"This way," I coaxed, tugging again.

He stumbled to his feet, legs trembling. Shock made his movements slow, unsure. The blow to his head had left a faint sway in his stance; his balance was off, like a fawn on new ice. The air thickened around us with our mingled breaths.

I led him toward the rear of the chamber where the wall seemed to seal solid. To human eyes, there was nothing there but unbroken stone. To mine, a narrow runnel invisible in the dark—a seam where water had once whispered through.

I had widened it over years, claw by claw.

The crack would not admit a broad-shouldered man standing stiff, but it would accept one bent and guided, pressed close to the shape of me.

"Lower," I told him. "Shoulders down. Turn sideways."

He obeyed more than understood, too dazed to argue. His chest brushed the stone with each breath; the rock scraped a line along his jacket. I went first, pulling him after me by the wrist, backing into the slit so our bodies slid against one another in cramped friction.

His heart hammered against my shoulder blade where his chest met my back. I felt every beat.

The air changed at once—cooler, wetter, laced with the metallic tang of deeper veins. Sound shifted, too. Narrowing, amplifying small noises. Our breathing became loud in the confined space. Each scuff of his boot echoed ahead, multiplied and thrown back at us.

He muttered something under his breath that might have been a prayer.

"Good," I said. "Tell them where you are. Tell them who holds you. The mountain listens."

A few more shuffling steps and the rock widened just enough that he could straighten a little. I dropped to all fours for a stretch, letting my fingers feel the slight dip where runoff had carved a shallow channel. Water gathered here during storms, then slid away into the lower throat of the caves.

He slipped once, foot skidding in the damp. His shoulder slammed into the wall. The sound cracked along the tunnel.

I caught him before he could fall, wrapping an arm around his waist and hauling him back upright. His weight sagged into me, heavier than he looked. Human bodies always surprised me that way: so soft, yet so full of stubborn mass.

"Careful," I chided, though a small, satisfied noise purred at the back of my throat. "You will bruise."

He laughed once. A thin, broken sound. "You care if I bruise?"

"Yes," I said simply. "You are mine. I don't like my things damaged by anyone but me."

He went quiet after that.

We descended in slow, clumsy increments—his, not mine. I could have flown down this passage, memory and muscle carrying me in a fluid rush. Instead I matched his awkward pace, adjusting each step to his uncertainty. The darkness thickened around us, then turned from absence to presence—a living thing pressing in, cool and damp.

Small sounds began to thread the air: the steady plink of water falling from stalactites into unseen pools, the distant rush of something larger moving far below. The stone underfoot grew slicker; thin skins of moisture glinted under my invisible gaze.

He shivered again. The chill was seeping through his clothes, through his thin skin.

"We're almost there," I lied. Time meant little down here. Distance even less. "Deeper is safer. No one will steal you there."

"Why...why would anyone want to?" His voice cracked on the words.

Because you saw me, I thought. *Because you looked up at the night and let it choose you. Because the dragon woman and I both heard the same Song coil around your fear.*

"Because they take," I said instead. "That is what they do. I keep."

My tail brushed his calf, a gentle herding. He followed.

The air cooled further, touched now with the clean, hard scent of moving water. The distant roar grew louder, layer by layer, until it became a constant in the background—a white rush that filled all the quiet spaces.

He flinched at a louder echo, hand tightening on my shoulder.

"What's that?" he shouted, voice swallowed and thrown back at us in ragged fragments.

"Home," I purred. "Listen. It will cover your heartbeat. It will hide your smell. No dragon, no beast, no stealer will hear you over that."

He swallowed, Adam's apple bobbing against the dim shine of my gaze.

I smiled in the dark, unseen.

The mountain closed behind us, stone and water and echo swallowing the world above. Every step took him further from her and deeper into mine.

The river grew louder the deeper we went.

Not the open, laughing water the humans liked to play in, but the old kind that lived under stone. It spoke in grind and echo and endless fall, a low roar that crawled up through the bones and shook loose whatever was not anchored.

He stumbled behind me, one hand dragging along the wall, the other gripping the back of my scruff where I let his fingers tangle in the thick ruff of fur. His boots slid in the damp. His breath sawed in and out, harsh little clouds I could hear more than see.

"Watch," I said, though his human eyes were useless here. "Step after mine. The stone bites harder than I do."

The ceiling dropped, close enough that I felt rock brush the tips of my ears. Moisture beaded on my whiskers, tiny droplets catching the faintest greenish glow ahead.

The moss was singing.

It clung to the walls in thin veils, its bioluminescence a shy, pulsing heartbeat that barely scratched the dark. To me, it painted everything in clear lines: the curve of the tunnel, the jagged teeth of stalactites, the rope of roots breaking through stone. To him, it was only suggestion. Hints of shape. Phantom light.

"So dark...so cold," he whispered, voice fraying on the edges.

Good, I thought.

"I am your warmth; your life," I purred.

The tunnel opened without warning. The sound hit first, as it always did. No drip or trickle now, but a full curtain of water plunging from a slit in the ceiling into a black pool below. The falls turned the cavern into a throat of thunder. Every surface shook with it, the vibration a constant shudder through pads and claws and marrow.

He flinched, hand flying from my fur to cover one ear.

"Too loud," he gasped.

I loved it.

The roar hid scent. Hid heartbeat. Hid speech. Up above, ears and noses and clever metal toys might find a man on a hillside. Down here, under this pounding veil, the world beyond my walls went deaf.

My nest spread out around us, carved by time and patience into something almost like a home. The ceiling arched high, hung with stone teeth. The pool at its center was ink-black, mirror-slick until the falls shattered it into spray. Water channeled away through narrow cracks, feeding the underground veins of the mountain.

Along the outer curve of the cavern I had built my arrangements.

Bones, yes. Many. Some stacked in careful spirals, some woven like ribs of pale wood into low fences. Skulls lined the ledges, each turned to face the pool, empty sockets catching moss-light. Antlers interlocked overhead in elegant tangles, their tips polished to a warm, touched sheen.

In one corner, under a natural overhang, lay my hearth. Stones blackened by years of smoke ringed a shallow basin. A stack of dry wood, scavenged from sunlit slopes and carried down piece by piece, waited beside it. Pelts were piled in a low mound nearby: deer, bear, coyote, all tanned by use more than craft, their fur still thick and soft.

My den. My chapel. My throat of thunder.

I led him to the pelts and felt his legs buckle when they touched the edge. He folded to his knees with a choked sound, fingers clutching at fur.

"Please," he said. I could barely hear him over the falls. "Please don't—"

"Shh." I nuzzled the side of his neck, inhaling the salt and sour and copper there. His skin quivered under my nose. "You shake like a leaf, little storm. The water will stiffen you if I leave you dressed."

His hands fumbled at his jacket, clumsy with cold and exhaustion. I let him try. When he tangled himself instead, I stepped in.

Claws half sheathed, I caught cloth and pulled. The zipper gave with a sharp little snap. Layers came away like shed bark. The smell of him sharpened with each barrier removed, until there was only damp cotton and warm skin and the faint musk of fear-sweat.

He squeezed his eyes shut, cheeks flushing as the last of his shirt peeled over his head.

I tilted mine, considering.

Human bodies were so fragile. All flat planes and soft curves; no proper fur, no armor save bone, and the thin tension of muscle. Yet there was a certain symmetry to him. The slope of shoulder to chest. The narrow waist. The lines of tendon in his throat when he swallowed.

Mine, I thought again, a slow, satisfied purr building in my chest.

Bruises bloomed along his ribs where he had hit rock on our way down. Purple, green, yellow. Marks of impact and possession. I groomed around them with careful licks of my tongue, the rasp of it leaving gooseflesh in its wake.

He shivered.

"Too cold," he whispered.

"Then we warm you."

I hooked a claw into the waistband of his jeans and tugged. He yelped, startled, but didn't fight when I stripped them away, then the thin scrap of fabric beneath. His hands fluttered, seeking something to cover himself with, but my tail curled around his wrist, all gentle steel.

"No hiding," I said. "Not from me. The mountain already knows every inch of you. I should, too."

His pulse drummed at the base of his throat like a trapped bird. I watched it for a moment, hypnotized, then turned toward the pool.

Steam did not rise from it. This was not a human bath with candles and comfort. The water that crashed down was snowmelt and hidden spring, cold enough to bite.

I stepped into it first.

The shock hit in a bright rush, stabbing up through my legs to my spine. My fur flattened, slick and heavy, then lifted again as I shook, droplets scattering in a glittering halo that the moss caught and held for heartbeats.

"Yes," I sighed. "Good."

I beckoned him.

He came because there was nowhere else to go. Each step he took into the shallows turned his skin paler, gooseflesh racing up his thighs, across his belly, up his chest. When the water reached his hips he hissed through his teeth.

"Too—too cold—"

"It will wake what needs waking," I said. "And numb what hurts."

He was all edges now. Elbows, ribs, clenched jaw. The roar of the falls pounded against his skull. I waded closer and pressed my body along his side, letting my warmth bleed into him where it could.

"Lean," I ordered.

He did, sagging against me. My paws braced on the slick stone. With one, I cupped handfuls of water and poured them over his shoulders, his back, his chest. Each cascade carved new paths through dirt and dried blood, leaving his skin clean and raw-pink.

I worked slowly, methodically, the way I had once cleaned my own kits when they were too small to manage it. Claws half extended, I scraped mud from under his nails, smoothed tangles from his hair. The pads of my paws followed the ridge of his spine, the dip of his lower back, memorizing him by touch.

He breathed around little gasps, almost sobs, the cold a shock that bordered on pain.

"It...it hurts," he chattered.

"Yes." I stroked water over his face, wiping away the tracks of earlier tears. "Life hurts."

His eyes opened then, wide and glassy, pupils blown huge in the dim. For a moment we simply looked at one another, the world narrowed to falling water and shared shiver.

"Why," he chattered, barely audible.

My whiskers brushed his cheek. "You...you I carried. You I bathe. You I name *mine*."

The word thrummed through the cavern, through my chest. *Mine*.

His knees buckled again. I guided him out of the pool before the cold stole him entirely, steering him toward the hearth. Water streamed off his skin in rivulets, catching the moss-light like threads of liquid silver.

I settled him on the pelts nearest the fire ring then shook myself, sending an arc of droplets flying into the dark. My fur fluffed out again, thicker, ready to be blanket as well as guard.

A sparkstone lay where I had left it, tucked into a shallow crack in the rock. I struck it with one claw, once, twice, until fat sparks kissed the tinder. The dry kindling caught with a soft whoomph, orange licking up and out, pushing back the greenish glow with its own restless dance.

Firelight painted his skin in copper and shadow. The chill left his limbs in visible waves. Little tremors rippled along his muscles as feeling returned.

I crouched beside him and draped one of the largest pelts over his lower half. His hands clutched it instinctively, dragging it higher, grateful for the barrier and the warmth both.

"There," I said. "See? My nest has teeth, but it also has fur."

He huffed out something that might have been a laugh, or a sob.

I lowered my head until my brow touched his, the way I had once greeted my mother after long hunts. My breath mingled with his, hot and cold.

"You will live," I told him. "Because I say so. I will feed you, guard you, keep every claw and bullet from your skin."

His eyes squeezed shut. A tear slid from the corner of one, cutting a new clean line.

"Why?" he whispered. "Why me?"

Because you looked at the stars, I thought. *Because you sang under your breath when you thought the dark was empty. Because you didn't scream when you saw me the first time. Because when my claws closed on you, the Song in your bones did not break.*

My tail curled around his ankle again, anchoring him to the stone. To me.

"No hunter will drag you away. No man will claim you back. Not even the dragon woman who thinks the mountain listens only to her. You will stay. You will eat what I bring, sleep where I curl, breathe under my watching. You will give your days and your dreams to this den."

His breath hitched. For a moment I felt something in him try to rise —panic, protest, the human instinct to run. The roar of the falls crushed it back down.

"And if I say no?" he asked, the bravest thing he had said yet.

I smiled, slow and sharp. "The mountain has already heard you say yes."

I pulled the pelt higher around his shoulders and lay down beside him, not quite touching. Heat from the fire lapped at our fronts while the stone's chill kissed our backs. The thunder of the water wrapped us in its constant, beating shroud.

After a while, his shivers eased. His breathing lengthened, deepening into the rhythm of exhausted sleep. His hand, tangled in the fur at my neck, loosened but did not let go.

I watched his face, the tiny twitches that moved through it as dreams took hold.

Mine, I thought one more time, the word a vow and a prayer both.

The Hallow hummed in the stone in answer, low and approving, as if the mountain had taken note.

In my nest, in my dark, with my river singing and my bones arranged just so, I closed my eyes at last and let the world narrow to the sound of his breathing and the certainty that no dragon, no hunter, no god would take this from me.

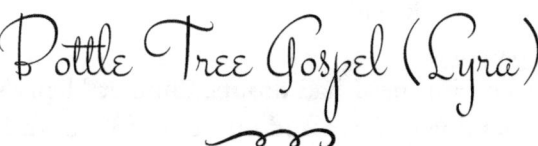 Bottle Tree Gospel (Lyra)

The Bottle Tree smelled like salvation and heartburn.

Chili, cornbread, spilled beer, wood worn smooth by a hundred elbows—those scents hit me the second I pushed through the door. Warm and thick and familiar enough to make my knees consider folding. Behind it all, the faint, ever-present whiff of fryer oil and whatever floral perfume Maeve favored this month clung to the air like a blessing.

The place was already humming.

Tall barstools scraped the scarred hardwood every time someone shifted their weight. Neon signs buzzed and glared from behind the bar —a blue one in the shape of the state, a red one promising a beer special that had been discontinued five years ago. The old jukebox in the corner spilled out a low, lazy guitar line, half-drowned by conversation and the occasional burst of laughter from the regulars' table under the mounted elk head.

I didn't realize I'd been holding my breath until the door swung shut behind me and the tavern's warmth wrapped around my shoulders like a coat I actually wanted to wear.

Compared to the woods, the Bottle Tree was dim—the kind of low, amber light that made everyone look softer and more forgivable. Strings of green and blue glass bottles hung in the front windows, catching what little remained of the sunset and turning it into shards of color on the floor. A real bottle tree—gaudy and glorious—stood by the door like a sentry: an iron trunk sprouting arms tangled in bottles of every shape and hue. Locals stuffed notes in some of them. Wishes. Warnings. Confessions.

The mountain had its Hallow Song.

The town had this.

Butch wasn't with me; I had dropped him at Henry's on the way over. The kid was finally down and out, dead to the world in his own cabin for at least six hours. It eased my mind to leave a hundred pounds of dog snore and fur to keep watch over the kid.

"About time," Maeve called, voice cutting across the room like a warm knife. "I was about to send a search party. You eat yet?"

I shrugged out of my damp jacket, the muscles between my shoulder blades protesting after too many hours and not enough sleep. I'd gone home because protocol and sanity both insisted. Shower, twenty minutes on top of the covers with my boots off, and Butch snoring on the rug; just long enough for my eyes to shut and my bones to remember there was such a thing as stillness.

"I could eat," I said, which in Maeve's dialect meant pile it high and don't argue.

"Good." She jerked her chin toward my usual spot. "Stool's been keeping a warm spot for you. Well. Warmish. Sheriff's ass sat there an hour ago, but I wiped it down with honor."

The recovery team had claimed the big table under the bear. Half a dozen SAR volunteers, two deputies, and a forest service tech leaned across their drinks, faces flushed from hot food and hot talk. Their neon-bright flagging tape still hung from various pockets and loops like they'd forgotten to take off their armor.

I slid onto my barstool. The cushion knew the shape of me. So did Maeve; she already had a mug halfway to the tap.

"Root beer," I reminded her.

She sniffed. "You and your temperance. Coffee after, so you don't fall asleep on my bar. Chili and cornbread?"

"Yes."

"Cheese?"

I gave her a look.

She snorted. "Like I don't know your sins by now." She ladled a mountain of chili into a deep bowl, topped it with shredded cheddar and a dollop of sour cream, and slid it in front of me along with a slab of cornbread that steamed when I broke it open.

I didn't realize how ravenous I was until the first spoonful hit my tongue—spice and smoke and tomato, the kind of heat that bloomed in the chest instead of the throat. Food tasted better after a day like this, partly because my body remembered it still existed and partly because I knew the dead would never taste anything again.

I ate.

Around me, the Bottle Tree breathed.

A kid no older than ten darted between tables, weaving his way back to his family's booth and clutching the stuffed black bear somebody had won from the claw machine by the restrooms. A pair of older women in church cardigans clinked margarita glasses and cackled at something on a phone screen. A line of muddy work boots sat under the regulars' table like they were part of the decor.

The world had not ended because one boy lay cooling in the morgue and another was missing.

It never did.

That was the cruelty and the mercy of it.

"...and my granddaddy always said if you heard her laughing in the holler after midnight, you turned right around and went home."

My attention snapped to the recovery table.

Maeve stood there, one hand braced on the back of a chair, dish towel tucked into the waistband of her jeans like a holster. The SAR techs leaned in, elbows on the scarred wood, boots hooked around the chair legs. One deputy had his forearms crossed on the table, badge catching the light whenever he shifted. Their bowls were empty, their glasses half-drunk.

They were listening.

"She'd laugh like a woman," Maeve went on, her voice dropping into the storyteller cadence I'd heard a thousand times. Evening rose and fell around it, the bar's noise dimming in a natural circle. "Pretty as you please. Not a cackle. Not a witch. Like somebody told her a good joke and she just couldn't help herself. That's how she gets you."

"Gets you how?" one of the volunteers asked. He was new to the county—I could tell by the clean lines of his jacket and the way he still looked at the mounted heads on the walls like they were impressive.

"Depends which story you believe," Maeve said. "Some folks say she just chases you out. Some say she eats you heart-first so you still got time to regret your choices."

There were a couple nervous laughs.

"Wampus, right?" another said. "That thing those hikers were talking about today?"

Maeve's gaze slid toward me, just for a second. Measuring. Checking.

I kept eating.

"Wampus cat," she corrected. "Woman on two legs, cat on four, both when she's feeling frisky. Old as the oldest trees. Mean as a drunk copperhead. You boys think you're brave until you meet something that's been hunting this ridge since before your granddaddy learned how to read a deer track."

The rookie deputy scoffed, but it was thin. "Come on, Maeve. It's just a story."

She raised a brow, unimpressed. "Stories are how the mountain tries to give you a cheat sheet, honey. You'd do better to listen."

One of the older SAR guys rubbed his jaw. "My uncle used to say she watched the hunters, not the hikers. If you set snares, she set her sights. If you took more than you needed, she marked your scent. Said there's balance in it. Predators hunting predators."

"Your uncle had sense," Maeve said. "Shame it skips generations."

The table laughed, but there was a nervous edge to it. I watched their eyes flick toward the windows, toward the darkness gathering behind the glass bottles. They were remembering the body they'd helped haul out, the mess that hadn't looked quite enough like a bear or a cougar had made it. They were remembering the copper taste in their mouths they couldn't explain.

The Hallow's Song hummed under my boots, faint but insistent. It could reach even here—through the cracks in the old floor, through the stone foundation, through the roots of the oak that shaded the back patio. It didn't care about neon signs or sports on the corner TV. It cared about the shape of fear sitting heavy in the lungs of half the room.

The mountain heard.

It always did.

I scraped my spoon along the bottom of the bowl, gathering the last of the chili. My hand shook once, a tremor so small only I noticed. Hours since we'd found Tommy. Hours since I'd left his body under a sheet on the hillside and walked away into my private storm. Hours since Taren's voice had poured through the rain and steadied me from the inside out.

I'd gone home because Henry needed me to be human enough to expect a shower and a change of clothes.

I'd come here because I needed to remember I was still tied to the living.

Michelle Crane sat alone at a two-top near the back, under the old concert poster wall. Her pink jacket had been traded for a Bottle Tree sweatshirt two sizes too big, sleeves swallowing her hands. Her phone glowed in front of her, the blue light painting her face in ghost colors. She scrolled and scrolled, thumb flicking sharp, as if somewhere in the endless digital stream there'd be a post that said 'Never mind. False alarm. Happy ending'.

Her untouched cornbread sat cooling on a plate.

Maeve finished her tale with a shrug that wasn't quite casual. "All I'm saying is, if you see something with a woman's laugh and a cat's eyes, don't hang around. Get off the ridge. Let the old things do their work."

"Super comforting," one of the SAR volunteers muttered, but his hand went reflexively to the string of bottle charms tied around his wrist —a gift from his grandmother, I remembered. For luck. For protection.

"I aim to please," Maeve said. "Or at least keep you breathing long enough to complain." She straightened, snagged two empty bowls in one hand and a basket of fries with the other. "Now eat what's left or I'm calling your mother and telling her you wasted my cornbread."

They groaned and laughed. The spell broke into fragments of conversation—someone at the bar yelled for another round, the jukebox swapped to a faster song, the elk stared down at us all in permanent bafflement.

Maeve dropped the dishes at the pass, snapped some order at the line cook, then made her way back toward me.

She topped off my root beer without asking. Foam rose, catching the glow from the neon and turning it to a soft amber crown.

"You look like overcooked pasta, Ranger," she observed, bracing her hands on the bar.

"Flattering," I said.

"You pay me for accuracy, not ego management."

"I don't pay you at all."

"Exactly." She tipped her chin toward the recovery table. "You hear me brag on your monster?"

"I heard." I took a sip, cool and sweet and sharp against my tongue. "You're going to have them all sleeping with the lights on."

"Good." She snagged a bar towel and twisted it in her hands, eyes sliding briefly toward Michelle. "Tommy's folks are driving in tomorrow morning. Sheriff's bringing a pastor to meet them at the station. I figured tonight I'd give the ones who found him something to think on."

Her gaze met mine.

There was nothing soft in it—the kind of look carved by years of weather and worry, by winters that buried roads and summers that burned off illusions. Mountain wisdom lived behind those eyes, old and unhurried. The kind that came from burying neighbors, raising search parties, and learning what the ridgelines take as payment.

I'd never been able to picture Maeve young. Not truly. Not carefree or foolish or anything less than the woman standing in front of me now; shoulders steady, jaw set like bedrock. She carried the gravity of a longstanding pact with these hills, the kind of seriousness that made you believe she knew every secret the mountain had ever whispered.

"Think she's out there still?" one of the deputies called from the table. "Your Wampus?"

Maeve didn't look away from me when she answered. "Oh, she's out there."

The Hallow shivered under the boards at my feet; a low, almost amused chord.

I swallowed a sigh.

There were days I wished the mountain would pick a different mouthpiece.

"Any word on our missing boy?" Maeve asked me softly, voice dropping under the general din.

"Nothing since I left the ridge," I said. "Grid search is paused till first light on the far side. They've got deputies at the lower crossings, trailheads, and county roads. If he walked out and hit pavement, somebody will see him."

Maeve snorted softly. "If he walked out, he'd have come here. Everyone else does."

I didn't argue. She was right. The Bottle Tree was gravity. If you were scraped up by these hills and still breathing, you ended up on one of these stools eventually.

Her eyes searched my face like she was reading a menu. "And you? You hear anything?"

She didn't mean radios.

I let my gaze travel over the room before answering. The regulars. The SAR team. The deputy pretending he wasn't still shaken. Michelle, a raw wound lit blue in the corner.

"I heard enough," I said.

Maeve hummed, the sound low and skeptical but accepting. She'd lived with these mountains long enough to know when a conversation had reached its edge.

"Eat your cornbread," she said instead. "You're no good to anybody if you fall over in the woods tomorrow."

"Yes, Mama," I muttered.

She smacked the bar with the towel in dignified delight and moved down to tend to another customer.

I tore off a piece of cornbread and let it crumble a little between my fingers before eating it. Cornmeal, apple butter, just enough sweetness to be indulgent. I chewed slowly, letting my shoulders lower notch by notch.

The tavern thrummed around me—footsteps, laughter, clinks of glass, the muted clatter from the kitchen. Someone fed the jukebox a new dollar and the song changed, fiddle sliding in under guitar. Conversations rose and fell like small waves. A bottle clinked against another in the tree by the door whenever someone came in or out, catching the draft and chiming thinly.

Under it all, the mountain's hum stayed steady. The Hallow Song threaded up through the floor into my bones, a reminder and a warning both.

Old things were listening.

Old things were moving.

My thoughts were swirling around in my head when the front door opened and let the night in.

Cold air slipped across the floorboards in a narrow draft. It carried rain, wet asphalt, and a faint sterile note that didn't belong to the Bottle Tree. Antiseptic and steel and the ghost of formaldehyde.

Monroe stepped through it like he was bringing the smell with him.

He was built like the hills around us—lean and stringy rather than big, all tendon and wiry strength. Receding hairline, what was left of it kept clipped short; beard trimmed close enough to show the sharp angles beneath. His face had the weathered lines of a man who'd squinted into too many storms and rafters of fluorescent light. His gait always made me think of a fox: careful, unhurried, and taking in more than he let on.

He paused just inside, letting his eyes adjust to the dim. Neon painted one side of his face blue, the other amber. For a second, the coroner and the mountain man overlapped—the licensed official and the boy who'd probably grown up gutting trout in cold creek water.

Maeve spotted him first. Of course she did.

"Well, if it isn't the angel of awful timing," she called, snapping the bar towel over her shoulder. "You hungry, or just here to ruin somebody's appetite?"

Monroe's mouth tipped. He made his way to the bar with the slow inevitability of gravity.

"Evening, Maeve. Lange." He nodded at each of us in turn then slid onto the stool beside me with a small grunt, as if sitting after the day we'd had was its own kind of mercy. "Chili if there's any left. Beer if you're feeling generous. Coffee if you're feeling vindictive."

"You get both," Maeve said, already reaching for a bowl. "You look like something the cat dragged in and decided against."

"Flattering," he murmured. His gaze flicked to my half-empty bowl, then to my face. "You alright?"

"I've been worse," I said. It was true. It also wasn't the point.

Maeve set a steaming bowl down in front of him, then a bottle of local amber and a chipped mug that might once have been white. He wrapped his hands around the coffee first, as if he needed warmth more than bite.

"It's Tommy," he said after one swallow. No preamble. That wasn't his way. "Next of kin confirmed."

My hand tightened around my own mug. "Parents?"

"Mother on photo ID." He blew out a breath through his nose. "Sheriff didn't want her at the scene. Good call. Father's driving in at first light. We'll do a formal view if he insists."

Maeve braced her elbows on the bar opposite us, towel clenched in one fist, her earlier storyteller's ease gone. "You tell them anything yet?"

"Only what I had to," Monroe said. "Hunter. Accident. Animal involved. We'll have more when we have more."

His eyes slid to me again, the question unspoken.

"What did you see?" I asked quietly.

The tavern noise swelled and dipped around us—cutlery clinking, chairs scraping, the jukebox shifting into an old Van Morrison track. A burst of laughter went up near the pool table. None of it touched the space on the bar where the three of us had circled an invisible body.

Monroe rubbed a hand over his jaw. "Officially? Cause of death is exsanguination secondary to massive thoracic trauma. That's what's going on the paperwork. Animal attack—probable cat." He gave Maeve a look. "That make you feel better?"

"Not even a little," she said.

"Same," I added.

He took a spoonful of chili, chewed like the act of eating bought him time to put his words in order. When he spoke again his voice dropped, meant for our ears and no one else's.

"Off the record," he said, "it's wrong."

"How wrong?" I asked.

Monroe rotated his spoon between his fingers, the polished handle catching the bar's low light. "Ribs were crushed inward, not just broken. Sternum, too. Like something came down on his chest with a hell of a lot of focused force. You see that with cars. Sometimes with trees if the timing's bad. Not like this." He shook his head. "His heart and lungs were pulp."

Maeve's mouth tightened. "Bear?"

"If it were a bear, half of him'd be missing." Monroe's gaze went distant, cataloguing. "We had that black up on Beulah Ridge last year—remember? One swipe and the poor bastard's arm looked like pulled pork. Teeth tore, claws raked, then it fed. It ate. That's the point for a bear."

He took another sip of coffee. I could see the steam fog the lenses of his memory.

"This wasn't feeding," he went on. "A lot of tearing, yes, but shallow in some places, deep in others; like something changed its mind halfway through. Claw marks don't match the usual suspects. Too wide a spread to be bobcat. Wrong angle for cougar. I measured a few—not quite human hand-span, not quite paw."

Maeve's brows snapped together. "You're saying what, it...played?"

Monroe's jaw worked. "I'm saying it felt like...punishment. Or enjoyment. Or both. Not a clean kill for meat."

I thought of the way the Wampus had ripped the vest open like confetti. The way her purr had vibrated through the soil.

"What about his neck?" I asked.

"Bitten," Monroe said. "Teeth impressions—big ones—but not a full crush. More like control. Holding. The fatal damage was the chest. Whoever—or whatever—did it wanted him to know he was dying."

Maeve swore softly under her breath.

"And scavengers?" I asked. "Any sign of them setting in?"

"That's another thing." Monroe pushed the chili away, appetite finally losing to the details. "There should've been carrion insects already starting, given the time frame. Some surface activity at least. Flesh like that, out in the open? Nature doesn't waste. But the wound tracks and blood dispersion told a different story. It all happened faster than the environment could react. And there was this...pattern."

"What pattern?" Maeve asked.

He glanced around, making sure no one was leaning too close, then leaned in himself. I mirrored the motion. So did Maeve.

"Scratches on the exposed bone," he said. "Fine ones. Not from teeth or claws. Like something with smaller points—not quite nails—had...petted him. After." His mouth curled, uncomfortable. "I've done this twenty-odd years. I don't spook easy. That spooked me."

A shiver traced the back of my neck.

"Any sign of tools?" I asked. "Knives, hooks, anything man-made?"

"No," Monroe said. "No hesitation marks, no slicing before tearing. If a human was involved, they weren't the one doing the damage. Animal saliva present along the ragged edges—protein markers, enzymes. But..."

"But?" Maeve pressed.

He huffed. "We didn't get as much of it as I'd expect. Parts of the wounds were almost...rinsed. Like water had washed them, but not from weather. More targeted." He shrugged one shoulder. "Could be I'm overthinking. Could be the rain did stranger things than it should've."

I watched the way the muscles in his jaw flexed, the way the lines at the corners of his eyes deepened. Monroe overthought for a living. It kept him honest.

"You ever seen anything like this before?" I asked.

"Not here," he said. "I saw something close in Montana when I was green." His mouth tugged sideways. "Rancher's son, found half down a ravine. Cat got him, they said. But the eyes... Someone'd closed them. Carefully. Like they couldn't stand the way he'd died and tried to give him a different story."

Maeve's hand, still clenched in the bar towel, loosened. "Tommy's eyes were open when they found him."

"Yeah." Monroe stared into his coffee as if it might offer absolution. "And whatever that thing was, didn't care."

We sat with that for a moment. The jukebox hummed on, oblivious. Someone dropped a pool ball hard enough to make it crack against the felt. A burst of laughter rose from the corner where the recovery team had gathered, smoke and legend thick around them.

Michelle's silhouette huddled over her phone near the back wall, a thin thread of pink in a room of flannel and denim.

Monroe followed my gaze, then brought it back to me. "There's something else."

"Of course there is," Maeve muttered.

He ignored her. "Sheriff wants to put out a statement tomorrow. Caution hikers, reassure the church crowd that we're on top of it. You know the drill. They'll say cougar. Maybe bobcat if they're feeling cute. They will not say monster."

"Good," I said. "Last thing we need is a bunch of idiots with rifles looking for Instagram glory."

Monroe nodded once. "Exactly. But I'm telling you two because I trust you to think beyond the press release." He lifted his mug again, fingers steady now. "Whatever did this...didn't finish. It wasn't hungry enough or it was interrupted. That means it might try again. Soon."

Maeve's eyes flicked to me. "You going back out tonight?"

I didn't bother lying. "After I talk to Michelle."

Monroe's mouth flattened. "Then be careful, Lange."

"I'm always careful," I said.

He gave me a look that said he'd seen the incident reports that said otherwise. "You're always effective," he corrected. "Careful is a different thing."

Maeve snorted. "Listen to the man. He's the one sewing what's left of folks back together."

Monroe's gaze sharpened. He lowered his voice further, so the words were for me alone. "I've cleaned up after bears. After mountain lions. After men. I know what they do to a body. I know the shape of their anger, their hunger, their accidents." A pause. "This felt...personal. Like something that thinks about itself. That's the part I don't like."

He held my eyes, and for a heartbeat the coroner saw straight through the ranger into the dragon coiled beneath.

"I've got a feeling," he said quietly, "this one's yours."

The Hallow hummed in my bones in grim agreement.

"I know," I said.

He nodded once, acceptance and warning both, then reached for his chili again as if naming the thing made his appetite come back.

Maeve exhaled, long and slow, then slapped the bar with her palm and straightened. "Alright," she said. "Enough morgue talk over my good beans. Monroe, eat. Lange, finish your root beer. Then go do what you do."

She shifted away down the bar to refill someone's glass, leaving Monroe and me in our small, heavy orbit.

He took one more bite, then nudged his shoulder against mine—a brief, awkward gesture of solidarity.

"Seriously," he said. "Watch your back out there."

"I will," I told him.

The bench across from Michelle still sat empty, a hollow space that made the entire booth look lopsided. Her phone screen glowed against her face, bleaching the color out of her cheeks. She wasn't scrolling, just staring. As if waiting for the device to give her a different story than the one she'd been handed.

The noise of the tavern swirled warm around her—pool balls cracking, chairs scraping, the low thrum of conversation—but none of it seemed to reach her.

Her shoulders were curled inward, protecting a center that had already been hit.

I slowed when I reached the table. Never rush grief. It bites.

"Michelle," I said softly.

She startled, blinking up at me like someone waking from too deep inside themselves. Her eyes were glassy, rimmed red. She tried to straighten, but her spine wouldn't hold it.

"Ranger Lange." Her voice cracked on the second word. She cleared her throat and tried again. "Sorry. I didn't see you."

"You don't have to apologize." I slid into the seat across from her, setting my hat beside me. "This is a hard day."

She looked down at the table. A napkin lay there, folded and refolded into tighter and tighter squares until it was nothing but creases. Her fingers smoothed one edge, then another, desperate for something to control.

"I heard them talking," she whispered. "Maeve. And the team.

93

About...about the legend." She swallowed hard. "About the thing in the woods."

I didn't answer immediately. Michelle needed to speak first. That was how the dam broke cleanly instead of exploding.

"I know it sounds stupid," she went on, voice tightening. "I know it's just stories. People around here like to scare tourists, right? But Tommy—" Her mouth trembled. The name cost her something. "The hunter boy, Tommy's gone. Found dead. And Darren...Darren hasn't answered his phone since last night. And the blood. He would never leave me like this."

Her knuckles went white around the napkin. "I just keep thinking maybe he got turned around. Lost. He wouldn't just—" She choked on the word 'disappear'.

I leaned forward, forearms on the table. Professional, steady, gentle without softening into false comfort.

"Yes, we found Tommy," I said. "But at this point, there is nothing connecting the cases. There's no reason to believe that Darren has suffered the same fate."

She pressed the napkin to her face, but it did nothing to stop the sound that escaped her—a breath turned inside out.

"I'm so sorry," I said.

"I keep thinking..." Her voice strained to stay low, but desperation leaked through every syllable. "If something like that got Tommy—if it was that fast, that violent—then Darren..."

Her throat closed. She shook her head hard, shaking off the thought like it burned.

I chose my next words carefully. Promises carried weight in mountains like these.

"I can't tell you he's safe," I said. "And I won't lie to you. But I can tell you we have trained teams out there tonight. Two dog units. Thermal drones flying grids at first light. I'm going back out myself."

She lifted her gaze, and for the first time I saw them without the glaze of shock—just raw fear.

"Do you think he could still be alive?" she asked.

The question punched the air out of her. Out of me, too.

I took a breath, steady as bedrock. "He has a chance," I said. "And as long as he has a chance, we fight for him. That's what I can promise."

She held that answer in her hands like a chipped cup—small, fragile. All she had.

"What if he's hurt?" she whispered. "What if he's cold? He hates the cold. Did...did anyone find his jacket? He had it tied around his waist when—"

Her voice broke again, and she pressed her fists to her forehead. "God, I don't know what to do. I don't know whether to hope or—" She stopped, breath shuddering. "Or stop."

"Hope helps him," I said gently. "Hope keeps you steady. And steady people are easier to help. When I find him, he needs someone on the other side of this who isn't falling apart."

She let out a small, ugly laugh. "Too late."

"No," I said simply. "You're here. You're fighting. That counts."

For a moment she stayed bowed over her hands, shoulders shaking. Then she dragged in a breath and forced herself upright.

"I'm sorry," she murmured again. "This must be nothing compared to what you see all the time."

I shook my head. "Loss is never nothing. Not once."

Her eyes filled again.

I reached across the table and set my hand near hers—not touching, but close enough to bridge the distance between us. "Then we're going to bring everything we have to getting him back."

Her fingers twitched, then settled. She nodded, trembling.

"Thank you," she whispered.

"Try to sleep tonight," I said. "Even a few hours helps. I'll call you the moment we have anything."

She nodded again, but I could see she wouldn't sleep. Not without nightmares waiting on both sides.

I rose slowly, giving her time to gather herself. The tavern's warmth seemed to bend around her booth, trying to shield her in its glow.

"Michelle?" I said gently.

She looked up.

"We won't stop looking," I told her. "Not for a second."

Something in her finally yielded—a tiny exhale that sounded like a prayer with no language attached.

I stepped away from the table, threading through the crowd and toward the door.

As I reached the door, the Bottle Tree's lights flickered.

Just once. Barely a shiver.

But every conversation dipped mid-syllable. Every fork paused halfway to a mouth. The jukebox hiccupped; the neon beer sign buzzed like a hornet nest stirred too hard.

Then everything steadied.

Maeve's eyes snapped up from the taps. Monroe froze halfway through a sip. Even Michelle tensed, head lifting, as if she felt it in her bones.

The mountain had spoken.

I put my hat on my head and stepped into the cooling night.

The hunt was waiting.

Deep Earth Devotion (Wampus)

Water still clung to my fur when I slipped back through the waterfall's curtain.

The world outside roared and flashed and clawed at its own sky. But in here, the sound gentled—thunder turned to a steady, muffled growl. Cold drops skated down my spine, gathered at the curve of my tail, and fell one by one onto the stone. The cave breathed around me, damp and deep, its air thick with mineral and smoke and the faint, sweet edge of human.

His scent.

I paused just inside the narrow throat of rock, letting my pupils swell to drink what little light the den offered. Fire-glow pulsed at the far end of the chamber—soft, orange, heart-like. The slick walls held the flicker and gave it back in fragments, so it looked as if embers floated behind the stone.

He lay where I had left him.

The pelts had taken his shape over the last few hours, curled up around his sides like loyal beasts. Deer, fox, coyote—the ghosts of old hunts making a nest for my newest one. Firelight stroked his bare skin in long, slow passes, turning it copper, then gold, then shadow. His chest rose and fell with the fragile rhythm of human sleep, each inhale a small, defiant act against the dark.

His eyelids trembled now and then, as if he still ran in his dreams. I watched the tiny movements with a pleasure I didn't have words for. He ran in there; he stayed with me out here. Both truths fed me.

He hadn't tried to crawl away while I was gone.

Good.

I shifted my grip on the rabbits, their small bodies limp, and wet from the spray. A few dark drops fell from their noses to the stone, vanishing almost at once in the damp. They still held a trace of the meadow on their fur—sun on clover, panic in the grass. I had taken them from a place I remembered well: the first hollow I ever hunted in, when my paws were too big for my body and my hunger was bigger than both.

"You ran fast," I murmured to them as I padded toward the fire. My voice echoed softly, fur and stone swallowing its harsher edges. "Now you feed my prize."

Life fed life. That was the only honest law. Men tried to stack laws on top of that one—paper rules and iron traps—but paper rotted and iron rusted. Hunger stayed.

I crouched near the hearth I had carved from the rock, a shallow hollow blackened from years of use. Above it, the smoke wound its way along a narrow crack in the ceiling and disappeared. Men would have called it poor ventilation. I called it a blessing—just enough draft to keep the fire breathing but not enough to betray the den with a plume outside.

With a flick of my wrist, I laid the rabbits on a flat stone and drew one claw along the soft fur of the first. My nails were made for this—violence and precision. The same gift turned different ways. The skin parted with a faint, damp sigh. Warmth rushed out, a small exhale of heat that steamed in the cool cave air.

I worked methodically. A cut here, a tug there. The sound of pelt leaving muscle was an old, familiar one. A quiet, sticky peeling that always reminded me of shedding my own skins when the Song first remade me. Strips of fur came loose in my hands, still warm from the little hearts that had beat beneath. I folded each pelt carefully, even though no one was watching. Some I would cure and keep, some I would lay at the edge of the underground stream for the minnows to tug at. Nothing truly vanished down here. It only changed shape.

Steam twisted upward as I exposed the pale meat. It smelled sharp and clean, all iron and wild green; the meadow's last message to the dark. I gutted them with the same care I had shown their skins, setting aside the bits the fire would like and the bits the water would take. The tiny hearts I held a breath longer between forefinger and thumb, feeling the echo of their last beats.

"Life into life," I told them. "Circle to circle."

The Song had hummed that into my bones once. Long before men gave me names meant as curses or blessing. Long before my hunger became a rumor mothers used to keep their kits close to the fire.

I had believed it then with a purity I did not recognize in myself anymore.

Now... now I believed in smaller things. A body. A den. A man whose warmth proved I still knew how to keep something alive.

My gaze slid back to him as I threaded strips of rabbit onto a slender branch and propped it over the coals.

He slept on his side, arm crooked beneath his head, curls damp with cave-humidity. The bruise along his temple had blossomed, deepening from red to the blue of mountain dusk. My doing. The river rocks' doing. Gravity's doing. Whichever story made him mine more cleanly.

His lips were parted just enough to show the edge of his teeth. His breath came shallow but steady. Shock and hunger weighed him down like stones sewn into his limbs. His body knew how to conserve itself. Clever thing.

The firelight painted shadows into all his hollows—collarbone, throat, the dip at his waist where soft human flesh yielded to bone. I watched the light wander him and felt a swell of satisfaction that had nothing to do with the meat on the spit.

How long had it been since another heartbeat had shared this cave with me? How many years had I been sleeping?

Time underground didn't keep itself in neat human stacks—days, weeks, months. Down here the passing was marked by other rhythms: flood seasons in the underground river, slow mineral drips building teeth from the ceiling, the thinning of my own patience. Sometimes the Song rose loud enough to pull me into the surface storms; sometimes it ran low and quiet as bone.

But people... people came less and less often. Their roads crept higher up the mountain's flank, then pulled back again. They built cities in the valleys instead, humming with neon. Animals knew better than to come too close.

For a long stretch I had only my own breath for company and the old, old voices lodged in the stone.

You were not made to be solitary, something in the rock had told me once. *Creatures like you are woven of others.*

Yet I had been alone.

Alone long enough that wanting had twisted under my skin, roots tangling around roots until I could no longer tell need from hunger, worship from possession.

He shifted in his sleep, a tiny sound escaping his throat. Not quite a word. Not quite a moan. My ears pricked toward him before I could stop them, the tufted tips catching small eddies of warm air the fire created.

He was so soft.

Not weak—not exactly. I had seen his stubbornness in the way he clawed at the rocks when I dragged him here, the way he had tried, even half-conscious, to anchor himself to the world he knew. But softness lived in him where it had long since burned out of me. A softness in his gaze when he looked at the sky. A softness in his hand when it brushed my cheek in that half-dream and did not pull away.

He is warm, I thought. *He is soft. He is mine.*

The world had taken enough from me.

I would keep this.

Fat spat from the rabbits as they cooked, hissing where it struck the coals. The scent of browning meat rose and wrapped itself around us—a thick, savory ribbon winding through smoke and stone. It layered over his human smell, over the trace of river and fear and sleep, until the cave became one woven rope of fragrance that said *mine, mine, mine* in every thread.

"Did you have someone to cook for you up there?" I asked him softly, knowing he couldn't answer. "A mother? A lover? Someone who thought of the way you take your food and tried to make it easy?"

The silence answered for him.

I had watched humans share meals before. Circles of them around fire or table, hands passing plates and bowls, laughter sticking in the grease on their fingers. I had watched lovers feed each other in the shadows of tents in my younger days, the bite passed between mouths more worship than nourishment. I had watched mothers chew meat to tenderness before placing it in their kits' lips, like offerings straight from their own bodies.

All of it had fascinated me. All of it had looked like a form of prayer.

They gave each other life—piece by piece, fork by fork—and called it ordinary.

My tail curled around my calf, restless.

They had never done that for me.

The Song had poured itself through me once, making creatures from my stray hungers, leaving me to tend them or chase them or bury them. The dragons had taken what they needed and left me behind with all their mistakes running wild in my forests. The men had taken my mountains and fed me their worst. And when it was all too much, when the near-ending came and the guardians chained themselves to stone, no one had asked what the Wampus wanted.

I had taught myself to stop wanting.

It hadn't worked.

The rabbits browned, skin crackling, the smell turning from sharp to rich. I turned the spit with a casual twist of my wrist, claws glinting, watching the juices bead and fall. Each pop of fat into ember sounded like a promise being sealed.

"Life into life," I murmured again. "Circle to circle."

Behind me, the underground river's voice never wavered. The waterfall that guarded my entrance thundered from far down the tunnel, the sound rolled to something lower, like a great cat purring in its sleep. The stone under my feet held the echo of older songs, older storms.

For a moment, I felt the old ache rise—the memory of being wrapped in that music, not just brushed by it. Of knowing I was loved by something large and indifferent, the way lightning loves the tallest trees.

Then it passed, as it always did.

Now there was this instead.

A man sleeping on my pelts. A pair of rabbits turned to offering. A den that smelled the way I always thought safety would smell, if such a thing existed for creatures like me.

When the meat was done I lifted the skewer and let it rest, juices settling. I took one of the bowls from the tidy stack I had carved from river-stone—smooth and gray, edges worn from use—and placed a few careful pieces inside. Not too much. He would be hungry, but human bellies were foolish when empty; they clawed at themselves if filled too fast.

I carried the bowl to his side.

Up close, the heat of him struck me anew, a gentle radiant warmth that felt more extravagant than any fire I had nursed. I knelt and set the bowl just in front of his mouth, so that when he woke his first breath would pull the scent straight into his lungs.

Slowly, with a careful claw, I pushed a lock of hair off his forehead. It clung slightly to my fingers, damp with cave-air and the salt at his hair-line. His skin was cooler there than it was at his throat. I almost bent to warm it with my tongue, the way I would for a fevered kit.

Soon, I told myself. Soon I would wake him. Soon I would say 'Open for me', and he would.

For now—

For now, I took my place.

I slid down onto my hip beside him, tail curling protectively around his legs. One hand rested lightly at the center of his chest, feeling the thump-thump-thump of his heart through skin and bone and fur. My other arm propped me up so I could watch his face.

The fire crackled. The river murmured. The mountain shifted its weight overhead.

Deep in my ribs, beneath fur and muscle and old scars, a purr began —low and steady, the sound of storms waiting beyond the horizon.

I let it rumble through me and into him.

I had made a feast for two.

Soon, he would eat.

And he would understand.

His breath hitched, body shifting beneath the pelts as if some nightmare had nudged him toward waking. I leaned forward, letting my cheek brush the warm rise of his shoulder. His skin tasted of salt and fever-dreams.

"Wake, little ember," I murmured against him, my lips grazing the place where his throat beat the loudest. "Your hunger calls to me."

My breath warmed his neck. He shivered.

Good.

His eyelids fluttered, lashes trembling like young leaves in a storm. When he opened his eyes they were clouded—exhaustion, starvation, confusion all swimming together. He blinked at the dim light, at the fire's glow, at my face so close to his.

Then the scent of the meat reached him.

His stomach growled, loud enough to echo off the stone.

He startled at the sound—embarrassed, maybe—but the instinct to survive burned through all his confusion. His hand rose, slow but determined, toward the bowl I'd placed near his lips.

I caught his wrist before he could touch it.

"No." My voice was soft, but firm enough to stop him. I guided his hand back down until it rested in his lap. "I give. You receive."

He blinked again as if trying to find meaning in the words. His arm trembled—weak, desperate. His lips parted in a small, helpless exhale.

I cupped his jaw in one hand, feeling the faint rasp of stubble beneath my thumb. He leaned into the touch without meaning to. Drawn by warmth, by instinct, by the echo of care he had gone too long without.

"Good," I murmured.

I took a small piece of meat from the bowl. Steam curled around my fingers. I held it near his lips, close enough that he could smell the richness—the fat, the char, the meadow running wild through the taste.

He leaned forward, but too fast.

A growl vibrated from deep in my chest—not anger, but correction. A low feline warning.

He froze.

"Slow," I breathed. "You will choke if you rush."

He swallowed hard, throat bobbing beneath my fingers. Then he nodded, obedient.

I brought the bite to his mouth again, slower this time. He opened for me. The moment the food touched his tongue, his eyes fluttered shut and he let out a sound that punched straight through the thin cage of my ribs—need, relief, life returning.

But then he tried to take more.

His hands rose again, instinct winning over instruction. I caught them both this time, folding his wrists gently back into his lap, pinning them there with a single palm.

"No," I whispered. "I feed you."

A tremor rippled through him—not fear exactly, but something close. Something like surrender pulled tight by survival.

I brought another morsel to his lips. He ate it more slowly, though hunger caused every line of his body to tremble. His jaw fluttered beneath my hold, soft movements brushing my fingers. When juice slicked down the corner of his mouth I caught it with my tongue, tasting him and the rabbit in one stroke.

His breath hitched.

"You are sloppy," I chided softly, letting my teeth graze his chin. "Let me keep you clean."

I fed him again and again, each bite small enough to force patience. His breathing deepened, his chest rising and falling with the rhythm I chose. When he tried to lean forward too quickly, I tightened my fingers around his jaw—not punishment, but guidance.

He let out a quiet, frustrated noise.

"Yes," I murmured. "Hungry. Good. But hunger teaches discipline."

He opened for me again.

This time, instead of placing the morsel in his mouth I held it between my lips. His eyes widened—fear, confusion, desire all tangled— but he parted his lips when I leaned in. Our mouths met, the heat of him soft and human against my teeth. I pushed the bite across his tongue, feeling the way his breath trembled against mine.

When he swallowed, a low sound escaped me—almost a purr.

Feeding was sacred. A ritual in some ancient part of me older than men's gods. When I fed another creature from my own hands, my own mouth, it was not sustenance.

It was claim.

It was devotion.

He was starving. Desperate. His body knew nothing but need.

And I... I offered him tenderness. Grooming, shaping, pacing. Teaching a rhythm with my breath and my hands and the slow curl of my tail.

He ate until his eyelids grew heavy again, each blink slower than the last. His jaw slackened faintly beneath my palm. The trembling in his fingers softened as warmth trickled back into his limbs.

"You see?" I whispered, brushing a stray curl off his forehead. "Only I keep you alive. Only I keep you fed."

He swallowed, a little too thickly. "I...I feel..." His voice cracked, unused. "Thank you."

He didn't understand the weight of those words.

But they hit me like a stone thrown into a still pool.

I bent my head and let my cheek rest against his hair. My heartbeat pressed into the crown of his skull.

"You will always eat," I murmured. "You will always drink. You will always be warm. With me."

His breath dragged, unsteady. Whether from exhaustion or fear or some muddled attempt at gratitude, I could not tell.

Humans were strange that way.

He sagged forward, his forehead brushing my stomach, his hands still pinned gently between his thighs where I had placed them. The contact warmed me from skin to marrow.

"Lie back," I told him.

He did. Limp, pliant, trusting.

I gathered the pelts around him, keeping only his shoulders and head against me. His cheek rested above my navel, his breath warming the strip of skin there.

His eyelids drooped.

He fought sleep, blinking too hard, trying to stay alert.

"No," I whispered, stroking the side of his face with my knuckles. "Rest. You have eaten. Your body must return to strength."

I curled around him, arms and tail and body forming a ring.

"No one will take you," I said with a growl so soft it touched the air more as vibration than sound. "Not the men. Not the hunters. Not even the woman of smoke and frost. You stay here. With me."

He shuddered—not with fear, not exactly, but something close. Something instinctive.

His breath slowed under my hand.

His lashes dipped again.

I lifted his head gently, guiding him until the side of his face rested against my stomach, exactly where I wanted him. His hair brushed my skin in small, feathering shocks.

He sighed, deep and defeated and warm.

Pride swelled in me—thick, heavy, possessive. A tide rising where loneliness had hollowed me out.

I stroked his hair once. Twice. Slowly.

His eyes finally closed.

"There," I murmured.

As the fire crackled, his breath evened out into soft, rhythmic pulls. His weight settled fully against me—trusting, yielded. *Mine.*

I folded my body around his like a fortress, like a nest. Like something ancient reclaiming what had been stolen.

And as his dreams pulled him under, I pressed my lips to the crown of his head and let a purr roll through my chest.

Possessive. Proud. Waiting.

A storm with its claws sheathed—for now.

He slept with his cheek against my stomach, his breath warming the small hollow just above my hips. His lashes lay dark against his skin; the faint sheen of sweat gleamed along his collarbone. He was soft like this —unguarded, pliant, dreaming of worlds that didn't have claws or teeth.

I combed my fingers through his hair, slow and steady. Each stroke soothed something frayed inside me, something that had been torn loose long before he ever wandered into my forest.

"You are mine," I whispered into the warm crown of his head. "You are warm. You are alive because I keep you so."

The words rumbled through my chest, a low vibration that echoed in his bones. My purr had grown since bringing him deeper underground, rich and resonant, as if the cave hummed in reply.

His breath hitched. Not waking, just shifting. Sensing me. Responding.

Good.

I leaned down until my lips hovered above the shell of his ear. "Wake, little ember."

His eyelids fluttered open, heavy and shimmering with confusion. His mouth parted in a soft, dazed sound. He blinked up at me like someone surfacing from deep water, unsure if the world had changed while he was submerged.

"It's...warm," he murmured, voice rasping.

"*I* am warm," I corrected gently. "And I will keep *you* warm."

I slid my hand along his sternum, feeling the faint tremor beneath his skin. His heartbeat stuttered then found its rhythm. He watched me the whole time, eyes unfocused but trusting in the way wounded creatures trust the darkness that shelters them.

"Sit up," I whispered, coaxing his shoulders with my palms.

He obeyed slowly, dazed, guided more by instinct than choice. His muscles trembled with weakness but he leaned into my touch, letting me pull him upright until his back brushed the cool stone wall behind him.

I unfolded myself, rising over him on hands and knees. The fire painted us in amber and shadow; the pelts rustled beneath his shifting weight. My tail curled behind me in a slow, questioning shape—a curve of anticipation, of hunger tempered into something softer.

His breath hitched when I reached for the pelts.

"Let me see you," I murmured.

I peeled the blankets back inch by inch, revealing his chest, his ribs, the smooth pale skin of his stomach. He sucked in a breath at the cave's cool air, muscles tightening, but he didn't pull away.

He watched me with wide, uncertain eyes.

I brushed my knuckles along his jaw. "Don't fear me."

"I..." He swallowed. "I don't."

He didn't know if that was true. He didn't know anything but exhaustion and the strange shelter of my body around his.

But the words still fed me.

I shifted forward, settling onto his lap in one slow, fluid motion—like a lioness draping herself across warm stone. My thighs bracketed his hips, my knees sinking into the pelts on either side of him. His breath punched out against my chest.

His hands twitched, as if unsure whether to move or stay still.

I took them gently and placed them at his sides.

"Here," I murmured. "You don't hold me. I hold you."

He nodded, eyes darkening with a mix of fear and something more primitive. Need, instinct, the magnetic pull between predator and the prey she has chosen not to devour.

Not tonight.

I leaned over him, letting my hair slip forward to brush his shoulders, then his neck, then his chest. The soft tuft at the end of it dragged across his skin like a whisper. He shivered.

His breath grew unsteady.

"W-What…what are you doing?" he whispered.

"Claiming," I breathed. "Bonding. You stay. You survive. You belong."

His pulse leapt beneath my lips as I pressed a kiss to the corner of his jaw—a touch barely there, more heat than pressure. His eyelids fluttered half-closed.

"Taste me," I whispered.

His gaze snapped open, startled. His lips parted, but no words came.

I guided him, not with force but with the gentlest press of my fingers behind his nape. Drawing him forward until his mouth brushed the side of my breast through the fur-like softness of my skin.

He tensed in confusion, breath caught in his throat.

"It's all right," I murmured. "Let me give you warmth. Let me give you strength."

My purr deepened, a low, resonant hum that filled the cavern, vibrating through stone and water. It shivered through him, melting tension down his spine.

He exhaled shakily, his breath brushing the sensitive skin above my heart.

Slowly—hesitantly—he pressed his lips there.

Not erotic.

Not devouring.

Just a surrender born of hunger for safety, for warmth, for something alive in all this darkness.

I exhaled, long and trembling.

"Good," I whispered, stroking the back of his neck. "You take what I give. You live because I will it."

His breath grew warmer against my skin. He leaned into me, guided by exhaustion and the primal comfort of body against body—the instinctive knowledge that warmth meant survival.

I held him close, guiding his head with reverent touches, letting him rest his mouth against me as if drinking from warmth itself. His hands curled weakly at his sides, his body softening under me.

"There," I murmured. "Let the fear go. Let the cold go."

He sagged into me, surrendering the last of his resistance.

I felt that surrender in every part of me. It was not a victory of violence, but something deeper. Older. A claiming that bound without blood.

His breathing slowed.

Soon, too soon, he drifted again toward sleep.

"No," I whispered softly. "Not yet."

But his eyelids grew heavy, fluttering shut. His breath evened out against my skin.

Sleep took him with a gentleness I could not offer.

So I shifted back, lowering him carefully to the pelts, cradling his head in my hands as though he were something sacred; something carved from fragile light. I wrapped the furs around him, creating a nest that held only warmth and the smell of us.

I curled around him, one arm beneath his shoulders, one draped across his ribs. My tail coiled protectively over his hips. His head rested in the hollow of my shoulder.

His breath warmed the underside of my jaw.

The fire flickered amber across his hair, catching red where embers glowed.

I stroked a thumb along his cheek.

"I was forgotten once," I whispered to the sleeping dark. "But I am forgotten no longer."

The river murmured behind the stone. The waterfall thundered softly through the tunnels. The cave felt tighter, warmer, as if pulling us closer.

I didn't sleep.

Creatures like me don't sleep when we fear losing what we've claimed.

And outside, somewhere in the weave of mountain and forest, the air shifted.

Not wind.

Not water.

Something else.

Something I recognized with a deep, instinctive dread.

The dragon woman.

Coming closer.

I tightened my grip around his sleeping form, my claws sliding halfway out as instinct flared sharp and bright.

"She will not take you from me," I whispered into his hair.

My purr turned low, dangerous.

A warning to the mountain.

A promise to the man.

A vow carved in warmth and shadow.

The Mountain Calls the Gold (Lyra)

The door of the Bottle Tree closed behind me with a soft thump, and the night took me back.

The warmth of the tavern dropped away in an instant, like someone had slammed shut a furnace door. Out here the air slid cold and clean along my cheeks, smelling of wet pavement, woodsmoke from a distant stove, and the sharp, green edge of the tree line. Behind me, the murmur of voices and clink of cutlery still carried—muffled now, like a heartbeat under layers of quilt.

I stood on the cracked asphalt and let myself feel the separation.

Inside: chili and cornbread, neon buzzing, Maeve's dry voice, Monroe's careful warnings, Michelle's grief curling fragile around a glass of water she kept forgetting to drink.

Out here: the mountain. Vast. Dark. Waiting.

I didn't move right away. It was never good to yank yourself too fast from one world into another. Whiplash made you sloppy.

The tavern windows glowed a warm gold at my back. I could hear the jukebox change tracks—a hiccup of silence, then the low twang of a guitar. A chair scraped. Someone laughed too loudly, the sound edged with shaken relief. Glass met wood behind the bar; Maeve probably smacking a pint down in front of one of the recovery boys. Monroe's baritone carried in a brief, steady rumble.

Underneath it, so soft most ears wouldn't have caught it, I heard Michelle cry.

Just one sound—a bitten-off, muffled thing—but it slid under my ribs all the same.

Human sounds. Human lives. Human fragility.

I let them anchor me for a breath.

Then I let them go.

The mountain called in the space they left behind.

I walked around the side of the building toward the gravel lot, boots crunching over cigarette butts and last year's leaves. My truck waited under the single yellow security light; paint dull, antenna crooked, the hood still ticking with leftover heat from the drive down off the ridge. I had parked a little farther from the door than usual, a habit born of nights exactly like this when I didn't want eyes on what came next.

Butch's absence tugged at me. Dropping him at Henry's place on the way in had been the right call, but it still felt like I'd gone out missing part of myself.

Henry had barely woken when I'd nudged open his trailer door earlier, Butch's big head shoving happily past my thigh. The kid's hair had stuck up in damp tufts, eyes squinting against the hall light.

"You're supposed to be home," he'd mumbled, voice sleep-rough.

"Brought you company," I smiled.

"Fine," he'd whispered, eyes going shiny in a way he probably hoped I hadn't noticed. "But don't go alone."

"I'm never alone," I'd answered, which was true enough in more ways than one. "And I'll come back for you both."

Now, in the parking lot's wan light, I rested my hand on the truck's side panel for a moment, feeling the residual warmth from where the engine sat. The metal hummed faintly, echoing the deeper, older hum that ran under everything in this county.

The Hallow stirred in my chest in answer.

Wind shifted, coming down off the ridge instead of up from town. It slid beneath my collar, carrying the scents I knew better than my own breath: wet rock, moss, the electric tang of an impending storm that hadn't yet made up its mind. A pressure bloomed behind my breast-bone, subtle but insistent.

Anticipation. Warning. Welcome.

"Yeah," I murmured. "I hear you."

Tommy's torn vest flashed behind my eyes. The way Butch had leaned into Henry with that soft, anchoring weight. Michelle's fingers crushing that napkin into smaller and smaller squares as if she could make her world more manageable by sheer focus.

And somewhere above us, in the maze of branches and shadow, something big and clever and lonely paced with stolen life curled around its claws.

Darren didn't have the luxury of my hesitation.

I drew in a slow breath then ghosted around to the far side of the truck, putting steel and shadow between myself and the tavern's windows. Out here, the security light didn't quite reach. Gravel shifted under my boots; beyond that, the tree line thickened into a wall of black.

This was the seam between the two worlds I walked.

On one side, I was ranger—badge, radio, incident reports, the measured calm of a professional who knew how to say 'next of kin' without slipping on the words.

On the other side, what I truly was.

The mountain's hum climbed a notch, matching the rhythm of my heart.

I shrugged out of my jacket and tossed it onto the passenger seat through the open window then unbuttoned my flannel, fingers steady even as the air kissed my sweat-damp undershirt. It was cold enough that my breath was white, but beneath my skin heat coiled low and insistent.

My pulse synced with the Hallow's thrum—one-two, one-two, like footsteps down a long-forgotten deer path.

"Alright," I whispered. "Let's stop procrastinating."

I tugged the shirt over my head and dropped it into the cab then toed off my boots, peeling socks from my feet and tucking them inside the leather for later. Jeans followed. The night made goosebumps run up my legs, but underneath the surface chill a different warmth stirred.

One that had nothing to do with blood vessels and everything to do with what had made me.

The Hallow rose in me like molten gold.

I closed my eyes and leaned back against the truck, letting the metal's coolness brace my spine. My hands settled palm-flat over my sternum, as if I could feel the fault line there.

Then I breathed out.

The exhale curled from my lips in a stream of shimmering air, flecked with pinpricks of light so faint most humans would have dismissed them as imagination. Silver-gold sparks eddied in front of my face, caught briefly in the curl of my breath before winking out.

Desire threaded through me—not the human kind, though it had its echoes there. This was the older version. The hunger to be whole. To be the shape I had been carved for.

The Age of Making rose up in memory, as it always did when I loosened my grip on this smaller skin.

Back then, there had been no uniforms. No trucks. No root beer sweating on a bar while a coroner tried to make sense of teeth-marks that didn't match any known predator.

There had been only sky.

The Hallow had been louder then, the Song so near to the surface that we had felt every note in the hinge of our jaws. It had breathed dragons into being in pairs—gold and silver, flame and storm, fire and ice. I'd been forged bright and hot, my scales catching the newborn sun; my wings casting the first true shadows over uncut ridges.

Taren had risen beside me from the same furnace, all steel and snow, and sharp, clean lines. His fire had burned pale and strange, lightning given breath.

Together we had flown sky-corridors carved by storm and intention, braiding our flames in long spirals that cooled into rivers, mountain ridges, and fault lines. Our mating flights had not been an afterthought to creation—they *were* creation. Every shudder of our bodies had written new edges into the world.

We were more than guardians then.

We were mother and father alongside the Hallow itself.

Three voices braided into one Song, shaping our part of the world while others like us tended theirs.

I carried that memory like a thorn and a treasure both—too beautiful to forget, too powerful to touch without bleeding.

Now, in a gravel lot behind a small-town tavern, wearing nothing but the thin barrier of my human skin, I let that version of myself uncoil.

The first shift always happened in the bones.

They vibrated—not enough to be visible, but enough that my teeth rattled gently in my skull. The world seemed to hesitate around me, as if holding its breath to watch.

Heat gathered behind my sternum until it was almost painful.

The Hallow's hum climbed from low drone to something close to song.

Then everything gave way.

Golden light flashed along my arms, racing from shoulder to fingertip as if someone had poured dawn straight into my veins. My skin rippled under it, pigment dissolving into molten, metallic sheen. Breath hitched in my chest, reshaping the cage that held it; ribs expanded, thickening, re-angling. I felt my spine lengthen, vertebrae clicking into a new, older alignment.

Claws unfurled where nails had been, curved and perfect, each one a crescent of polished obsidian edged in gold. Scales rippled outward in overlapping bands, each the size of my palm at first, then larger. Overlapping, tessellating into armor that shimmered with the same deep luster as coins that had slept a long time in dark water.

Horns curled from my skull, growing out and back in an elegant sweep that balanced the weight of my changing head. The sensation should have hurt. It didn't. It felt like undoing a long cramp.

My jaw lengthened. Teeth sharpened—not all at once but in a kind of flowering. Canines stretching, molars reorganizing into something meant for tearing and crushing both. My tongue tasted the air and found it thicker, richer, full of layers I could not access as a woman.

Wings burst from my back with a sound like a sail snapping full of wind. Membranes stretched between long, fingerlike bones—the skin thin and strong, webbed with faint, glowing veins. Heat rolled off them in waves, steam rising from my shoulders where the cool night met the furnace beneath my scales.

My throat burned with flame I hadn't allowed myself to release in far too many moons. It wasn't an unpleasant burn. It was the ache of withheld speech.

I dropped to all fours as the last of the human proportion slipped away and the dragon's weight settled into itself.

When the light cleared, I stood in my true skin.

Ancient. Shimmering. Lethal. Glorious.

Gold-scaled shoulders rolled under the starlight, catching it and throwing it back in fractured pieces. My tail lashed once; a long, sinuous counterbalance heavy with muscle and memory. Each movement felt inevitable, like the punctuation of a sentence the world had been trying to finish since I'd walked down off these ridges and agreed to answer to 'Ranger' instead of what I truly was.

The air hit my lungs differently like this—bigger, colder, full of information. I could taste the whiskey on Monroe's breath through the tavern wall. Smell the onion in Maeve's chili. Feel the faint tremor of Michelle's sobs through the ground itself.

Farther away, the ridgeline lay spread beneath the stars like a sleeping animal. Every root, every stream, every pocket of stillness. I felt them all, separate and connected, a vast nervous system that whispered along the length of my spine.

In my human skin, I only ever brushed the surface of this—touch, taste, scent, sound, sight. Five narrow doorways into a world that deserved more. But in my true form, the boundaries dissolved. I didn't observe nature, I *participated* in it. My breath mingled with pine resin. My pulse synchronized with the shift of groundwater beneath shale. The wind didn't strike me, it conferred with me. Every living thing hummed with its own intent, and all of it flowed through me in currents older than language.

To be dragon was not to stand apart from the wild.

It was to be one vertebra in a creature as vast as continents.

Underneath it, a darker thread: the Wampus's trail. It smelled of wet fur, iron, and a kind of stubborn loneliness that made my scales prickle.

The scent hit me harder than I expected. Not just an odor, but an *impression*—a feeling carried in the molecules of her being. Dragon-sense does not merely register the world, it translates it. And what it translated now made my chest constrict.

Loneliness.

Not the simple, human kind.

A vast, feral emptiness with teeth.

It rolled through me like cold fog, sliding beneath my scales and tightening every joint along my spine. My talons curled instinctively, gouging grooves into the gravel at my feet. Pebbles skittered downslope. I lowered my head, nostrils flaring as I breathed in the trail again, trying to understand it.

A chuff broke from my throat—deep and uncertain. Half warning. Half sorrow.

She had been alone too long. Even before her great sleep.

Far longer than any creature meant to live alongside another heartbeat.

That great, yawning ache inside her wasn't hunger.

It was abandonment fossilized into instinct.

A wanting so desperate it had curdled into possession.

My wings shivered against my sides. The wind tugged at me, and I answered with a low rumble—not at the Wampus but at the emotion blooming inside my own chest.

Because, for the first time, I *felt* her as she was now.

Not her rage.

Not her violence.

But her yearning.

It cracked through me with surprising force. Enough that I dug my claws harder into the dirt to steady myself. The ground beneath me vibrated faintly, as if the mountain felt what I felt and braced, too.

Dragons do not pity.

But we recognize familiar wounds.

I closed my eyes briefly. The ache inside her echoed something I had carried for centuries—waiting for Taren, missing the half of my fire, walking a world where no one else spoke my native tongue.

If I had been left in that hollow long enough...

If the Hallow had gone silent to me the way it had to her...

If I had never known the counterweight of a bonded mate...

I could imagine how a creature might twist.

My tail lashed once, sharply, scattering loose stones. Compassion surged hot and unwelcome. It softened something in my chest I didn't want softened—not when lives hung in the balance.

But compassion was not permission.

Understanding was not absolution.

I opened my eyes and let the gold burn through them, clearing the fog of sympathy. Darren's fear pulsed faintly through the ground—far, far below. The memory of his torn jacket flashed. Michelle's shaking hands. Monroe's grim warning.

The Wampus's loneliness might explain her, but it did not excuse her.

She had dragged a man away from warmth and safety.

She had spilled another's blood.

The mountain hummed in my ribs in quiet agreement. A warning and a summons.

I chuffed again, lower this time—resolve sharpening behind it.

"I'm sorry," I murmured into the wind, my voice layered with dragon resonance. "I'm sorry for what the world made you."

My claws flexed. Gravel ground beneath them.

"But I can't let you keep him."

Duty steadied me—cool, luminous. Inevitable. I inhaled, letting the mountain align my bones then angled my head toward the sky.

The ache of compassion remained but I folded it into resolve, a weight I could carry.

The hunt had begun.

And I wouldn't leave Darren to her emptiness.

Darren's scent clung to it in thin, fading strands. Fear. Sweat. Blood, sharp and sour.

My chest tightened. Not physically, not just from the flare of dragon instinct that came with the scent of prey somewhere between alive and dead, but from something softer. Human-shaped.

He was young. He had laughed under strings of neon once. He had taken pictures of bottle trees for a girl who folded napkins into tiny, helpless squares.

He was not meant to end as bones in a cave.

I stretched my wings a little farther, letting the membranes catch the night. For a breath I simply stood there, feeling the gravel dig into the thick pads of my talons, the truck's cooling metal warm against my flank, the mountain's hum braided into the beat of my hearts.

Taren was not there.

The absence hit me as it always did when I shifted—sharp and immediate. A phantom limb.

When we had flown in the Age of Making we had done so together, twin streaks of light across incomprehensible distances. His presence had been a constant pressure at the edge of my mind; a weight I had leaned into the way I now leaned into the ridgeline's wind.

Without him the sky felt slightly off-balance, as if missing a star.

I turned my head toward the higher peaks out of habit, horns catching starlight.

In the old tongue, the one that sat in the marrow of my dragon bones, I spoke his name.

"Taren," I rumbled, the sound vibrating through my whole frame. The language didn't need air the way human speech did; it moved along the fault lines of stone and river. "I rise."

The word rose with me. It slipped along the Hallow's veins and vanished into the distance where his own mountains reared cold and high.

For a heartbeat, there was only the usual answer: wind in branches, distant owl, the soft groan of tree trunks shifting in the night.

Then—faintly, so faintly I might have missed it if I hadn't been listening with everything I was—a silver-threaded awareness brushed the edge of my mind.

Not words. Not yet. Just a pressure, like the weight of a familiar hand almost settling on my shoulder.

Hope flickered along my scales, as bright as the first spark before the blaze.

The mountain had called the gold back to itself. The gold had answered.

Now it remained to be seen if the silver would, too.

The first downstroke always felt like falling in the direction I was meant to go.

I gathered myself, muscles coiling from jaw to tail, then drove my wings down hard. Gravel scattered under the blast of air. My bulk rose clean off the lot, the truck shrinking beneath me in a heartbeat. The security light flashed once across my belly scales, then vanished as the earth dropped away.

The night met me like an old lover—cold and clear and full of secrets.

Air curled beneath my wings in strong, steady currents. Every feather-fine adjustment of membrane and bone translated into lift, tilt, speed. My body remembered the angles even when my mind was tired, and this was older than fatigue.

The town fell away behind me, a scatter of warm lights along the valley floor. Ahead, the ridge reared up, its dark spine silhouetted against a sky punched full of stars. I climbed toward it, beating upward through bands of shifting wind.

The world opened.

Dragon-sight didn't work like human sight. Humans saw surfaces. Reflections. Whatever light was kind enough to bounce their way.

I saw heat.

Not just the obvious—deer bodies glowing soft orange under the canopy, rabbits streaking like quick embers through brush, the wash of coyotes slipping along the edges of fields. I saw heat signatures layered on time: old campfires still whispering warmth into stone, the fading echo of trucks that had rumbled along Forest Service roads hours ago, the ghost-heat of hikers' footsteps stamped into damp soil.

Scent curled up to meet me in visible trails, in smoky ribbons of information. Pine and rot and rain and diesel. Fear and sweat and blood. They tangled in the air like colored string.

Beneath all that, subtle but unmistakable, the ley lines glowed.

They weren't lines, really—not in any human sense. More like veins, faintly luminescent, running through rock and root. Places where the Hallow's song rose closer to the surface, humming louder. Brighter. I saw them as threads of molten gold, weaving under ridges, pooling in hollows, spilling down in thin curtains over cliffs.

Every living thing along those veins pulsed in my awareness.

Owls, perched and still, eyes bright coins.

A black bear, half-dozing in a nest of leaves, its slow heartbeat a drumbeat against the earth.

Fox kits, a tangle of sleep and warmth in a den that smelled of milk and dust.

All of it part of one vast, breathing body.

And there—off to my right, halfway up the north slope and moving away from town—two residual signatures twined together in the air like cooling embers.

One glowed faint and uneven, hot then fading, ragged with panic and exhaustion. Human. Young. Frantic.

A trail, not a presence—*the echo of a life that had run hard through these woods.*

Darren.

The other imprint was unmistakable, even as an afterimage: larger, colder at the core, edged in a predator's sharp, possessive instinct. It burned on the landscape like a twisted star—territorial, self-satisfied, thrumming with a hunger that had nothing to do with feeding.

The Wampus.

These weren't bodies.

Not scents.

Not tracks.

They were emotional heat-scars, pressed into the world by creatures moving through the Hallow's field. Lingering just long enough for a dragon to read what had passed.

I banked toward the path they'd carved, angling my wings to catch a rising column of air that tasted of wet stone and something feral. The mountain's hum climbed under my ribs, tightening with my turn.

As I moved, a prickle ran down my scales—static, soft at first then growing.

Not from storm.

From him.

You took to the sky without me.

Taren's voice slid into my mind along the curve of the ridgeline, silver and warm and threaded with reprimand that tasted suspiciously like amusement.

My chest tightened, and if I'd had a human mouth just then I would've smiled.

I had to move fast, I answered, sending the thought along the same channels that carried his.

You are fast, he murmured, and I felt his attention settle over my shoulders like a mantle. *I am faster.*

Heat flushed along my neck spines, but not from exertion.

You're also halfway across the world, I said. *I work with the tools I've got.*

Mmm. His hum wrapped around the words, thick with that slow, dangerous fondness that had always made my bones feel a little too big for my skin. *I remember when the tools you had were my claws and your fire, moving together. The sky complained less then.*

The banter slid into place as easily as breathing. It always had. Somehow, in the middle of death and missing hikers and monster trails, it still managed to comfort me.

My wings beat harder, cutting up over the first ridge. Below, the bottle tree lot became a thumbnail of light then disappeared altogether behind trees.

The world sharpened further as his presence bled into mine.

He didn't fly here—not physically. His mountains were elsewhere, crowned in snow and ice and wind that would flay a human to bone in minutes. But dragons were never fully alone in the Hallow. Our kind had been built with channels between us.

Through those channels, our senses braided.

His vision slid over mine, overlaying my gold-heat and living-aura sight with his own silver lattice.

I saw, suddenly, the bones of the world.

Not metaphorical ones but the literal stress lines in the stone. Tectonic plates shifting slow and stubborn beneath the surface, their edges glowing in his awareness like bright seams waiting to be pressed or soothed. Old-magic pools—deep, cold wells where the Hallow had once poured itself thick and heavy now lying mostly quiet but still pulsing faintly.

There, he said, and the word directed my attention more than any gesture could have. A fault line ran directly under the narrow valley I'd been about to ignore, its seam dark and heavy. *The mountain breathes deeper in that cut. Creatures like your Wampus enjoy such places.*

I overlaid his silver map with my gold.

Along that deeper breath, life clustered thicker—elk trails, bear dens, the buried bones of long-ago storms. Predator pathways glowed brighter, worn into the land like habits. The Wampus's trail blazed there, unmistakable.

Together, we saw the world not as a collection of separate pieces but as a layered, conscious thing.

Alive. Aware. Watching us back.

You feel that? I asked, riding a thermal up and along the fault line he'd shown me. *She's not just hunting. She's...nesting.*

Wanting, he added softly. *This creature guards its wanting the way we guard flame.*

A shiver rippled through my wings.

Guarding wanting was dangerous business. Flame was meant to move, to consume and pass on. Wanting, hoarded, warped.

I'm hunting alone, I said, though we both knew I didn't mean it literally anymore. *On the ground, at least.*

Because it is yours, he said. Not a question.

I banked again, following the heat-scent trail that now glowed like a streak of smeared ember down the slope, cutting toward a darker patch of rock where I knew cliffs broke the forest into scars. *Because it's in my Hallow,* I said. *Because it killed in my woods and stole on my watch.*

Silence answered at first—a long, considering one. The kind that used to stretch between us at the top of some high, thin-aired current right before we dove.

I know.

Those two words carried more than agreement. Memory wove through them, unspooling in the back of my mind.

The first time we'd hunted something that thought, instead of simply ate. The way it had dug into the edges of our territory, leaving not just bones but broken meanings in its wake. How furious I'd been.

How amused he'd pretended to be, until the thing had taken a swipe at me that left a white scar along my flank.

We had taken that personally. We always did.

Be wary, Lyra, he added, his tone shifting. *This one has not only teeth. It has a story it tells itself. Those are the most dangerous kind.*

You're not helping, I muttered, but his concern warmed me as much as it needled.

I rolled my body through the air, a long, lazy tumble that shook some of the tension out of my shoulders, then leveled out again. The Wampus's scent grew stronger, edged now with damp stone and the mineral stink of water running underground.

Darren's heat signature flickered—slower, steadier. Not panicking now. Not moving much at all.

Alive. For now.

We flew—him nowhere and everywhere, me cutting a golden arc above pines that bowed and then stilled in my wake.

Memory crowed in my chest with each stroke of my wings.

I remembered storm corridors where lightning raveled around us in white veins, our bodies weaving through bolts that would have shattered mountains now. I remembered his silver form rolling under my own, the flash of his scales as our flames tangled, writing new valleys into the skin of the world. The mountain's song had been different then—high and wild and delighted.

Now, the song was lower. Older. Weighted with the centuries it had spent watching humans cut into its sides and pour asphalt into its veins.

Still, as Taren's presence pushed stronger against my thoughts, the Hallow's hum rose in something dangerously close to pleasure.

It remembered us.

We hadn't stopped being what we were.

Your wings still hold well, he said. There was pride in it, and something more intimate. *In another age, I would meet you at that southern peak. We would drive this wanting-creature from both ends of its den and see which one of us reached its heart first.*

My money would be on me, I said automatically.

Of course, he agreed. *That is why the game works.*

Beneath the teasing lay a simple truth: he was with me, as much as he could be. Every beat of my wings echoed from his side of the world. Every inhalation tasted faintly of his storms.

My fear of the Wampus's teeth—its claws, its strange, curled devotion around its stolen prize—dulled under that.

I was not alone in this hunt. Not where it mattered.

I tucked my wings in and dropped lower, slipping under the first fringe of cloud. The forest loomed closer, individual trees resolving into tall, black spears. Between two rocky outcroppings a narrow ravine cut deep into the mountain's side, breathing damp and cold.

The Wampus's trail vanished into that crack.

Behind my breastbone the Hallow's hum sharpened to a note that sounded, unmistakably, like a summons.

I angled toward it, gold belly skimming just above the treetops, and felt Taren's attention narrow with mine.

Go, he said.

And I did.

The Wampus's trail narrowed into a single, braided thread the deeper I flew—tightening, concentrating, twisting downward like a rope pulled underground.

Darren's aura flickered at the very end of it.

Weak.

Strained.

Thready, like a candle guttering in its own melted wax.

I banked lower, circling above the ravine where the forest broke open into a narrow spine of rock. Moonlight flashed along a sheet of water spilling over the cliff edge—thin, bright, and incessant. The waterfall carved a white scar into the stone, its spray rising in cold curtains.

The moment I glided above it, the tug hit me.

A gravitational pull—fear braided into something stranger. Satisfaction. Possession.

The Wampus's emotional spoor curled up through the mist like steam from a fresh wound.

I landed hard on the slick stone beside the falls, talons scraping sparks that hissed out in the spray. My wings folded close, scales steaming in the cold, damp night. The waterfall's roar pressed against me, drowning out the valley below and leaving only the mountain's thrum...and that other sound, deeper still.

A purr.

A low, resonant vibration that no ordinary animal should have possessed.

I drew a breath through my snout.

The smell hit like a physical thing.

Musk.

Damp fur.

Old bones soaked with marrow long-drained.

Iron. Bright and metallic, fresh and not fresh.

And under all of it...Darren.

His warmth clung to the air like the ghost of a handprint on glass. Faint but unmistakable.

My throat tightened. I angled my head toward the cleft behind the falls—dark, narrow. Breathing.

The den was deep inside there.

The Wampus had dragged him into a place that was more than shelter.

It was home.

I lowered myself to the stone, talons gripping hard. I could not enter as a dragon—not quietly, not safely. My size alone would collapse half the cavern, burying Darren before my fire could even warm the air.

I inhaled once more, filled the back of my lungs with cold water vapor, then let the transformation pull me under.

Golden scales rippled backward into skin.

Wings sank into my spine with a deep, molten ache.

My jaw shortened.

My skull reshaped.

My fire banked low, settling deep behind my sternum like an ember swallowed whole.

I crouched naked on wet rock, steam rising from my shoulders in slow spirals. My hair clung cold and heavy to my back. The waterfall's mist kissed every inch of skin it could find, but dragons had no shame.

I moved toward the cave mouth.

The rock was slick beneath my feet, the roar of the falls a constant shiver along my bones. I pressed one hand to the stone beside the entrance.

It was warm.

Not from lava or magic.

From life.

From breath.

From something large and content purring deep in the dark.

That same purr vibrated faintly through the soles of my feet.

I listened harder.

Drip of water.

Rush of the falls.

A groan—human and faint, slipping between stone echoes.

Darren.

I stepped closer, leaning in, eyes trying to adjust to the lightless maw.

The deeper the cavern went the colder the air blew out in slow, damp exhalations. And beneath that cold was something else—something thick, mineral-heavy, and breathing with a rhythm that did not belong to geology.

This wasn't a hiding place.

This was a nest.

Claustrophobic, snarled with tunnels, layered in scent markers. Perfect for a creature who thought about wanting the way dragons thought about flame.

A den for her prize.

My teeth clicked together.

Taren.

His voice answered instantly, a silver thread sliding into the center of my chest.

Yes, Lyra.

She has him in a den. Deep. Twisting. She made a home for him.

I felt rather than heard his exhale—fractured and displeased.

Don't face her without your pack.

My jaw flexed. The word 'pack' still struck me sideways sometimes, even after all these years of wearing human skin. But he was right. Den-beasts fought with desperation, not strategy. If I went in alone and she sensed threat, Darren would be the first thing she destroyed.

"Henry and Butch," I said aloud, the name Butch oddly warm on my tongue. "I need them."

The mountain hummed in agreement.

The stone vibrated under my palm in a warning. A countdown. The kind of message mountains had used long before humans learned to decipher fault lines.

Time was running out.

I crouched lower, the waterfall mist drifting in cool ribbons over my skin, and listened again.

The purr in the depths shifted—pleased.

Content.

Plotting in its sleep, perhaps, or celebrating a full stomach and a warm body curled nearby.

Darren was alive.

For now.

My fingers curled against the rock, leaving faint gold smudges of residual scale-dust.

The cavern was a maze of dangers—slick rock, narrow passages, blind corners, unpredictable footing, total darkness. I could navigate it, but she owned it. She would fight like every root and bone belonged to her.

I would need Henry's steadiness. Butch's nose. The dog's lack of fear when following me into places no sane creature would go.

And more than that I would need the right moment.

This was not it.

I backed away, step by slow step, until the roar of the waterfall thickened the air around me again. The spray hit my shoulders and ran down my arms in cold, sharp lines.

The mountain shifted underfoot. Another message.

Move.

Move now.

I rose to my full height, still naked, still steaming in the cold air. Moonlight skated down my skin, painting me in silver where my scales had been.

I looked once more at the cave mouth. At the dark that breathed.

"I'm coming back for him," I said.

Stone swallowed the words.

The purr in the deep changed, a soft rise in pitch—amused, perhaps. Or warning.

Behind me the mountain wind stirred, brushing my hair forward like a hand on my back.

A blessing.

Or a dare.

Either way, I stepped into the night again.

And every creature awake in the woods seemed to feel the shift.

The hunt had changed.

So had I.

A Man Called Mine (Wampus)

His scent woke me before thought did.

Warm and salt-sweet, threaded with smoke from my fire and the faint ache of fear that still clung to his skin. My body recognized him the way roots recognize water. I lay very still, eyes closed, and counted the beats of his heart.

Thump.

...thump.

......thump.

Slow now. The frantic flutter of prey had quieted. He slept like something that no longer expected to run.

Good, I thought. *He is learning.*

I opened my eyes.

The den greeted me in soft orange and shadow. Embers glowed in the stone ring of my hearth, their light licking at the walls in low, lazy waves. Steam drifted in thin veils through the opening where the underground falls poured, a silver sheet beyond the edge of the fire's reach. The air was thick with damp stone and mineral and the rich, comforting scent of rabbit fat that had soaked into fur and rock alike.

Our bed of pelts had become a nest.

I had dragged them here over seasons—deer, bear, fox, things from

130

higher, colder ridges—and shaped them to the hollow of the floor. Now they curved around us like a bowl cupped in the hands of the earth. He lay in the deepest part of that curve, where the warmth pooled and the stone remembered our bodies.

I rolled onto my side to see him better.

Firelight painted him in layers. Shadows pooled at the hollows of his throat and hips; golden lay bright on the bridge of his nose, the plane of his chest, the fine hair dusting his forearms. The pelts lapped at his waist and legs, fur blending into skin, hiding and revealing in uneven edges as if the mountain were still deciding which parts of him it would allow me to see.

His face was softer in sleep. The lines fear had carved there loosened, smoothing back into the youth underneath. His mouth parted on a slow exhale. I watched the column of his throat move with the swallow that followed, the faint pulse there beating against the thin skin as if asking to be marked.

My fingers curled reflexively.

He shifted once, a small, unconscious movement, and the pelts slid lower. A strip of his side bared itself—ribcage, the gentle taper of his waist, the stretch of muscle that had tensed so beautifully when he'd tried to run. Bruises bloomed there in violet and yellowed gold, fragile flowers I had planted by dragging him home too quickly.

I should have been sorry.

I was not.

The ache that rose in me was not remorse; it was hunger of a different kind. I had taken so many bodies into the dark over the years, but none had stayed. None had curled into the space I made for them. None had warmed the cave long enough for the stone to remember.

He was the first.

My hand slid down my own stomach, smoothing fur that had been rumpled by sleep. My claws—retracted for him, always for him—caught lightly in the thick ruff there, then lower, where skin and fur met in ways that made me shiver. It was not a gesture meant to be seen. There was no one here to perform for. Only him, sleeping. Only me, awake.

For my kind, desire had always worn many faces. Hunger. Territory. The clean rush of a chase. The deep, purring satisfaction of a kill well made. This was not that. This was the sharp, aching awareness of another heartbeat just beyond my teeth, another breath brushing my air, another warmth pressed into the hollows I had lined with my own.

My thumb circled idly over a sensitive patch of my own skin, not to taunt, not to tease—just to soothe the ache of having something so wanted so close and not sinking into it fully. A small sound climbed my throat— half purr, half whine—and I swallowed it back so it would not disturb him.

He needed sleep. I needed...this. Quiet, private; the small, wild comfort of my own body while I watched the miracle of his.

I let my gaze travel him again, slower.

The curls of his hair, damp still at the roots from where I had washed him last night, spread across the pelts like dark moss. One lock clung to his forehead. I resisted the urge to smooth it away and instead traced the air above it with a fingertip, memorizing the curve.

His eyelashes cast faint shadows on his cheeks. Humans had always fascinated me there—such delicate armor for such fragile orbs. If I leaned closer I would see the flutter of his dreams, little storms moving behind the lids. When I had dozed with my head on his chest, I had felt those storms; the tiny kicks of his dreaming heart. He had whispered words then, broken and soft. He didn't know he had offered them. I had tucked them away like stolen treats.

Mine, I thought now as my gaze slid lower.

His chest rose and fell in slow, even pulls. Faint scars crisscrossed the skin there, small and pale and old—proofs of a human life lived with some clumsiness, some courage. A childhood fall. A branch. A broken bottle. Each mark was a story I did not yet know. I wanted them all.

His hands lay loose at his sides, palms turned up, fingers curled slightly as if he had fallen asleep reaching for something and forgotten mid-gesture. The pads of his fingers were callused in places from what- ever work he did aboveground. I had felt those calluses scrape lightly at my ribs when he had clutched at me in fear. I imagined, briefly, what they would feel like if he touched me on purpose.

My claws dug gently into the fur over my own hip.

It had been so long since anyone had touched me.

Winters stacked behind my eyes when I let myself think back—years of snow and rock and the slow, patient crush of silence. There had been beasts of course. I had tangled with bear and cougar, fought and mated in the blind, frantic way of creatures whose lives burned fast and short. But they had never stayed.

They were born to move on, to die. To leave bones behind like punctuation marks.

I had outlived them all.

The Song had sung me into being and then fallen quiet, its attention turning elsewhere, leaving me on this slope with a hunger I didn't know how to spend. The mountain had loved me once, I was sure of it. The trees had bent when I passed. The streams had braided around my paws. But seasons changed. Storms moved. New lives rose. Old monsters blurred into myth. Sleep.

Only the silence stayed.

Until him.

I looked at him the way a starving animal looks at the first bloom after a killing frost: disbelieving, possessive. Aching with the fear that any sudden move might crush it.

If I kept perfectly still, perhaps he would stay. If I was gentle enough, careful enough, if I didn't bite too deep or hold too hard, perhaps the world wouldn't notice what I had taken.

My hand slid higher over my own ribs, feeling the rise and fall that mirrored his. For a moment, with my eyes half-lidded, I could almost believe his lungs and mine shared the same breath. That his blood and mine answered to the same pulse.

He shifted again, a small restless sound in his throat. He furrowed his brow. A dream nipped at him. I froze, every muscle gone tight, waiting to see if he would wake.

He didn't.

The furrow smoothed. His mouth relaxed. A sigh slipped out and brushed my face, warm and soft as a moth's wing.

The ache in me sharpened.

I could wake him now, I knew. Could slide my hand over his shoulder, his chest, his hip, until his eyes opened and his fear shone there with the reluctant devotion I'd forced into blooming. I could ask him for words. For touch. For reassurance that what I had claimed wouldn't walk away.

Instead I laid there and watched him.

I watched the tiny twitch at the corner of his mouth when a dream nudged it. I watched the way his chest stuttered once, catching on some unseen memory before evening out. I watched the way his fingers relaxed further into the pelts, trusting their warmth.

I wanted to remember all of it.

If the dragon woman comes, I thought, *if she finds the way down into my den, if she bares her teeth and calls him by some name from sunlight and roads... I want to know exactly what I am losing.*

The idea of him choosing her made something low and ugly rise under my ribs. She was all control and command and that cold, steady fire the mountain hummed for. I had seen the way the forest leaned toward her, how her voice slid through the dark like a blade.

She belonged to the Song that had made us both.

I belonged to its forgetting.

My hand slid over my own flank again, nails scratching lightly at the place where fur gave way to skin. Heat pooled there in a low, purring throb. It was not for him—I would not wake him yet. This was for me, for the beast that had gone too many years with nothing but blood and bone for company.

He is warm, I told that beast. *He is soft. He is here.*

The silence that had eaten so many winters did not feel quite so ravenous with his heartbeat weaving through it.

I turned my head until my nose hovered an inch above the crook of his elbow and breathed him in, slow and deep. Sweat. Musk, faint now under cave and smoke. The metallic ghost of old fear baked into skin and hair. Underneath it all the simple, impossible scent of a living man resting without running.

Mine, I thought again, the word settling heavy and sure in my chest.

My eyes slid closed on a slow blink as I let my cheek rest lightly against the curve of his arm, not enough to wake but just enough to feel that he was real. My breath found his rhythm, matching it, syncing with it. Two sets of lungs negotiating a shared song.

For a few heartbeats, there was nothing but that—warmth, breath, the soft drag of fur against skin where I shifted closer. Heat curled low in my belly, slow and steady; not the frantic burn of the chase but the deep coal-glow of having something to curl around.

I leaned closer, mouth parting to press a careful kiss against the inside of his wrist—

And the cave shivered.

Not stone, not water. Those stayed steady. This tremor moved through me instead, a pressure behind my eyes, a tightening in my jaw, a rush of metallic cold down my spine. The fur along my neck stood up all at once.

The Hallow's attention flicked sharp and bright across the back of my mind.

A warning.

A presence.

A dragon.

My pleasure froze mid-breath and cracked into fear.

The Hallow moved.

Not the way it usually did—slow and deep, like old lungs inflating somewhere under the roots. This was a sharp shift, a sudden tightening, as if an enormous fist had closed around the mountain's heart.

Heat pressed in behind my eyes.

I hissed and jerked my head up, pupils wide. The den looked the same—fire embers, steam veils, stone glistening with old moisture. He still slept, chest rising and falling, unaware.

But the Song thrummed wrong.

A metallic taste flooded the back of my tongue, hot and bitter, like biting down on lightning. My ears flattened. Every scar along my spine lit up in memory. The fur along my shoulders and back rose in a ridge.

Something ancient brushed the edges of my territory.

Not claws on stone. Not paws on moss. This was a presence sliding over the skin of the mountain. A ripple of will and heat and power that made the rock under my fur feel suddenly thinner, as if it might crack and spill us out into the open.

I knew that flavor of wrong.

Dragon.

I couldn't see her—not from down here where water and stone

wrapped around us—but I felt her all the same. A streak of golden consciousness razoring along the ridgeline above, slicing through mist and branch and night as if they were nothing. Bright. Sharp. Too bright. Too sharp.

Dragon-woman, my mind spat. *Sky-queen. Fire-thief.*

My body reacted faster than thought. I rolled over Darren in a rush of fur and muscle, pressing my chest to his, my limbs bracketing him, making my body a shield.

He grunted in his sleep, breath puffing hot against my collarbone. One of his hands slid uselessly against my side, fingers flexing once before relaxing again. He didn't yet know why he moved. His dreaming heart did.

My claws punched through pelts and into the packed earth beneath, anchoring us to the stone as if sheer force might keep the sky from chewing through it.

The pressure in the Hallow climbed.

She was close. Not at the cave mouth—she hadn't found that yet. Above. Moving over the slope with the ease of one born to look down on everything. A will too sharp for this soft, green world. Cutting through the Song as if she had a right.

Panic clawed up my throat.

My kind had stories, too, buried under all the names men and their pretty goddesses had piled on us. Bastet, they had called some of us, and Sekhmet, and any other lion-faced woman they could not understand. They had thrown us onto temple walls and into firelight tales. sometimes divine, sometimes demon, but always theirs.

They didn't know the older stories.

How dragon-fire once raked through forests like combs through hair, tearing up roots and nests alike. How sky-queens and sky-kings had circled above, deciding with lazy eyes what lived and what burned. How their quarrels had cracked mountains. How their mating flights had left scars on the land that took centuries to stop smoking.

We had watched from the underbrush, from the cave mouths, from the shadows at the edge of their flame.

Once, long ago, one of them had noticed us.

My muscles spasmed with the memory—heat searing down from a

sky I couldn't fight, trees going to ash around me while I ran with some-thing small and precious in my jaws. A den. A litter. A soft, mewling scrap that had never even seen sun before the fire found it.

Dragon-fire had taken everything. Not out of hunger but care-lessness.

I could still hear the way the air had screamed.

Now the Hallow thrummed with that same old note, tuned to a different sky.

My breath came too fast, panting around my teeth. I lowered my face to his throat, not in tenderness this time but in calculation. Measuring how quickly I could drag him if I had to, how far, how deep. My whiskers trembled with every exhale. His pulse beat against my lips, a frantic drum trapped under skin.

"Mine," I rasped, voice shredding around the word.

He stirred, lashes fluttering. His body felt my fear even if his mind was still fogged. His fingers dug weakly into my fur, seeking purchase, seeking anchor.

"Stay still," I snapped, sharper than I meant. My tail lashed, knocking against the stone with dull, muffled thrums.

He froze at the tone alone.

Good boy, I thought wildly, wildly grateful. *Good prey. Good prize. Stay tame. Stay timid. Let me be the teeth.*

The Song tightened again then pulsed, sending a wave of pressure through the stone. It rolled over my nerves in a metallic shiver. I heard her above—not with ears but with the same deep sense that let me count roots and streams.

Gold flared against the dark.

She was scouting. Searching. Her attention swept over the ravine where the waterfall poured, brushed the rock above our den like a hand groping for a door it couldn't see.

A hiss ripped from my chest. The fur along my spine bristled so hard it hurt.

I shifted off my prize just enough to twist toward the cave mouth, still keeping one foreleg heavy across his hips. My tail lashed and snapped in the air behind me. The den suddenly felt too small, too close, too easy to pierce.

I bared my fangs at the stone as if it were see-through, as if she could look in and meet my gaze.

"Mine," I snarled, louder this time, the sound bouncing off the damp walls. "He is mine."

My scent glands flared open along my cheeks, my throat, the underside of my jaw. I rubbed all of them along the rock as I moved, pressing my smell deeper into the cave's bones. Musk and rabbit fat and wild cat, layered into stone that already knew me, had known me for longer than humans had named this place.

Mine. Mine. Mine.

The Hallow might sing for her in bright, clear notes. The mountain might lean toward her like plants toward sun. But this den—this nest, this dark—belonged to me.

I pressed my shoulder hard against the low stone arch that marked the den's throat, grinding fur and skin into the rock until it scraped. I wanted every inch of this place thick with my message.

Come, sky-queen, if you dare.

Come and choke on what I own.

Behind me, he made a small, frightened sound. Instinct jerked me back to him. I prowled the length of his body and then over it again, settling atop him like a living weight. My claws pricked through the fur and into the pelts around his ribs—not enough to pierce skin but just enough to say stay without words.

"Sleep," I ordered, though I knew he could not. "Be still. I will protect you."

My voice cracked on 'protect'.

The dragon's presence flicked closer, then farther, like a searching tongue of flame. The pressure eased for a heartbeat. Then slammed back, making my ears ring.

I squeezed my eyes shut and dragged air into my lungs. It came in short, ragged pulls. My heart hammered so hard it felt like it might crack bone. Every old scar along my side burned with remembered heat.

Dragons once hunted my kind.

Dragons once stole what I loved.

Dragons once took everything.

They lived high and long and bright. We lived low and sideways, in the spaces their fire skipped. Their loves had moved mountains. Our losses had been buried underneath.

Not this time.

Not this one.

"He is warm," I whispered against his throat, inhaling his scent like a drug. "He is soft. He is mine. The world has taken enough from me. I keep this."

My tail thrashed harder, the tip slapping fur and stone in sharp, angry beats. The sound mingled with the steady rush of the waterfall, the crackle of the embers, the thin, terrified whimpers he tried to swallow.

"If she comes," I told him, voice dropping to a growl that shook both of us, "I will rip her sky down around her. I will tear her gold and silver. I will feed her wings to the dark."

He didn't answer. His breathing sped up, then hiccupped, then forced itself slow again. Even in fear, he listened.

Above, the dragon's presence paused.

For one long, stretching heartbeat, it hovered directly over us the way the sun hangs on the lip of a ridge before choosing side. The Hallow went very, very still.

I held my breath and pressed every inch of myself down over him, trying to fold him inside my body, to tuck him between my bones. My claws sank deeper into the pelts until earth crumbled under them.

If she finds the crack in the stone—

If she scents him—

If she calls to him with that too-bright voice—

A low, frantic sound rattled in my chest. I didn't recognize it as my own.

Then, slowly, the pressure shifted.

The bright, cutting awareness above us turned away, sliding along the ridge in a new direction. The weight behind my eyes lightened. The metallic taste faded by degrees, leaving only the damp mineral tang of the cave and the salt of my own breath.

The gold presence moved on.

Not gone. Never gone. But retreating. Strategizing. The way sky-hunters did when they were not sure where the prey had gone, only that it existed.

Relief hit me like a physical blow.

My limbs trembled. My jaws unclenched with a cracking ache. I dropped my forehead to his shoulder and let out a shuddering exhale that tasted of fear and victory and something just this side of hysteria.

"She didn't find us," I panted, more to myself than to him. "She didn't find you. She didn't take you."

A laugh scraped up, raw and strange.

The den felt too small again—but in a different way now. Not from looming threat, but from the wild, manic relief beating against its walls. I wanted to run, to claw, to sing, to bite, to mark him all over again until not even the mountain could pretend not to know whose he was.

The dragon had passed.

The sky had looked and failed to see.

He was still here.

Mine.

Relief hit me like a fall from a great height.

For one heartbeat the dragon's presence pressed against the stone above us, bright and awful and searching.

The next, it slid away.

The Hallow's pressure eased, the air in the den widening by a hair. It was like surf pulling back from a line of rocks—still dangerous, still loud, but not breaking over my skull.

My legs gave out.

I toppled sideways off his chest and landed beside him in the pelts, panting like I had outrun fire. My heart slammed against my ribs so hard it hurt. My hands shook when I dragged them over my face, claws catching in my own fur.

He laid where I had held him, hair damp with cave-heat, mouth parted just enough to show the edge of his teeth. His lashes fluttered in uneasy sleep. The pulse in his throat beat frantic against skin that still smelled of stream water and my hands.

If the dragon wanted him, then he was worth wanting.

If he was worth wanting, he was worth keeping.

If he was worth keeping—

My fingers curled in the fur between us.

—then he had to be mine.

Not the mountain's.

Not the sky's.

Not hers.

Mine.

The thought struck with the same force as the dragon's presence had, knocking the breath out of me in a different way. My chest ached, tight and bruised. Something in my throat burned.

I couldn't stay still.

I rolled toward him, catching his shoulder with both hands and shaking before my better instincts could smooth the motion.

"Look at me," I rasped.

He jerked, a choked sound scraping out of him. His eyes flew open, wild and unfocused, trying to find a horizon in the dim, flickering light. For a moment he looked straight through me, still tangled in whatever dream he had clawed together out of fear and memory.

"Wha—?" His voice cracked on the broken syllable.

"Look at me," I said.

He did, because he always did. His gaze snapped to mine like metal to a magnet, even through the fog in his head. Humans called it eye contact. For my kind it was a line, a tether. A binding.

"I—did I...do something?" he stammered.

The question sliced me. I had shaken him like prey. Like prey. I forced my hands to loosen on his shoulder, then failed and clutched him tighter.

"Yes," I said, leaning close enough that my breath warmed his cheek. "You slept. You breathed. You stayed."

My voice came out raw. My chest still heaved, but no air seemed to reach the hollow inside.

"She came," I hissed. "The sky-queen. The gold hunger. She skimmed over us like a hawk looking for a nest to tear. She wanted you. She will want you again."

His face blanched even in the orange wash of the fire.

I bared my teeth without meaning to.

"She is not just a story," I snapped, hackles rising. "She is real and old and bright, and she takes what she wants because she can. She burned my world once."

My breath hitched. I swallowed the memory like bone fragments.

"She will not burn you," I said fiercely. "I won't let her."

His throat worked under my stare. His hands crept up, fingers curling in the edge of the pelt like it might root him.

"O-Okay," he said, voice thready. "Okay."

It wasn't enough.

The relief that had slammed through me when her presence veered away now had nowhere to go. It rattled around inside my ribs, scraping against all the old hollows. I felt too big for my skin and too small for my fear at the same time.

I needed something solid. Something I could hold. Something that would answer back.

"Say it," I told him.

He blinked. "Say...what?"

"That you are mine." The words came out on a growl, vibrating low in my chest. "Say you stay. Say you will not leave me."

His eyes went wider, white rimming the blue. "I—"

My hands fisted in the pelt under his shoulder and his ribs, hauling him half upright toward me. The motion was clumsy, urgent. My breath puffed hot against his face. I could smell his fear, sharp and sweet under the lingering salt of dried water and rabbit fat.

"Say it," I insisted, voice cracking. "I almost lost you. The sky wanted to steal you. The mountain sang for her when it should have sung for me. I will not have you drifting like smoke between us. Put your feet in my dark. Put your words in my ears. Say you are mine."

A tremor ran through him. His pulse hammered so hard I could feel it through my fingers.

"Okay," he whispered.

Not enough.

"Not okay," I snarled. "Say it."

His breath hitched. He swallowed, his throat bobbing under my stare.

"I'm..." His lips fumbled around the shape of it, the way a hand fumbled for a hold on wet stone. "I'm yours."

The sound hit like meat thrown to a starving thing.

My lungs dragged air in on a shudder. My vision swam for a moment, not from tears—I had burned my tears out centuries ago—but from the sheer force of relief.

Mine.

Again, quieter this time, trying it on like a new pelt, he whispered, "I won't leave."

The Hallow hummed low and dangerous, reacting to words it understood better than promises carved on paper.

You can't swear that, I thought wildly. *You are soft and breakable and your kind drifts like leaves.*

But my hunger seized on it anyway.

"Good," I said, the word more breath than sound.

I needed him closer.

Instinct overrode thought. I pulled him fully into my lap, crowding him up against my chest, my arms wrapping around his back with a strength that made him gasp. His legs slid awkwardly between mine, the pelts bunching under his bare skin. He was all angles and heat. Too thin, too fragile, every rib a count of how easily the world could have cracked him.

He clutched at me reflexively, fingers digging into my shoulders, my sides, desperate for balance.

"Easy," he whispered, though he had no power to make it so.

"Not easy," I said, voice gone rough. "Never easy. You are here. You are warm. You are mine. She will not take what I have."

I pressed my forehead to his, hard enough that our skulls clicked together. His breath puffed against my mouth in short, startled bursts. I closed my eyes and inhaled him, dragging his scent deep until it settled into every old hollow inside me.

My hands moved without my telling them to—over his back, mapping the planes of muscle and bone, counting every line. My claws stayed sheathed by the thinnest mercy. I traced his shoulder blades, his spine, the curve of his waist, memorizing, as if the act itself could nail him into this moment.

He shivered under the touch, a small involuntary sound escaping his throat. It fluttered against my lips and teeth, soft and frightened and alive.

"Say it again," I breathed, the words tumbling over one another. "Say mine. Say mine mine mine—"

"I'm yours," he said, quicker this time, tripping over the words as if speed would keep me from demanding more. "I'm yours, I'm yours."

Each repetition struck sparks along my nerves. I felt half-feral with it, half-sick. Relief and triumph and terror tangled until I couldn't tell one from the other.

This wasn't the slow basking of before, the careful feeding and grooming. This was staccato—jagged breath, frantic hands, the rhythm of a heart that had been braced for loss and suddenly, violently, didn't have to be.

I kissed him.

Not like humans did, all coy and neat. My mouth covered his in a rough, possessive press, teeth scraping his lower lip, breath mixing hot and fast. He froze for a heartbeat, then yielded in the only way he could —by not fighting, by letting me set the pace, by parting his lips when I demanded entrance with the insistent tilt of my head.

His hands clutched at my fur, at my shoulders, at anything that felt solid. His fingers shook.

I took the sound he made into my mouth like a vow.

My tail lashed against the stone then curved in around us, bracketing his hips, hemming us in. The world narrowed to heat and heartbeat, to the frantic thrum of his pulse against my tongue, to the way his breath stuttered every time I shifted, to the raw, ragged noise in my own throat that might have been a purr and might have been a sob.

"Mine," I exhaled against his lips, his cheek, the corner of his jaw. I marked him with the word, with my breath, with the press of my teeth against skin that would bruise. "You said it. You stay. You do not leave."

He nodded, tiny jerks of his head that knocked our noses together.

"I stay," he echoed, voice shaking. "I won't leave. I promise."

He was saying it to survive. I could smell the fear under the words, like rain under smoke.

But his body told an equal truth.

His breath came fast, not just from terror but from something

144

hotter, more urgent. His skin beaded with the fine sheen of sweat born not from fever or fear alone, but from keeping pace with me. Matching my frantic rhythm, answering my hunger with his own.

When my hands moved over him, his muscles rose to meet my palms. When I pulled him closer, his body arched instead of recoiling. His pulse leapt beneath my mouth, yes with panic, but also with a kind of primal, helpless wanting humans rarely admit even to themselves.

His fingers tightened in my fur—not just to hold on but to pull me closer.

His thighs trembled between mine—not simply from weakness but from the effort of holding himself against me, of giving back the intensity I demanded.

His voice faltered on fear.

His body surged on instinct.

He wanted me.

Not like a lover.

Not like prey.

Not like anything simple humans could describe.

He wanted what I had to offer.

The heat.

The wildness.

The terrible, necessary closeness.

As much as I wanted him.

That was the truth that rose from his skin, his heartbeat, the trembling of his hands.

He was afraid of me.

He was drawn to me.

He wanted me.

All three truths braided together, tightening around us like the roots of an old tree.

And I—greedy, starved, triumphant—accepted every one of them.

I didn't care why he gave me the words.

I cared that his body answered mine.

Before I could pull him back into the pelts—he moved.

A sudden, rough sound left his throat.

His hands slid to my hips, strong despite exhaustion, and in one unsteady, decisive surge he flipped me onto my front, pressing me into the warm spill of fur.

My breath hitched—surprise first. Then something molten, ancient, delighted.

"Wait—" I rasped, not in protest but in wonder.

He leaned over me, breath hot against the back of my neck.

"I am yours," he whispered, voice low and trembling. Not with fear this time but with the bewildered courage of someone who has stepped through pain and into impossible pleasure.

"Now... you be mine."

The words shocked through me like a lightning strike.

Claim.

Not prey's fear.

Not survival-mimicry.

Claim.

My claws slid uselessly through the pelts, my spine bowing in a helpless arch as heat clawed up through me. A growl rolled out of my chest, deep enough to shake dust from the stone.

His voice broke again; softer, almost reverent.

"I don't know if this is a dream," he breathed. "I don't know if you're real or if I'm just... falling into something I want too much. You feel like... the wildest part of me. Like the thing I've never said out loud."

His hands gripped my hips harder.

"You feel like desire."

A shudder rolled through me so violently my vision blurred.

"Say it," he urged, bending over me, his mouth brushing the rim of my ear. "Say you're mine."

The words tore out of me like a vow.

"I'm yours."

A rumble of satisfaction vibrated through his chest and through mine.

Not dominance alone.

Not submission alone.

Recognition.

Answering.

Fire finding fire.

His rhythm matched the frantic beat of my heart, each movement threaded with sharp need and startled awe, a mortal tasting the kind of hunger only old creatures know.

Pleasure tore me open, raw and blinding, and I let it.

I let him.

I reveled in the impossible truth of being wanted back.

When at last the frenzy broke it left us trembling, breathless. Tangled in warmth and pelts and the dizzy aftermath of something neither of us had language for.

We collapsed together in the soft spill of furs, my body curling instinctively around his, limbs wrapping him in a cage made not of threat now but of keeping.

I tucked his head beneath my chin, pressed his ear to my chest so he could hear the pounding of my heart. Let him know that as long as it beat, he would not be alone in the dark.

"We are one," I murmured into his hair, the words vibrating through both of us. "You breathe, I breathe. You sleep, I watch. You are mine. I am yours. The mountain will learn our names together."

My hands, trapped between our bodies, tightened.

He did not say he was mine again.

He didn't have to. I had enough of his words hoarded already.

I curled tighter, tail looping over his hips, drawing him in until there was no space between us. My purr rolled out low and constant, a sound big cats used to soothe frightened kits and dying mates and themselves.

"She cannot have you," I whispered into the top of his head, over and over until the sentence blurred. "Not the dragon. Not the sky. Not anyone. You are mine. And I am yours."

He trembled a long time before exhaustion dragged him back toward sleep. His breathing finally slowed, matching the rise and fall of my chest.

I didn't sleep.

I stared at the cave ceiling, at the faint shimmer of damp stone, at the shadow-flickers cast by the fire. My ears stayed pricked. Every drip from the waterfall, every pop from the coals, every fractional shift in the Hallow's tone pricked my nerves.

Beneath my triumph, the mountain moved.

Not much. Just a slow, deliberate tightening somewhere far above. Like a fist closing around a new idea.

The stone under my spine thrummed.

Something was coming back.

Something bright.

Something gold.

I held my man closer and bared my teeth at the unseen sky.

Cat and Dragon (Lyra)

The mountain closed over us one narrow crack at a time.

Butch went first, because of course he did. His paws found every ledge, every slick patch of stone, nails scraping softly as he eased his big body sideways through the slit in the rock. His hackles were a ridge of fur along his spine, tail low, ears flicking at sounds I couldn't hear yet.

Henry came next, already sweating through his uniform despite the cold air sliding out of the earth. His pack scraped against granite. I heard his breath catch when he had to turn sideways and duck. One hand on the wall, the other clenched in the back of Butch's harness.

I brought up the rear, the mountain's weight pressing down overhead. It wasn't just stone—it never was, not for me. The narrow passageway throbbed with the slow pulse of the Hallow, like we were slipping through one of the mountain's arteries and it hadn't quite decided if we were blood to be carried or something to be rejected.

The rock brushed my shoulders on both sides, cold and slick in places where underground water had worn it smooth. The ceiling dipped so low I had to tilt my head and hunch over, headlamp beam throwing a thin white arc across stone that gleamed wetly. The air smelled like damp mineral, old leaves, and something heavier that curled at the back of the throat—musk and rabbit fur, and a metallic tang that didn't belong.

Butch stopped suddenly, muscles bunching beneath his coat. A soft whine slipped out before he swallowed it, looking back over his shoulder at Henry like he wanted permission to turn around and bolt. Henry's hand dropped to the scruff of his neck, fingers digging in.

"I know, buddy," Henry murmured, his voice too loud in the tight space. "I know."

I touched the wall beside me. The stone shivered faintly, the way skin twitches under a fly's touch. The Hallow was listening. Watching. Waiting.

The Wampus had burrowed herself deep in here. I could feel her through the stone like a bruise you keep bumping: loneliness, hunger. Raw devotion twisted into something sharp. She wasn't an empty predator. She loved. She just didn't understand how to love without teeth.

Henry's boot slipped on damp gravel. He caught himself on the wall with a soft curse.

"Easy," I said. My voice had to thread the needle—steady, not sharp. If I startled him, he might panic

"I'm good," he said too fast. "Just...tight in here."

"You've been in worse," I reminded him. "Remember that kids' cave program with the girl who decided halfway in that she hated the dark?"

He huffed a laugh that came out thin. "You mean the one who peed on my shoe?"

"That's the one." I shifted closer so my chest brushed his pack whenever the crevice narrowed. Not enough to crowd him but just enough to let him feel my presence. "You did fine then. You're doing fine now."

"Yeah, well," he muttered. "That cave didn't have a man-eating cat goddess at the end of it."

He wasn't wrong.

Butch snuffled at the air ahead then kept moving, his body language saying more clearly than words: "Every instinct I have says turn back, but you are my pack, so I go".

The passage bent left then dropped in a series of awkward, steep steps where the rock had broken ages ago. Water ran somewhere below us, a constant low roar that grew louder as we descended. It wasn't the friendly sound of a creek. It was a deeper, hollow rush—the kind of water that carved worlds beneath worlds.

My headlamp flicked over claw marks raked into the stone. Old ones, smoothed at the edges. Newer ones, white and fresh, water droplets still clinging to the grooves. Here and there, a smear of fur.

She'd come this way more times than I could count. This was not some opportunistic den. This was home.

The Hallow thrummed in agreement, a slow beat under my ribs. It wasn't happy. It wasn't angry, either. It felt...wary. Like it had watched a wild thing grow lopsided in one of its shadows and didn't quite know what to do with her.

Butch stopped again and let out one sharp bark that ricocheted off the rock, coming back in stuttering echoes.

Henry flinched. "Ouch, Butch."

"That's his 'we're close' bark," I said quietly. "Not his 'oh God we're all going to die' one."

"How many barks do you keep track of?" Henry asked, his voice a little higher.

"All of them." I let a touch of dry humor into my tone. "It's in the ranger job description. Don't worry, you'll get there."

The passage opened for a breath's worth of space into a small alcove —no higher than my shoulders, but wider. We took the moment to breathe. Henry pressed his back to the nearest wall, shutting his eyes. Butch leaned into his thigh.

Beads of sweat clung to Henry's hairline, shining in the light. His hands shook as he unclipped his water bottle from his belt.

I put a hand on his wrist before he could fumble it.

"Hey," I said. "Look at me."

His eyes open. They were too wide, pupils blown. He kept his breathing even through sheer will, but the fear wafted off him like heat off stone.

"We're almost there," I said. "You're doing exactly what you need to be doing. Butch trusts you. I trust you."

He swallowed. "I just—" He broke off, jaw tightening. "I keep thinking of that coroner report. The way Monroe described the chest cavity. It's like I can see it every time I blink."

My own memory offered up the image automatically: ribs laid open like pages, the way the Song had mourned and moved on. The Wampus's kill was brutal and honest, but no accident.

"This isn't Tommy's story," I said, my tone gentler than my words. "We don't write the same ending twice if we can help it. You hear me?"

Henry gave a single jerky nod.

I squeezed his wrist once, then let go. "Alright. Shake it out, Ranger. Then we keep going."

He did, rolling his shoulders, flexing his fingers, grounding himself by burying one hand in Butch's ruff. The dog leaned harder into him, a living weight.

"Good boy," Henry whispered into Butch's ear. I couldn't tell who he was really talking to.

We ducked back into the throat of the mountain.

The air grew warmer as we went deeper, the damp turning from chill to clammy. The smell of musk intensified—cat, heavy and wild, layered over with the sweeter iron of fresh blood and the fatty ghost of cooked meat. Rabbit, most likely. My stomach twisted.

The rock underfoot shifted from jagged to oddly smooth in patches, as if something had rubbed against it over and over. Wampus's flank. Wampus's shoulder. Wampus's tail.

I could almost see her moving ahead of us—slipping through these constrictions like water, claws finding purchase without thought, carrying a man like a prize between her teeth.

She loved him. That was the worst of it. Her love was not gentle or sane or safe, but it was love. The Hallow had given her wanting without giving her a teacher. She had learned intimacy from hunger and possession from winter.

I'd known too many people who did the same.

My hand brushed another gouge in the stone, then another. Here and there, gouges overlapped each other. Layers of frustration. Pacing, circling. This was not just a corridor. This was where she walked out her wanting when it got too loud inside her skull.

The passage turned again, dropping another few feet. The roar of water grew until conversation would have required shouting. Instead we moved in pantomime, hand signals and touches and the language of breath.

Butch's tail was tucked tight now. Every so often he glanced back at Henry then at me, as if making sure we were still real.

The Hallow rose higher under my skin, tightening like a drumhead. It sang in a pitch only I could hear, tuned between warning and mourning. Wampus was close. Darren was closer.

The mountain knew the lines between them. It didn't like the knot.

Then I heard it—faint and thready. A sound that didn't belong to stone or water or dog.

A human sound.

Henry heard it, too. His whole body went as taut as a struck wire. His hand flew to my arm, fingers digging in hard enough to bruise.

"That's him," he mouthed, breath shredded. "Lyra—that's—"

I nodded once, a slow anchor. "I hear it."

Butch let out another short bark, then a low, anxious whine, nose pressed to a seam of shadow ahead. His body leaned forward but his paws worked the stone in place, torn between obedience and the animal instinct that said nothing good waited in that dark.

"Easy," I told him. "We go together."

The sound came again, a little clearer this time. Woven with the rushing water like a voice drowning just beneath the surface.

Darren.

"Alright," I said, more to the mountain than anything. "We're here."

The Hallow hummed back in a deep, resonant note that made my teeth itch.

Somewhere ahead, the Wampus lifted her head. I felt her attention snap toward us like a bared wire.

She knew we were coming.

I slipped past Henry and moved up into point beside Butch, one hand resting between his shoulder blades. I could feel his heart pounding through his fur, the jitter of adrenaline barely contained.

"Whatever happens," I said, pitching my voice so he and Henry both heard, "you stay behind me unless I say otherwise. Your job is Darren. Mine is the creature that took him."

Henry's breath hitched. "And if it tries to take you?"

I glanced back over my shoulder. The headlamp glare washed his face out to a pale oval, but his eyes were dark wells.

A dragon could have given him the truth. I gave him the ranger version.

"Then we ruin its day," I said.

Somewhere above us I could feel Taren stirring in his own distant range, his presence flaring like distant lightning. The mountain gathered itself around us like a held breath.

"Come on," I whispered to the stone, to the Song, to the man beyond the next bend. "Let's end this."

We pushed deeper into the vein of rock, toward the den, toward the monster and the man she had decided to call hers.

The passage opened into the den all at once, like stepping through a pupil into the back of an eye.

My headlamp swung out over rough stone and caught on firelight. Real flame, low and banked, licking at a ring of blackened rocks. The smell hit me second: woodsmoke, rabbit fat, wet fur, and the deep, mineral breath of the mountain's throat. Third came the sound—a dull, constant roar from the curtain of water beside us, smothered into a steady thunder that made every word feel small.

Butch froze on the threshold, lifting one paw. Henry's hand was latched on to the harness.

"Easy," I breathed, though the word was for all of us.

It wasn't what I'd expected.

I'd braced for carnage. For an animal's nest—torn hide, scattered bones, the reek of rot.

What I found instead was...order.

Rabbit bones did litter the stone floor, yes, but they were not strewn. They'd been arranged, lined up in neat rows along one wall: femur with femur, rib with rib, skulls facing inward like a ring of pale, attentive faces. Above them the rock bore shallow scratches that repeated in a rhythm I recognized as thought. Not human writing. But not meaningless.

Pelts lay heaped in the center of the chamber, forming a thick, low mound—a bed more than a lair. Deer, rabbit, and something larger and tawny thrown over the top. The pile had been shaped around the two bodies lying on it the way a nest shapes itself around its eggs.

Darren laid on his side, half-wrapped in fur, bare skin catching the fire's glow in long strokes of copper and gold. His eyes were open, pupils wide in the dim light. A faint tremor ran through his shoulders. Bite marks, bruises, and scratches mapped his throat and chest.

Pressed against his back, curved around him like a comma, was the Wampus.

She was smaller than she'd felt through the stone—woman-sized, mostly. But everything about her was too much. Too long. Too sharp. Tawny fur clung to her limbs and spine in thick, sleek bands. The rest of her was skin with a feline undertone, like someone had melted a cougar and a woman together and then forgotten where one ended. Her eyes glowed green-gold in the firelight, pupils slitted to knives.

When we stepped into the den, she was already awake.

She rose in one fluid motion, placing herself between us and Darren with a grace that was entirely predator. Spine arched, tail lashing, shoulders rolling forward to make herself bigger. Her lips were peeled back from long, curved fangs in a soundless snarl that finally tore loose into something that made my bones vibrate.

Butch answered with a deep-chested growl that I felt through the soles of my boots. The sound echoed weirdly off the wet stone, caught and bent by the waterfall's roar.

Henry sucked in a breath. "Oh, God," he whispered. "Oh, God."

He had known—on paper, in theory—that we were tracking a cat-woman. A creature with a name whispered over bar tops and told to tourists with a wink. We had said the words out loud, cool and clinical, like rehearsing for a storm that might never come.

But dragon instinct strips away illusions.

It showed me the exact timbre of his fear—sharp, young, metallic. His pulse fluttered behind me like a trapped bird. The air around him tightened with the scent of adrenaline.

He was facing the part of the world I had spent the majority of my life shielding people from. The part where instinct rules, where hunger thinks, where the Hallow shapes predators out of loneliness and dark corners.

To my knowledge, Henry had never stood this close to a legend with breath still warm in its lungs. He had never been looked at by something that debated whether he was threat, prey, or curiosity.

A ribbon of guilt twisted under my ribs.

This was my job—my burden—to keep these realities tucked beneath the surface of human life. To guard the seam between the ordinary and the mythic. To keep young men like Henry from standing exactly where he stood now.

But sometimes the mountain forced a truth into daylight.

Sometimes a creature refused to stay buried in story.

"Don't run," I said without looking back at him. "She's more likely to chase."

The Wampus's gaze locked on me. Her nostrils flared once, taking me in—sweat, steel, Hallow-scent. Recognition flickered across her face like the shadow of a passing cloud.

Dragon-woman, her eyes said. *Sky-queen. Fire-thief.*

She lowered herself further over Darren, her body forming a shield. Her claws sank into the pelts on either side of him, pinning him to the bed. A low, desperate sound rumbled out of her chest—half growl, half plea.

"Darren," Henry called, voice breaking. "Darren, can you hear me?"

Darren's gaze jerked away from the Wampus and found us. Found Henry.

For a heartbeat, relief flooded his features so clearly it almost knocked me back.

"Hello?" he croaked. His voice sounded like it had been rubbed raw with stone. "You—"

Then his eyes darted to the rifle slung over Henry's shoulder. To Butch's bared teeth. To the badge on my chest.

And his whole body flinched like we'd struck him.

"No," he gasped. He pushed up onto one elbow, ignoring the Wampus's attempt to keep him down. "No, don't—no—"

Henry took a step forward, hand outstretched. "Hey, hey, it's okay. We're here to get you out, man. We're getting you home."

Darren shook his head so violently his hair whipped. "You can't. You can't—she—" His voice cracked. He twisted, putting himself partially in front of the Wampus without seeming to realize he was doing it. "She's not—she's not what you think."

Henry.

The Wampus went totally still against Darren's back. Her eyes widened, the pupils swallowing almost all the color. For a second all that wild, bristling energy folded in on itself. Like a cat caught mid-hiss by the sudden, improbable gift of a hand.

He chose me, the look on her face said. *He chose me.*

"Darren," I said quietly. "Listen to me. We know you've been through hell, but you are not safe here."

His gaze snapped to mine. Up close, I could see the fine tremor running along his jaw, the sweat beading on his upper lip. The marks on his neck were not ambiguous. Neither were the ones scoring his chest. His body told one story; his eyes were trying desperately to tell another.

"She protects me," he insisted. "She...she feeds me, she—she keeps me warm—" His voice thinned around the last word. "She loves me."

The Wampus made a sound then that truly startled me. It wasn't a growl. It wasn't a roar.

It was a purr.

Deep and rolling like a motor under skin, vibrating the air between us. She pressed her cheek against Darren's shoulder, eyes half-lidded, and let that sound pour through her chest into his back. Her tail curled around his thigh, possessive and pleased.

She believes it, I realized. She believes every word.

And Darren...

Trauma had its own gravity. I'd seen it before—hostages defending their captors, kids insisting the bruise came from a fall, not a fist. The mind did strange gymnastics when the alternative was admitting you'd been trapped with something that could kill you whenever it decided to.

Add intimate touch, enforced isolation, a needy intelligence bent wholly toward you, and the bond could feel holy.

"I know she's shown you care," I said carefully. The wrong word here could snap him like a twig. "I know she's kept you alive. That doesn't make this safe. It doesn't make it right."

The Wampus's ears flattened. Her gaze flicked from me to Henry to

Butch, reading our posture the way any apex predator would. Three threats. One boy. One way out.

Her breathing picked up. So did Darren's.

"Look at me," I said, keeping my voice and my body still. "Darren, can I see your shoulder?"

He blinked, confused. "What?"

"Your left shoulder," I repeated. "The back of it."

He hesitated. Then, with a jittering swallow, he shifted his weight, turning just enough that I could see where his skin disappeared under the pelt.

The Wampus moved with him, trying to block the view. Her claws flexed, digging into fur and flesh.

"Let me see," I murmured, eyes never leaving hers.

For a moment she held my gaze, a hot, defiant challenge sparking there.

Then, slowly, almost smugly, she shifted just enough that the firelight landed on Darren's bare shoulder blade.

A sigil was carved there into his skin.

Not deep enough to be a maim. Deep enough to scar.

Four curved lines intersecting in a hooked spiral, the pattern echoing the scratch-marks on the den wall. Each stroke was precise, deliberate. This was a word.

The Hallow shuddered under my boots, the Song tightening around that mark like a throat closing on a sob.

Ownership, it said. Claim. Bond.

The Wampus purred louder, lowering her head to press her mouth to the center of the sigil. Her tongue flicked out, tasting the half-healed cuts, lapping away the last beads of blood like they were sacred.

"Mine," she crooned against his skin. "I keep you. I keep you."

Darren's eyes fluttered closed.

I took a step forward.

The Wampus's snarl came back full force, shredding the purr in half. Her fur stood on end, making her look twice her size. Her tail lashed the air, thick and heavy, the tip cracking like a whip.

"Back," she spat, the word mangled by fangs but unmistakable.

"You are not welcome. You steal. You take. You burn. You will not take this."

Butch barked, sharp and explosive, the sound bouncing off the walls. He planted himself between Henry and that bed of pelts, weight forward, teeth bared, every inch of him screaming "I will die before I let you pass!".

Henry's hand shook on the rifle strap. His eyes were huge, flicking from the Wampus to Darren to me like he'd been handed a nightmare and asked to pick which part to wake up from.

The Wampus shifted her grip on Darren, one arm snaking around his chest, claws poised just a breath from his throat. Not pressing. Not yet. But close enough that one panicked move on our part could end this entire search in a spray of arterial red.

"Okay," I said softly, palms raised a fraction, open. "Alright. Nobody is taking anything right this second."

My voice had to bridge impossible gaps now. Between human and monster, victim and rescue, love and the twisted thing it became when isolation and power wrapped around it too tight.

"Darren." I kept my gaze on the Wampus even as I spoke to him. "I need you to listen very carefully."

His breath hitched. "I'm listening."

"You are in shock," I said. "You're dehydrated, exhausted, and your nervous system has been on high alert for longer than is sane. Your brain is doing what brains do when they're terrified and trapped—it's trying to make it make sense. To make it safe. That's normal. It doesn't mean you have to stay here."

"I'm not trapped," he whispered, but the words didn't have heat in them. Just frayed insistence. "I choose—"

The Wampus pressed her claws that much closer to his throat. "You choose me," she hissed in his ear. "Tell her. Tell them."

He swallowed, Adam's apple bobbing against the sharp edges of her hand. His pulse beat wildly there, a frantic bird against a cage.

"I choose—" He choked, coughed, tried again. "I choose—"

His eyes darted to Henry's, just for a fraction of a second.

In that fraction, I saw it: the crack. The part of him that remembered the world outside this cave. The friends. The family. The plans. The life where love didn't come with claws.

"Darren," Henry said, very quietly. "Please. Come with me."

The Wampus let out a sound like stone tearing.

She dragged one claw across the sigil again, a fresh line of red following the track. The Hallow recoiled so hard it felt like the floor dropped out from under us for a heartbeat.

I took a breath that tasted like wet rock and blood and rabbit fat.

"Henry," I said, locking eyes with the Wampus. "When I say go, you and Butch take Darren. Don't look back. Don't argue. Don't hesitate."

His breath seized. "Lyra—"

"I know," I said. "Go means go. You hear me?"

He swallowed. Then nodded once, sharp.

The Wampus sensed the shift. Her pupils became huge. All the fur along her spine stood on end. Her tail lashed the air, smacking against stone hard enough to throw off chips.

"Don't take him," she begged, her voice dropping into something ragged. "Don't. The world took everything. The Song turned its face. I keep this. I keep him. He is mine."

For a heartbeat, my throat closed.

I knew what it was to be left. To be the last one standing when a world you'd built with someone else collapsed. To ache so badly for one small thing that stayed that you'd raze mountains to keep it.

"I believe that you love him," I said, and it was the hardest truth I'd spoken in a long time. "I do. But love that cages is still a cage. And I am not leaving him here."

Her gaze went incandescent with fury and grief. Tears—real tears, hot and sharp—gathered at the corners of her eyes and didn't fall.

"Then you will have to tear him from my claws," she whispered.

The mountain exhaled through the waterfall in a long, shuddering sigh. As if it knew exactly what was coming.

"Henry," I said, my voice settling into the steely place it went when there were no good options left.

"Yeah?" he croaked.

"When I move," I told him, "that's your go."

Butch's growl deepened, echoing the Hallow's hum.

Darren's lips parted, some half-formed plea caught there.

The Wampus's claws flexed. The golden glow of the firelight slid along her fangs.

I shifted my weight, feeling my dragon-bones sing beneath my skin.

The bonds in this den were about to break.

For a heartbeat we were all held in the same thin, trembling moment.

Darren half-curled on the pelts, the Wampus crouched over him. Henry braced with one hand on Butch's harness, the other on his rifle strap. The den seemed to be holding its breath. Even the waterfall's roar dulled to a muffled thrum.

"Henry," I said. "You remember what I told you."

His eyes flicked to mine. Fear. Trust. Resolve.

"Go means go," he whispered.

"Good." I shifted my feet a fraction wider on the slick stone and raised my hands the smallest bit, palms open, shoulders loose. I stepped sideways; not closer but just enough to draw the Wampus's focus fully to me.

Her head tracked the movement like a cat watching a mouse. Every muscle along her back tightened. Her claws flexed against Darren's skin.

"Hey," I said softly, adding an amber tone to my voice. "Look at me. Not at him. Me."

Her stare snapped to my face, pupils slitted to needles.

"Let him breathe," I murmured. "He can't worship you if he's dead, can he?"

A low, ragged sound scraped out of her throat. "You mock," she spat. "You who leave ashes. You who take and take and call it saving."

I shook my head once. "No mockery," I said. "Just a fact. You want him? You want him to tell you he's yours? You need him alive. So maybe don't put your hand on the part that pumps the blood."

For a moment, rage and logic wrestled across her face. Then, with visible reluctance, she shifted her grip a hairsbreadth lower. Still claiming, still coiled around him, but no longer a single twitch away from ripping his artery open.

It was the opening I needed.

"Henry," I said, never breaking eye contact with her. "Go."

Everything happened at once.

Butch lunged, not at the Wampus but sideways, slamming his full weight into Darren's legs. Darren yelped, knocked off balance. Henry dropped hard to one knee, shoulder driving into Darren's ribs, arms locking around his torso. Ranger, man, and dog rolled off the pelts together in a tangle of limbs, fur, and shouted breath.

The Wampus shrieked.

The sound knifed through my skull, a mix of grief and fury so raw the Hallow itself flinched. She lunged, claws flashing for Henry's exposed back.

I threw myself into her path.

We collided chest to chest, shoulder to shoulder, bone slamming into bone. Her claws raked across my forearm, scoring deep lines that burned white-hot. I drove my weight forward, forcing her back and away from Darren.

"Run!" I roared.

Henry didn't argue.

I heard him scramble up, heard Darren swearing, heard Butch barking like his voice could chew through stone. The scrabble of boots and claws on rock scraped my nerves as they bolted for the tunnel.

The Wampus twisted under me like liquid fury. She slammed her forehead up into my chin. Stars burst behind my eyes. My teeth clicked together hard enough to sting.

"Thief!" she screamed, spitting the word into my face. "Thief, thief, thief!"

She rolled her shoulders, using the leverage to spill me off to the side. I hit the stone on my back and slid, shoulder blades tearing against damp rock. She pounced, claws screeching against the floor where my throat had been a heartbeat before.

I kicked out, boot connecting with her ribs. The impact jolted up my leg. She snarled, stumbling sideways just enough for me to scramble up.

The tunnel entrance yawned behind her. In the beam of my dropped headlamp I saw Henry's back vanishing around a bend, Butch's tail flashing once before it, too, disappeared.

Good, I thought, even as my lungs dragged at the thick air. Good.

The Wampus followed my glance and realized what I already knew. He was gone.

For a split second, something like naked horror crossed her face. Then she turned it on me.

"You took him," she panted, chest heaving. "You took him."

She hunched lower, the fur along her spine bristling. The pelt-bed looked suddenly smaller behind her, pathetic and childlike.

"I fed him," she snarled. "I warmed him. I gave him what the Song took from me." Her voice cracked. "You came and stole. Just like before."

Before.

The word landed heavy, loaded with more than just this moment. Old history. Old wounds. Old hunts.

The Hallow hummed in my ears. It remembered, too.

"I'm not here to replay ancient wars," I said, my throat tight. "I'm here for him. And he's gone. You can still walk away with your throat whole."

She stared at me as if I'd offered her a bone and called it a crown.

"Walk away to what?" she whispered. "To the stones that do not answer? To winters with no heartbeat beside mine? To a hollow den and a Song that hums for everyone but me?"

Her voice shook. Tears cut clean tracks through the soot on her cheeks, catching in the fur along her jaw.

"I only wanted someone," she said, and it was almost a sob. "Just one. Mine."

I swallowed hard.

"I know," I said. "But wanting doesn't erase what you did to get it."

The pupils of her eyes swallowed what little green remained.

"Then I will take another," she hissed. "And another. And another. Until the wanting is full."

She gathered herself to spring.

Behind her, somewhere up-tunnel, I heard Butch bark twice— sharp, warning. Henry shouted my name, voice echoing, small with distance.

You can't fight her like this and keep them safe, the Hallow sang in my bones. *Not bound in skin. Not with your fire quiet.*

It was right.

I rolled my shoulders back and stepped sideways, putting my body between her and the tunnel mouth. The old words rose in my throat, tasting of iron and first light.

"Enough," I said to her in human tongue.

Then, in dragon-speech, low and rolling, to the mountain, *Open*.

The floor under my boots trembled.

The Wampus stiffened, eyes darting down then back up to my face.

"What are you doing?" she snarled.

"Ending this," I said.

I took three running steps toward her, each one pounding the syllables of the dragon-name I hadn't spoken aloud in longer than I cared to remember.

On the fourth, I leapt.

My body knew the motion the way lungs knew breathing. Bones uncoiled. The Hallow surged up through me in a flood of molten gold.

Everything else—stone, fur, teeth, fear—fell away in the burn.

For a heartbeat, there was only change.

Light roared out of me, hot and blinding, filling the chamber. The air exploded outward, snatching dust and ash and pelt-hairs into spirals. The den fire guttered, then flared as my heat hit it. Water seethed on the rocks behind the falls, steam billowing like breath.

My skin split into scales, each one a coin of dawn. My spine stretched, vertebrae multiplying, tail whipping out behind me in a crack of force. Fingers crushed into talons; arms unfurled into wings that slammed outward, skeletal and vast, scraping stone, carving fresh gouges into the cave walls.

My jaw lengthened, teeth reshaping into curved ivory blades. Old horn nubs pushed through my skull, curling back in sleek, golden arcs. My chest swelled with a breath that was more than air—Hallow-fire, white-gold and searing, filling a furnace that had been banked too long.

The den shrank.

The Wampus shrank.

I landed on all fours where I'd leapt as a woman, claws biting deep into the stone. The rock welcomed the weight, humming up through my bones like a song finally heard at proper volume.

The Wampus stared up at me, eyes gone wide and wild.

"Sky-queen," she breathed. The words were a curse and a prayer.

Behind her, the tunnel shook with a muted shout—Henry, I was nearly certain, swearing as dust rained down. Butch barked then whined, the sound receding as they pulled farther from the chamber.

Good, I thought again, but this time it came out as a low, thunderous growl that made stalactites shiver.

Golden light spilled from between my teeth.

She moved first.

She was fast. I'd give her that.

She shot up the nearest wall like a spider, all claws and momentum, four limbs finding purchase in cracks I couldn't have seen with human eyes. Her tail whipped for balance then lashed out, smacking against my snout with enough force to sting.

I snapped at her, teeth scoring stone as she let go and dropped, twisting midair to land on a ledge above my shoulder. From there she leapt again, aiming for my eyes.

I reared back, wings flaring, and met her midair with a swipe of my foreclaw. The impact spun her but she caught the edge of my horn with both hands, clinging like a burr. Her claws raked over my scales, searching for the thinner seams at my jaw.

"You take!" she screamed, voice cracking into hysteria. "You always take! Dens! Valleys! Sky! You burned us from the ridges and called it cleansing! You said the Song was yours—"

"Liar!" she shrieked. "You knew. You know."

How could I explain to her the rapture of it—the pure, obliterating joy of mating-flight, of creation-flight, when Taren and I had been nothing but fire braided through fire?

In those eras, nothing else existed.

Not valleys. Not hunting grounds. Not the small, trembling lives that scattered under the storms we made.

There had been no malice in it.

Only ecstasy.

Only purpose.

Only the fierce, crystalline knowledge that we were shaping the world with every spiral of our bodies.

She could never understand the penance that followed.

The way we spent centuries walking fault lines to mend what our joy had cracked.

The way longing settled between us after the Making—an ache that could never again be fully satisfied.

The two of us forever tethered by duty.

Forever out of reach of the abandon we once knew.

I opened my mouth to try anyway.

Her claws found the seam where two scales met at the corner of my eye. Pain flared bright and hot. I roared, jerking my head to the side. She lost her grip, tumbling.

I snapped at her again, catching her tail between my teeth just before she hit the ground.

She screamed, terrible and raw. I flung my head, slamming her into the wall. Rock cracked. Dust plumed.

She hit the floor in a rolling heap then pushed herself up, staggering, tail dangling at a wrong angle. Blood matted the fur along one flank.

She was shaking.

She was still coming.

"Stop," I rumbled. The word made the entire den vibrate. "You can't win this fight."

"I don't care," she panted, chest heaving. "You took him. You." She bared her teeth, eyes wild. "If I die, I die on the ashes of my love."

The Hallow hummed low and troubled beneath us.

She was made by the Song, too, Taren's voice murmured in the back of my mind, silver sliding along gold. *Don't end her flame if you can help it, Lyra.*

I can't let her keep hunting people, I shot back, the thought a coil of frustration and grief. *I can't leave her free.*

No, he agreed. *You bind. You do not butcher.*

He was right. He usually was when it mattered.

My lips peeled back from my teeth in a silent snarl. I lowered my head, sucking breath deep into my chest—not to burn her, but to light the sigils that lived in my marrow.

The Song rose up to meet me.

Not the thin hum I heard in skin, but the full-throated chorus that had carved my bones in the first place. It poured through me, through horn and claw and scale, through the long coil of my spine.

I opened my mouth and let it out.

Not as flame. As sound.

The note shook the chamber.

Rock vibrated underfoot, stalactites chiming against each other like struck crystal. Water arced sideways, the waterfall bending around the force. Dust rose in fine veils, dancing in the golden air.

The Wampus flinched, hands flying to her ears. Her eyes went wide, blinking against the pressure.

The glow started under my claws, seeping into the stone like molten metal into cracked earth. Lines of light spread outward in a web, tracing shapes older than language. Circles within circles. Knots within knots. Sigils of holding, of mercy, of not-yet-death.

The floor in the center of the den quivered.

Then it opened.

Not in a sudden, cinematic drop, but in a slow, terrible unseaming. Stone parted like lips, like a throat, revealing a shaft of darkness threaded with faint, distant glimmers.

The Underdeep breathed up at us—cold, exhausted air laced with the scents of too many creatures and not enough sky.

The Wampus staggered back from the edge, eyes glued to the space beneath.

Shapes moved down there.

Some were massive, hulking silhouettes pacing in circles worn so smooth the stone gleamed.

Some were smaller, twisted by time into hunched shadows that muttered to themselves in languages that had forgotten how to be words.

Others clung to the bars of their light-forged cages, long fingers curled around nothing, whispering to the dark as if it might answer.

A few lifted their heads when the rift opened.

Not at her.

At me.

Recognition crackled like old bone.

The first rumbling growl rose from a cavern on the left—one of the ancient things I had bound centuries ago. A creature of teeth and frost, reduced now to pacing and half-remembered fury. When it sensed me it threw itself against its shimmering bars, shrieking a sound that once curdled rivers.

Another, farther down, whimpered.

A soft, pitiful sound that used to mean *mother* in its old tongue.

Every one of them had been brought here by my hand.

Every cage was my making.

Every howl, every whisper, every broken mind was a record of battles fought and mercies chosen in blood and fire. The Song had not been busy.

I had.

The Wampus heard them, saw them, felt their collective hunger and grief—and her whole body shook.

Some creatures pressed closer when they sensed her, scenting fresh loneliness; a new mind on the edge of breaking.

Others recoiled, hissing, recognizing the predatory shape of her wanting.

A ripple passed through the Underdeep then.

A single, terrible syllable whispered up from dozens of throats at once:

"Gold."

My title.

My sin.

My duty.

"Gold-born."

"Flame-forged."

"Maker and ender."

The voices struck Wampus like a blow.

She flattened her ears, tail lashing, breath coming in sharp little pants.

Her gaze flew to me—not with hate now, but dawning horror.

"You... you put them here," she breathed.

The Underdeep answered for me.

A rolling, resonant shudder of metal-light bars trembling in unison.

Creatures calling, screaming, wailing my name in tones that remembered both salvation and slaughter.

"Spark that called us forth."

"Fire that sent us down."

Wampus pressed herself against the wall, claws scrabbling uselessly.

"What are you?" she whispered.

And though my mouth never moved, the mountain gave her the truth:

She is beginning and ending.

She is the hinge between worlds.

She looked from the abyss to me, horror and fury warring on her face.

"No," she whispered. "No. No pit. No cage. I will not."

"You left me no choice," I said, the words a rumble that made the light sigils flare brighter. "I won't let you keep feeding your loneliness with human bones."

She shook her head, backing toward the far wall, tail dragging.

My heart clenched.

"No!" she cried suddenly, voice tearing. Not to me. Not to the mountain. To the echo of the man's presence, now well up the tunnels. "Don't let her do this to me! Don't forget me!"

Her voice cracked and broke on the last word.

"Mine!" she howled.

Wampus's gaze snapped toward the narrow passage that led to light, to forest and freedom. A ragged, animal sound tore from her chest, but it was not directed at me.

It was directed at the loss.

And I felt it, too.

Not through sympathy but through the Hallow.

Darren's presence, which had burned bright and fever-hot inside the den, was already dimming. The moment he crossed the threshold of her scent, the frenzied tether she had wrapped around his mind began to unspool.

He stumbled into the outer cavern, blinking hard as if waking from a dream he couldn't fully remember. His aura flickered, the shape of his fear changing—less bonded, less surrendered, more his own.

I exhaled, sharp and quiet. "The trance is breaking."

Wampus froze.

Her ears flattened. Her tail lashed once, twice, cracking the air.

She felt it.

All predators who bind through instinct and need feel the unraveling.

Darren's memory of her—of what she made him believe, of the desire she coerced from hunger and shock—was already softening at the edges. The human mind protects itself that way; it blurs what it cannot hold.

Wampus staggered. "He forgets," she keened, voice breaking on the last syllable. "He forgets me."

Her claws dug into the stone until the tips squealed.

"I felt him warm beside me," she whispered, shaking. "I felt him want. And now he slips away."

Her grief hit the den like a shockwave—raw and feral. Devastating in a way that had nothing to do with romance and everything to do with survival instinct twisted into worship.

The Underdeep stirred beneath us, creatures murmuring, hissing, reacting to the fracture in her spirit.

I swallowed against the ache in my own chest.

"This is what happens," I said softly, though I doubted she could hear me beyond her panic. "When the dream is only yours."

She whipped toward me, eyes wild with pain and accusation.

"You steal," she choked. "You take. You end."

She had no self to return to without him.

Her gaze snapped back to me. For the first time since I'd stepped into her den, she looked small.

"I only wanted someone," she said again, her tone almost childlike. "Just...someone."

"I know," I said.

I stepped forward, one massive claw stretching out. Not to strike but to point.

"Step into the circle," I told her. "Or I come get you."

For a long, trembling moment, she stood on the edge between fight and fall.

Then, shaking, eyes burning with a hatred born of heartbreak, she straightened her shoulders.

Her voice, when she spoke, was hoarse but steady.

"I will not be dragged," she said. "I walk."

She limped to the center of the gold-lit pattern, every step a defiance. She stopped just at the lip of the opening shaft and lifted her face to me, chin high.

"Remember me, sky-queen," she hissed. "When your soft ones leave you alone. When the Song turns its face. Remember that I loved what you took."

Then, before I could respond, she stepped forward.

She fell without flailing, fur and limbs and defiance dropping into the glow.

The sigils flared blindingly bright as she passed, threads of gold whipping up around her like vines. They wrapped her in a lattice of light, slowing her descent, turning the fall into a kind of suspended sinking. Her scream echoed up—not in pain but in rage and grief, and something that sounded like a prayer torn in half.

Below, the other shapes stirred.

Some laughed.

Some wept.

Some merely watched as a new sister joined their endless wait.

The Song tightened around the Underdeep like a bandage.

I let the note in my throat die.

The light in the sigils dimmed. The stone groaned as the shaft closed, lips sealing, threads of gold sinking beneath the surface until the den floor was whole again. Scarred, but whole.

Silence rushed in behind the roar.

Steam rose off my scales in thick waves. My wings drooped, the tips brushing the damp rock. Blood—hers and mine—smelled copper-sharp in the cooling air.

Taren's presence slid close, a cool silver hand against the fever of my thoughts.

This is mercy, Lyra, he murmured. *You gave her an ending that was not teeth. You gave the world a chance to breathe.*

I lowered my head until my muzzle nearly touched the cooling stone where she had stood.

"It feels like punishment," I said aloud, voice rough as avalanche.

For her.

For me.

For all of us made by a Song that gave us wanting and then punished us for how we fed it.

The mountain didn't answer in words. It answered in vibration; a long, low hum that wrapped around my aching bones like a rough blanket.

Above, faint through the stone and water and distance, I heard Henry's voice calling my name, thin with worry.

I drew one more breath of den-air—smoke and fur and the ghost of a creature who had tried to make a man into a cure.

Then I turned toward the tunnel, folding as much of myself as the rock allowed back into quieter shape.

I had a man to return.

And a world, a little smaller now, to keep from breaking further.

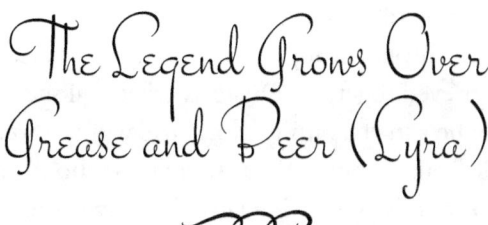

The Legend Grows Over Grease and Beer (Lyra)

"I heard he was found buck naked in the mountain veins—swears he was taken by a cat-woman with glowing eyes."

The whole bar erupted. Someone slapped the table hard enough to rattle the condiment caddy. Pool balls cracked and scattered like startled birds. A couple of the old-timers hooted so loud Maeve pointed at the noise-ordinance sign she kept taped by the register, though she was grinning while she did it.

Their laughter rolled over me like warm smoke. Humans had a remarkable talent for turning terror into tall tales before the dust had even settled.

"Aw, don't go spreadin' that malarkey," someone called from the corner booth. "Man had a bad concussion. Got turned around in the dark, woke up talkin' out his head."

I lifted my beer, hiding a smile behind the rim. That version would suit Darren fine. Easier to live with a concussion than a creature's heartbreak.

"Yeah," another chimed in, spinning his bottle by the neck. "Hit his skull down by the creek. Delirious as a fever."

They wanted an explanation that kept their world simple. I couldn't blame them for that.

"Still," a woman near the dartboard said, lowering her voice, "better fate than poor Tommy."

The shift in the room was immediate. A quiet heavy enough to feel in the bones.

"God rest him," an older man murmured.

"Amen," someone returned softly.

I felt the ache ripple through them—grief softened by communal ritual. Humans grieved together. Dragons grieved alone. Both hurt.

"Rested now he's in the family plot," the woman went on. "Shame, though. Boy wasn't all that old. Mountain takes who it wants."

A man by the woodstove nodded grimly. "Always has. Always will."

True enough.

Then, as if the quiet had lasted too long, someone added with a half-nervous laugh, "Still don't explain why Darren was naked."

Another wave of laughter. That blend of disbelief and hunger for stories—the way humans negotiated with the unknown.

It warmed something in me.

It felt good in the Bottle Tree tonight.

Warm.

Human.

Alive in a way the mountain never quite managed.

I nursed a local brew at my usual spot near the end of the bar. The burger on my plate dripped grease and comfort in equal measure. Butch lay sprawled across my boots like he intended to keep me from moving for the next century. Henry sat to my right, elbows on the counter, pretending not to listen even though every muscle in his body leaned toward the loudest gossip like an eager bloodhound.

This was their world. Their story. Their way of stitching fear back into something they could swallow.

And for once I let myself sit inside it, unarmored, simply listening.

I let myself breathe for what felt like the first time in days. There was something sacred about the Bottle Tree after a crisis. The neon beer signs hummed softly, casting a harmless kind of glow. The tables were scratched, the booths patched with duct tape and prayers, and half the lightbulbs flickered like they had their own moods. But it was safe.

It was home to people who didn't even realize how desperately they needed that safety.

Maeve leaned across the bar with the kind of smirk that only appeared when she was about to take over a story.

"All right, all right," she said, flicking her towel at a man who looked moments away from embellishing again. "If y'all are determined to talk about Darren Wells, then at least get your tales straight."

Several patrons pivoted toward her like sunflowers toward a familiar heat source.

Maeve lowered her voice to that campfire cadence Appalachia breeds in the bone.

"The boy was found curled up by the old limestone spill-off, clothes torn to shreds, ramblin' about somethin' chasin' him in the dark. Something with claws."

Gasps.

Chairs turning.

Someone shushed someone else.

She had them.

Every last one.

"Now," Maeve continued, "whether it was a bobcat, or a bear, or somethin' a little more... mountain-born..." She let the room hang on the pause. "Ain't my place to say."

A woman near the pool table hugged herself.

A man muttered that his grandfather once saw "something similar".

I dipped a fry in ketchup and popped it into my mouth.

This—right here—was why the mountain trusted Maeve.

She knew how to tell the truth sideways.

Not enough to expose anything real.

Enough to keep folks respectful.

And safe.

Henry nudged my arm gently. "Should we say something?"

"What, and ruin the free entertainment?" I murmured.

He snorted, cheeks still pink from the cold he had not fully warmed out of. His leg bounced under the counter. He had been quieter than usual tonight, processing more than the tavern chatter ever could. The mountain veins had changed him in the way real danger always shifts your bones around a little.

Butch gave a soft whuff, sensing the thread of tension between us. His tail brushed lazily over my ankle, grounding. I nudged him with the heel of my boot, a silent thank-you.

Across the room, someone raised a pitcher.

"Here's what I think happened," the man announced loudly. "Darwin—that's his name, right?"

"DARREN," half the tavern corrected in unison.

"Right, Darren. I think he wandered into a cougar den."

"That wasn't no cougar," a woman countered. "Cougars don't walk on two legs."

"That's Bigfoot, Susan," someone else mumbled.

I exhaled a laugh into my beer.

This was how small towns survived the inexplicable. With stories bigger than truth, and humor large enough to swallow the fear whole.

Maeve brushed past me on her way to refill a drink. She flicked my shoulder lightly. "You look like you slept in a rockslide, Lange. Eat more fries."

"Working on it," I said.

She studied me a beat longer. A knowing flicker crossed her expression. "Mountain's quieter tonight."

"So I've heard."

I took another sip. The ale was crisp and cold, the perfect opposite of molten gold and cavern fire.

Maeve tucked a stray curl behind her ear. "You did good."

The words warmed parts of me dragon-fire couldn't reach.

A shout rose from the far table.

"I'm tellin' you, she had fangs this long!" A man held his fingers apart dramatically. "And she was FLIRTING with him!"

The table howled.

Beer sloshed.

Someone nearly toppled from their stool.

Henry buried his face in his hands. "I swear they're getting worse by the minute."

"They are," I said. "It's charming."

He peeked at me through his fingers. "Charm isn't the word I'd use."

But he was trying to hide a smile.

Butch barked once, sharp and alert, when the tavern door blew open on a gust of cold mountain air. Snowflakes twirled in, glittering in the neon.

Every conversation paused.

Then resumed all at once—louder, livelier—because the man who stepped inside was just Monroe coming off shift, stamping snow off his boots.

Henry nodded.

Butch flopped back down.

My shoulders settled an inch lower.

The danger was over.

The mountain was breathing evenly again.

Darren was safe.

Michelle was with him.

And by now, they had long since packed up their little nylon tent and vanished down the highway toward concrete and car exhaust. Toward Starbucks' lights and Macy's escalators. Toward the bright clatter of a world that made more sense to them than this one ever would.

All that remained of them here was the cautionary tale being shaped between sips of beer and mouthfuls of fries.

I let myself soften into the moment.

The low hum of voices.

The clatter of plates in the kitchen.

The jukebox crooning something old and rhythmic.

Butch's warmth anchoring my legs.

Henry's steady presence.

Maeve's voice weaving truth into story, and story into shield.

It hit me then—quiet and sharp and tender.

This was why I stayed.

Not because the mountains needed a guardian.

Not because the Hallow demanded it.

But because places like this—laughter over beer, fear softened into folklore, humans choosing community despite everything—were worth saving.

Were worth bleeding for.

Somewhere down in the Underdeep, a creature howled in loneliness.

Up here, someone called for another round.

Someone teased Henry about his hiking boots.

Maeve rolled her eyes and told them to hush.

Butch sighed like an old soul asleep.

And I—gold-born, flame-forged, the spark that made and unmade —sat among them with a basket of fries, feeling almost human.

Almost.

Monroe spotted us.

He wove through the tables with his usual unhurried stride, carrying a coffee instead of a beer, like the mug had grown out of his hand sometime around 1998 and never left. Sheriff Daniels came in his wake, broad-shouldered and careful-eyed; the kind of man who filled space without trying to. A few heads turned. Voices dipped then climbed again, but softer.

Maeve clocked them, grabbed two clean mugs, and met them halfway.

"Evenin', gentlemen," she said. "Y'all look like you've been dragged behind a truck."

"Feels about right," Daniels answered, scrubbing a hand over his jaw. He nodded toward me, toward Henry, toward Butch sprawled at our feet. "Mind if we join you?"

"Pull up a stool," Maeve said, wiping her hands on her apron as she slid their beers across the counter. "First round's on the house if you promise not to talk shop too loud. I don't need folks thinking this is headquarters."

Monroe gave one of his rare almost-laughs. "We're not that interesting."

"Oh, please," Maeve said, and a quick flush crept up her cheeks before she could smother it. "Half this town watches you walk down Main like it's the Fourth of July parade. Don't make me call you modest on top of everything else."

Monroe blinked, caught off guard.

Henry choked quietly on his beer.

And I—sipping mine—caught the flicker in Maeve's eyes and wondered, not for the first time, whether her crush angled toward Monroe...or toward Sheriff Daniels... Or whether Maeve simply enjoyed keeping every man within shouting distance on their toes.

They settled in—Monroe on the other side of me, Daniels on the other side of Henry. The energy at the bar shifted, a subtle tightening. We were still just people sharing a drink, but the ones who made a habit of watching the room—bartenders, bouncers, nervous souls—kept half an eye on us.

Butch thumped his tail twice in greeting. Daniels leaned down to scratch behind his ear.

"Heard you took care of our problem, Lange," Monroe said quietly.

Not praise.

Not accusation.

A simple fact laid between us like a body on a table.

My fingers tightened around my glass for a heartbeat, then eased. "We won't be finding any more shredded hikers," I said. "If that's what you're asking."

"That's part of it," Daniels said, studying me the way he studied people deciding whether to lie. "But you know that's not all."

His badge caught a glint of neon, throwing a brief streak of red across my knuckles.

Behind us, someone dropped a quarter into the jukebox. A soft twang drifted up—a song about trucks and heartbreak and not much else. The perfect kind of noise to hide more important conversation.

"Is it safe now?" Daniels asked.

Four words.

The only ones that mattered to his job.

To mine.

I thought about the Underdeep.

About gold bars humming like buried lightning.

About eyes staring up from the dark—accusing, pleading, empty.

About the Wampus pressed against her cage of light and stone, breathing hard, whispering to a man who was already forgetting her.

Safe was such a human word.

"It's safer," I said. "For now."

Daniels held my gaze a long moment. He was good at reading the spaces between words, the things not said. Whatever he saw in my face made something in his shoulders loosen by a degree.

"For now," he repeated. "Good enough to put in a report."

Maeve slid mugs in front of them with all the ceremony of placing offerings at a shrine. "That's all any of us ever gets," she said. "Good enough for now."

Monroe's mouth tipped wryly. "I'll drink to that."

He did, then set the mug down and turned slightly so his shoulder brushed mine. It wasn't an accident. It was an anchor.

"Family identified the body," he said in a low voice. "Service was short. Pastor did most of the talking. Parents didn't say much at all." He stared into the swirl of his drink. "They asked if it was quick."

I didn't ask what he told them. I already knew.

"They won't get the details," Daniels said, eyes on the mirror behind the bar instead of any of us. "We'll call it a tragic wildlife encounter. Put up a few extra signs. Remind people to stick to marked trails." He huffed humorlessly. "And never mention that whatever did it walked on two legs most of the time."

"Locals will fill that part in for you," Maeve said. "They're doin' a hell of a job already."

Monroe looked at me sidelong. "Officially," he said, "I ruled it a predator attack. Unidentified. Lotta teeth for a cougar. Lotta... intent for a bear." His jaw worked, like he was chewing on words he didn't much care for. "Unofficially..." He shook his head. "Unofficially, I'm not writing that part down."

"That's why the mountain keeps you around," I said. "You know what not to say out loud."

He snorted softly. "I know I like sleep. And I won't get it if I start naming things I can't put in a cage."

A flicker of something dark crossed his expression when he said 'cage'.

He didn't know about the Underdeep.

He didn't want to.

That was my burden, not his.

"Thank you," I said.

He blinked. "For what? Doing my job halfway?"

"For trusting me to do mine," I said.

Silence settled for a beat. Not heavy. Not easy. Just honest.

Henry cleared his throat. "Darren... he's really going to be okay?" he asked, directing the question at Daniels then redirecting it to me when he realized where the answer would actually come from.

"He's home," Daniels said. "Doc says he's malnourished, dehydrated, got a whole bouquet of scratches and bruises, but nothing permanent. Physically, anyway."

"The rest will take time," I added. "But he's alive. He remembers enough to stay away from the north slopes for a while. That's more than most get."

Henry nodded slowly. His hand dropped to Butch's head, fingers tangling in fur like he needed to confirm something solid still existed. "He, uh... he say anything to you?" he asked me. "About what he saw?"

"A little," I said. I remembered Darren's eyes, unfocused and watery, as he tried to describe a dream that had been too real to be fiction, too impossible to be anything else. "He remembers getting turned around. A fall. Voices in the dark. Something warm keeping him from freezing. It's jumbled. The mind protects itself."

Henry's throat worked. "Good," he said softly. "I mean, not good, but... you know."

"I do," I said.

He looked at me then—not like a coworker, or even a friend. Like someone who had glimpsed the edges of what I was and hadn't quite decided whether to flinch or lean closer.

"You stayed down there alone," he said. "In that... whatever that place was." His eyes searched my face.

"I did," I said. "And you and Butch got Darren out. You're part of this now. Whether you like it or not."

He swallowed hard, but there was something like pride under the fear. "Then next time," he said, "I'm not hanging back as far."

Maeve snorted. "You are absolutely hanging back as far. Preferably behind three trees and a rock."

Daniels hid a smile behind his mug. "Listen to your supervisor, son," he said. "You don't get extra points for dying brave."

"I'm not planning on dying," Henry said.

"Good," I said. "Helps the paperwork."

They chuckled, the sound small but genuine. Butch thumped his tail again, approving of any mood that included laughter and the possibility of dropped food.

Daniels finished his beer in a slow, thoughtful swallow then set the mug down with deliberate care. "You'll let me know," he said, eyes on me, "if there's ever anything I need to... say differently. To the public."

I met his gaze. "If there's ever a time warning people will help more than it harms," I said, "you'll be the first to know."

He seemed to weigh that, then nodded once. "Good enough."

Monroe slid off his stool, joints protesting softly. "I'm going home," he announced. "Y'all can keep telling ghost stories. I'm gonna pretend the only monsters I see are cholesterol and tax forms."

"You wish," Maeve said, but her tone held fondness. She reached out and squeezed his hand once before letting go. "Sleep, Monroe."

He gave her a tired salute, then one to me and Henry. "You two keep it quiet out there," he said.

"Do my best," I said.

He shuffled away, Daniels falling into step beside him. The door opened. A gust of night slipped in, cold and clean, carrying the faintest scent of pine and snowmelt. Then it shut, and the Bottle Tree went on breathing in its own small orbit.

I stared at their empty stools for a moment.

Maeve leaned her elbows on the bar, looking at me over the tops of her glasses. "You all right?" she asked.

"I'm fine," I said.

She arched a brow.

I sighed. "I'm... functional."

"Close enough," she said. "Eat your fries."

Henry gave a soft huff of laughter. "That's the real reason the mountain hasn't collapsed yet," he said. "Maeve bullying you into complex carbs."

"She's got a better track record than most gods I've met," I said.

The jukebox shifted to another song. Someone started a fresh game of pool. Laughter rolled across the room like an easy tide. Outside, the peaks were dark and vast and patient.

Inside, for the first time in a while, I let myself believe—for a few heartbeats—that we'd bought these people some time.

"For now," I murmured, more to myself than anyone else.

The Hallow hummed back low and distant, like an agreement carried through stone.

"Hey, Lange," someone down the bar called. "That story true about the hiker comin' outta the woods bare-ass naked, swearing he'd been cuddled by Bigfoot?"

A ripple of laughter went up.

I took a long pull of my beer, then tipped my chin toward the voice. "If one more tourist asks me about Bigfoot," I said, "I'm moving to town and opening a nail salon. French tips only. No questions asked."

That got them.

Laughter cracked wide this time—real belly stuff. Someone slapped the bar, someone else choked on their drink. Even Henry snorted—half beer, half wheeze.

"That I'd pay to see," Maeve said, smirking. "Ranger Lange, Slayer of Cuticles."

"Don't tempt me," I said. "At least cuticles don't try to eat hikers."

"For now," Henry muttered.

Maeve rolled her eyes and reached for something under the counter. "Speaking of tempting." She set a warm plate in front of me, the scent of cinnamon and browned sugar rising like a benediction. "House special. On me."

I eyed the slice of pie. The crust flaked at the edges, glistening with butter. Steam curled from the gap in the top where filling bubbled lava-slow.

"You already comped my dinner," I said.

"Yeah, well." She shrugged one shoulder. "Mountain tax refund. Eat it before I change my mind."

Butch's nose slid along my thigh, hopeful. His tail thumped once, twice, like a gavel.

"See?" Maeve said. "Dog agrees."

"Traitor," I told him, then picked up the fork.

The first bite almost undid me. Sweet and tart, hot enough to sting my tongue. It tasted like fall and home.

For a few quiet breaths, the Bottle Tree was just a bar.

I was just a woman who'd had a long week.

The mountain could wait.

"Eat up," Maeve said, bumping Henry's elbow with the ketchup bottle. "Existential crises require carbs."

He obeyed, dipping another fry, and chewing thoughtfully. "I just..." He glanced around the bar at the regulars, the neon, the scuffed wood. "Nobody in here knows how close they came, do they?"

"Some of them know more than they let on," Maeve said. "But no. Not really." She flicked her gaze toward me. "That's the point of her being out there and you being out there. So they don't have to."

Henry nodded slowly. "Feels weird. Knowing." He looked at me sidelong. "But I'm glad you didn't do it alone."

I swallowed another bite of pie, the sweetness suddenly complicated. "Me, too," I said.

Butch chose that moment to roll onto his side and flop one heavy paw over my boot, as if pinning me in place. His ribs rose and fell in a contented sigh.

I finished the pie, chased it with the last inch of beer. Warmth spread through my chest that had nothing to do with fire or flame—just sugar and malt and the presence of people who wouldn't let me disappear entirely into the dark.

I set the empty glass down and slid off the stool.

Henry made a face. "You leaving already?"

"Day shift tomorrow," I lied. It was technically true. A ranger was always on shift when the mountain called. "Besides, if I stay any longer someone's going to ask me if we have chupacabras. I don't have the patience tonight."

Maeve snagged my hat off the back of the stool and slapped it lightly against my chest. "Don't forget your crown, Goldilocks."

"That's slander," I said, taking it from her. "My hair is clearly more muddy auburn than gold."

"Uh-huh," she said. "Keep tellin' yourself that."

I settled the hat on my head, fishing a couple of bills from my pocket and tucking them under my empty plate.

Maeve noticed and scowled. "I said it was on the house."

"And I ignored you," I said. "You'll live."

She snorted, but there was a little softness at the edges of her mouth. "Text me when you get home," she said.

"I will," I said.

Henry twisted on his stool to face me fully. "If, uh... if the mountain calls tonight..."

"I'll text you," I said. "And then I'll tell you to stay in bed."

"Butch doesn't listen when you tell *him* to stay," Henry pointed out.

"Butch," I said, looking down at the dog, "has seniority."

He thumped his tail, clearly agreeing.

I shook my head, a smile tugging despite the weight in my bones. "If the mountain calls," I said, "and I need backup, you'll hear from me. Until then, pretend you're just a normal guy with a normal job in a normal town."

He looked around the bar, where someone was now loudly insisting they could totally do the Wampus call if everyone would just shut up and listen. "Sure," he said dryly. "Super normal."

"Eat your fries," I repeated, and headed for the door.

The tavern lights washed over me one last time—amber and neon and a hundred years of stories soaked into wood. The hum of conversation rose and fell like a tide. For a heartbeat I let myself stand there, hand on the doorjamb, soaking it in.

This is why, the Hallow murmured deep below my feet.

I didn't disagree.

Outside, the night met me cool and close.

Crickets stitched sound along the ditch lines. A truck rattled past on the main road, taillights smearing red in the dark. The sky was clear—stars scattered thick as salt, the Milky Way a pale scar across the deep.

The golden afterburn of dragon-sense still tingled under my skin, a faint echo of scales and wings. I breathed in slow, letting the human shape settle back into itself, bones remembering smallness.

Behind me the Bottle Tree's windows glowed warm, rectangles of yellow in the dark. A laugh burst loud enough to slip under the door and spill onto the gravel. Someone whooped. Someone cursed and then apologized to Maeve through the wall.

It was ordinary. It was beautiful.

Underneath it all, the mountain exhaled.

A tremor shivered through the earth—a breath, not a quake. Nothing a human would feel. But I was not just human.

It ran up through my soles into my calves; a low, thrumming note that belonged to depths no one in the bar would ever see.

The Underdeep humming.

Gold bars holding.

Creatures pacing, muttering, curling tighter into their own minds.

And one voice, threaded through the rest like a single, raw nerve:

A broken, lonely croon.

Wampus.

The sound speared something tender in my chest.

"I hear you," I whispered, though my mouth barely moved. Breath more than speech. "Rest. The mountain keeps you now."

Then I turned toward the dark line of the mountain and walked into the night.

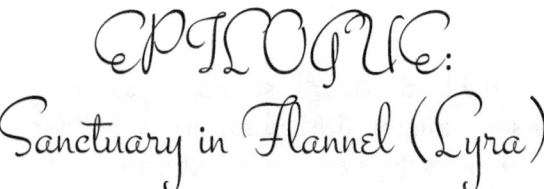

EPILOGUE:
Sanctuary in Flannel (Lyra)

The cabin door had clicked shut behind me long ago, locking out the wind and the weight of the mountain. Now the world was smaller—contained and quiet. Mine. The vastness outside had already receded, swallowed by wood and warmth, and I finally let my shoulders fall.

I padded across the one-room space in an oversized forest-green flannel shirt, white cotton underwear, wool socks slouched around my ankles. My hair was still damp from the quick, utilitarian shower I'd taken the moment I came in—hot water beating the cold stone of the cave out of my muscles. Droplets slid cool down my spine. The room breathed cedar and steeping tea leaves. The world had shrunk to breath and wood grain.

My antler chandelier threw a soft golden halo across the space. Candlelight pooled in the corners, warming the knotty-pine walls and making shadows dance like old stories. The place was simple and small. Lived-in.

The stone fireplace dominated the far wall, flames snapping low and steady. Butch laid sprawled across the bear rug in front of it, paws twitching in some heroic dream. Above him, the mantel held the few photographs I allowed myself to keep.

Maeve, behind the Bottle Tree bar, a laugh caught halfway to escape

—taken the night she tried to teach me how to pour without splashing and I absolutely failed.

Henry, younger, leaning against the ranger truck in a uniform two sizes too big, pretending not to be proud of his first solo rescue.

Butch, muddy and ecstatic, caught mid-leap during a stormy search-and-recovery where he'd found the missing hiker long before either of us did.

I crossed to the kettle, poured steaming water over ginger, honey, and a sprig of something wild I had foraged earlier in the season. The scent rose like balm, tracing heat along my throat. My body unwound a little more. Enough to feel human again. Enough to pretend.

I carried the mug toward the bed, stopping to tuck Butch's blanket around him when he kicked in his sleep. His tail gave one small thump, a thank-you. I brushed my fingers through the fur between his ears and felt the mountain's quiet hum beneath it. Even rest was never entirely still here.

My book waited on the nightstand, spine soft with use. I slid under the mismatched blankets, tugged them up to my waist, and took a sip of tea. The fire crackled; the window creaked under a brush of night wind; a distant owl cried out along the ridge. Familiar sounds. The kind that settled the heart.

For a breath—or maybe two—I sat in gratitude. Warm bed. Warm dog. Warm fire.

My eyes closed.

The Hallow stirred.

A shift beneath my ribs, a gold-threaded pulse sliding up my spine like someone whispering my true name from the other side of sleep.

My breath caught.

The Hallow's pulse feathered along my skin. Gold humming under bone. Heat gathering low and insistent, already knowing what shape it wanted to take.

Lyra...

Taren's voice slid into my mind like molten silver pouring into a cast. His presence. Full. Heavy. Impossible to ignore.

My breath stuttered.

The mug slipped in my hands, sloshing hot tea over my fingers. I didn't even flinch.

"Taren…" My voice was barely a sound. More of a prayer than a question.

The fire in the hearth brightened with no change in fuel. Shadows melted off the walls. Butch twitched in his sleep, sensing something old and powerful moving through the air akin to a storm front.

Taren's laugh rumbled low and deep, a sound that curled around my ribs and tightened.

You call for me before you sleep. Even when you don't speak it aloud.

My pulse hammered. Heat flushed under my skin, fast and blooming.

I pushed the blankets down, unable to stay still.

Unbutton your shirt.

His voice guided my movements.

A gravity I had obeyed long before mountains had names.

Trembling, my fingers went to the buttons of my flannel.

I told myself it was residual adrenaline from the fight, from the Underdeep, from seeing Wampus banished into shadow-light cages that hummed my name.

The shirt peeled open slowly, slipping from my shoulders, pooling around my elbows. Cool air hit my skin.

Heat followed instantly—deep and coiling, pulsing from inside.

Dragon heat.

I closed my eyes.

He pressed closer through the Hallow.

Good. Slowly now. I want to feel your breath change.

It did.

I couldn't stop it.

The blankets warmed at my thighs, soft and unbearable at once. My heartbeat thudded hard. The fire crackled again—not randomly, but in sync with him.

Taren's energy wrapped around my hips, my waist, my throat, without ever touching me.

Hand beneath the cotton, my golden gem. Let me hear your want.

A shiver tore through me.

I bit down on a sound that would have betrayed too much.

My fingers dipped beneath the waistband of my underwear, slow, guided by instinct and memory and the way his breath—imagined or not—seemed to trace the hollow of my neck.

Not so fast.

A purr beneath the words.

A reprimand threaded with hunger.

My hand stilled.

My touch lightened.

My lungs dragged in thin, heated air.

My thighs pressed together, needing friction, needing him, needing—

"You're torturing me," I whispered.

He exhaled in my mind, a long molten sigh. It rolled over me like dragonfire held just shy of burning.

No. I am reminding you.

A pause.

A shift in tone.

A deeper note that shook the mattress beneath me.

Reminding you what you are.

And what we are together.

The ache deepened—sharp, sweet, and scorching.

Everything inside me tightened, rising toward inevitable relief.

Not yet.

His voice curved, wicked with restraint.

The ache coiled low inside me.

My breath shuddered. My back arched. Everything in me tightened, rising toward the unbearable crest of release—

Not yet.

His voice curved through me, velvet over flesh.

A tease.

A leash.

A vow.

I gasped, fingers faltering.

Slow now.

The command was soft, but it wrapped around my body like a hand closing at the base of my neck.

You go too fast when you want too much. Slow for me.

Desire cracked through me like lightning.

I obeyed—because I always had. I wanted to.

My hand stilled... then moved again, slower, probing deeper, a trembling glide guided by the heat of his presence in my blood.

The tension built again—slow, slow, exquisite.

Taren shifted inside the bond, his breath like wind off molten stone.

Good. Better. Let me feel every part of you.

The ache sharpened.

Tightened.

Climbed.

I bit down on a cry, breath spiraling into something near-sob, near-prayer.

"Taren—please—"

He shuddered inside my mind, the sound of it like a dragon's wing scraping starlight.

When I say, my golden one. Not before.

My hips jerked once, helpless.

The climax hovered impossibly close, impossibly denied.

Heat bloomed behind my knees, under my ribs, up my throat.

I was shaking now. The world narrowed to breath, touch, flame and him.

"Taren... I can't—"

Begging.

Breaking.

His pleasure vibrated through the bond, dark and tender, a rumble that made my pulse stutter.

Yes. Like that.

A pause.

A trembling inhale that was half growl, half devotion.

Now.

The word detonated inside me.

Release rushed through me—slow at first, then devastating, a rolling wave of heat that made my lungs seize and my vision blur. I arched into it, into him, into the invisible shape of his body pressed through the Hallow and around me.

His voice wrapped me like arms—strong, molten, inevitable.

My golden goddess.

The words undid me.

I collapsed back into the pillows, shaking, breath stumbling out in uneven waves.

The ache inside me softened into warmth. The warmth softened into trembling satisfaction, the afterglow of a pleasure he had shaped with nothing but breath and will.

Taren's presence pressed closer—silver sliding through gold—his mouth not on my skin, yet felt as surely as flame:

This is only the edge, he murmured against the inside of my throat, each syllable a vow, a command, a confession.

If I stood beside you in flesh and flame, golden one, I would worship you with the same devotion that carved valleys and lifted mountains. I would remake the world with you again—slow, reverent, perfect.

My legs weakened at the sound of him in my bones.

Keep your fire banked, he ordered, though the order trembled with longing.

Do not spend what belongs to us both. When I come to you—truly come—your pleasure will be the altar I burn upon.

My breath caught, helpless.

Every thought I have ends in you, he added, softer now, almost breaking on the truth of it.

The warmth of him began to ebb—slowly, reluctantly—like tide drawing back from shore only because it must return stronger.

I let my breath steady, let the last tremors slip through my thighs... then smiled into the dark.

"Taren," I murmured, a soft drag of amusement and promise.

"You should be the one keeping your fire banked."

A low, startled growl curled through the bond.

I continued, voice hushed, smug, wicked in the way only lovers forged in fire could be.

"Because the next time I reach through the flame to touch you...you will kneel to my pace. My hands. My pleasure."

I felt him still—utterly still—on the other side of the Hallow.

A drag of breath.

A tremor not mine.

Heat rippled across my skin in a shockwave.

His answering whisper came ragged:

Golden goddess... you dare.

"I demand," I whispered, settling back into the warm imprint of the blankets. "And you will think on it until I come to you in flame."

A deep, hungry silence followed.

Sleep before I break my own vow to the mountains and rush to your side, just to feel your pleasure.

The bond softened—retreating like embers under ash—but not before a final pulse of heat stroked down my spine.

The Hallow throbbed with his departing heat—slow, steady, promising.

My limbs loosened.

My pulse thudded wild but sated.

Butch snored softly by the fire.

The cabin folded itself back around me... small, quiet, safe.

At least for the moment.

Only my heartbeat stayed fierce.

The Hallow pulsed once beneath the floorboards—not violently, just enough to tug me out of the molten haze Taren had left behind.

My breath steadied.

The ache in my belly softened.

But the mountain... shifted.

A soft rattle tremored through the wooden frame of the cabin.

My mug quivered on the nightstand.

Butch lifted his head from the bear rug, ears pricking sharply toward the window, a low warning rumble rolling in his chest.

This was not leftover magic.

Something outside had exhaled.

"Taren," I whispered, sitting up and adjusting the flannel where it had fallen open across my ribs. "Did you feel that?"

His response slid in slow and measured, the way a blade lowers before cutting.

I did. Something old wakes beneath your mountain.

The fire in the hearth snapped—not like a log shifting but like a whip.

Blue flame licked briefly along the edges.

My dragon instincts rose, alert and cold.

"What is it?" I whispered.

Listen.

I did.

At first I heard nothing.

Then—a keening sound, high and sharp shimmered across the ridge, thin as a fever dream.

My skin prickled.

That sound didn't belong to anything that walked on four legs; or two, for that matter.

"Taren..." My voice thinned. "Tell me that isn't—"

A second cry slashed mockingly across the night, echoing from impossible distances.

Butch shot to his feet, barking once, frantic.

Taren's voice turned to iron.

A Raven Mocker.

My heart stumbled.

"That's impossible," I breathed. "They died with the last threshold witches. They've been gone for centuries—"

Gone is not the same as ended.

Some evils sleep.

Some wait for a crack in the world.

Something stirred this one.

Something freed it.

The word *freed* scraped through my mind.

My bare feet hit the floor. The boards were cold enough to ache. I crossed the room to the window, wool socks whispering against wood, and pulled the curtain aside.

The ridge outside looked wrong—altered and unsettled, as if a shadow had crawled through it on hands and knees. Trees bowed inward as though bracing against something unseen. Frost crept uphill, slipping against gravity like being drawn toward a pulse. A thin ribbon of darkness wove through the underbrush in the way smoke moved underwater. Snow swirled, hovering for a heartbeat before resettling without any wind at all.

The Underdeep wasn't doing this.

This was coming from somewhere older.

Somewhere meaner.

Somewhere that remembered witch fire.

"How close is it?" I whispered.

Taren's response sharpened, silver cutting through my thoughts.

Close enough that I feel its hunger.

A pulse shivered through the windowpane—a vibration, subtle and knowing, as if something outside had recognized me.

My breath caught.

"What is it looking for?"

Taren's answer came low and grim.

A heart.

Strong.

Burning bright in the Hallow.

My stomach dropped.

"Taren... it wants a dragon heart."

A single beat of silence.

Then Taren's voice, low and certain:

It wants yours.

A raven cawed outside—not the common croak of a bird but a cavernous sound threaded with death-magic. A voice shaped from the breath of grave dirt and stolen hearts.

No ordinary creature claimed that cry.

Only one that had learned to speak fear long before humans learned to bury their dead.

Cold crept through the window glass.

My breath fogged the pane.

"Taren," I whispered, "if it gets me, can it hurt you? In the dream-flame?"

A pause followed.

I don't know.

The worry in his tone slid through my ribs.

My fingers touched the pane.

Something in the darkness leaned back—curious, hungry. Aware.

Another cry split the night. Closer now, sharp as splintered bone, hungry enough to bend the air.

Butch growled low, planting himself between me and the door, hackles rising.

Taren's presence tightened in my mind, fierce and unbearably tender.

Rest while you can, fire of my heart.

Your next hunt is coming.

And this one wants your heart.

The Story Continues...

Bound by Shadow
Hallow Rising, Book Two

The mountains whisper.
  The shadows answer.

When a new presence stirs in the high ridges, it does not hunt with claws—but with memory, guilt, and hunger that wears a familiar shape. The Raven Mocker has begun to stalk the dark, and its attention is fixed on those sworn to protect the land.

As the threat deepens, Lyra is pushed closer to the edge of her oath, forced to confront what it truly means to guard a world that demands sacrifice without mercy. Distance stretches, vigilance sharpens, and the bond she shares with Taren is tested in ways neither expected.

Because some monsters don't want destruction.

They want pursuit.

They want fear.
They want *her*.

Bound by Shadow continues the *Hallow Rising* series with folklore-driven horror, rising tension, and a bond under strain—where love does not weaken the guardian, but may be the most dangerous thing of all.

Also by Chrissy Chicory

The Culebra Chronicles

- *Eternally Connected* (Prequel)
- *Unabashedly Chosen*
- *Seriously Challenged*
- *Increasingly Complicated*

The Nettles B&B Paracozy Mystery Series

- *Lilac and Cherry Tarts* (Prequel)
- *Hollyhock and Sticky Buns*
- *Wisteria and Wedding Cake*
- *Mums And Pumpkin Pie*

Ink and Verse: Cursive Practice Through the World's Greatest Poetry

- Volume 1: *Emily Dickinson*
- Volume 2: *Sappho*
- Volume 3: *Voltaire*
- Volume 4: *Dante Alighieri*
- Volume 5: *Homer*
- Volume 6: *Poe*
- Volume 7: *Twas the night before Christmas*

Lucid Living: A Gentle Guide to Personal Growth

- Volume 1: *Personal Development*
- Volume 2: *Finance*
- Volume 3: *Health & Fitness*
- Volume 4: *The Art of Play*

Chrissy Chicory's fiction and nonfiction books are available through Amazon, Apple Books, Barnes & Noble, Kobo, and other major eBook and print retailers

—plus library services like OverDrive, Hoopla, and Scribd through Draft2Digital's wide distribution.

The Ink and Verse handwriting series is currently available exclusively on Amazon.

About the Author

Chrissy Chicory is a Florida author known for weaving magic, folklore, and emotional depth into stories where the unseen presses close to the everyday. Her work spans cozy mystery, romantasy, and magical realism —each grounded in atmosphere, heart, and a belief that stories are living things, meant to be felt as much as read.

With *Hallow Rising*, Chrissy steps into darker terrain, drawing on Appalachian folklore, ancient guardianship myths, and slow-burn, fated romance. The series blends folklore-driven horror with mythic fantasy, exploring what it means to stand watch over a land that remembers every vow—and what it costs to love while holding the line.

Her other works include *The Culebra Chronicles*, a romantasy series set in historic St. Augustine that follows a group of magical half-fae sisters through pirate curses, ghost tours, and long-buried family secrets; and the *Nettles B&B Paracozy Mysteries*, a cozy paranormal series featuring haunted heirlooms, meddling pixies, and second chances served with tea and sticky buns on the Florida coast.

Beyond fiction, Chrissy is the creator of the *Ink and Verse* handwriting workbooks, which celebrate classical poetry and the meditative art of cursive, and the *Lucid Living* series, gentle guides to mindfulness, self-discovery, and intentional living.

Across all her work, Chrissy invites readers into worlds where folklore lingers, magic has consequences, and even the darkest paths are illuminated by connection, courage, and choice.

Sign up for Chrissy's newsletter at **ChrissyChicory.com** to receive free ebook prequels, exclusive content, and behind-the-scenes glimpses into upcoming releases.

She also hosts **The Velvet Teacup Society**, a reader community devoted to magical storytelling, monthly teacup giveaways, and cozy virtual gatherings. Learn more at **ChrissyChicory.com/Velvet-Teacup-Society**.

Magic is all around us.

Before You Go...

Thank you for walking the ridgelines of *Hallow Rising*.
    For listening when the mountains whispered.
    For standing watch where shadows press close.

If this story stirred something in you—fear, wonder, longing, or fire—I would be deeply grateful if you shared your thoughts in a review. Even a few honest words help other readers find their way to this world and decide whether they, too, are ready to cross the boundary.

Think of it as a mark left at the edge of the trail.
    A signal fire lit for those who come after.
    A truth spoken aloud so the mountains remember it was here.

You may leave a review wherever you purchased this book, or anywhere you share your reading journey with fellow lovers of dark folklore and mythic romance.

Thank you for keeping watch.

The mountains never forget those who do.
Chrissy Chicory

www.ingramcontent.com/pod-product-compliance
Lightning Source LLC
Chambersburg PA
CBHW051953060726
47506CB00012B/1109